MAFIO$O
PART TWO

Melodrama Publishing
www.MelodramaPubishing.com

FOLLOW
NISA SANTIAGO

FACEBOOK.COM/NISASANTIAGO

INSTAGRAM.COM/NISA_SANTIAGO

TWITTER.COM/NISA_SANTIAGO

Order online at
bn.com, amazon.com, and
MelodramaPublishing.com

Mafioso - Part Two. Copyright © 2018 by Melodrama Publishing. All rights reserved. No part of this book may be used or reproduced in any manner whatsoever without written permission except in the case of brief quotations embodied in critical articles or reviews. For information, address info@melodramabooks.com.

www.melodramapublishing.com

Library of Congress Control Number: 2017909508
ISBN-13: 978-1620780817

First Edition: January 2018

Printed in Canada

BOOKS BY
NISA SANTIAGO

MAFIO$O

PART TWO

NISA SANTIAGO

Max stepped off the bus at the Port Authority and merged with the masses of people coming off buses from across the country. She immediately felt out of place, even though this was her hometown. While following the crowd to the exits, she gazed at the ads plastered all over the tunnel. NYPD cops were situated everywhere. Max noticed a change in their uniforms. Back in '94, their holstered weapons were less threatening, and they wore a lighter blue with a softer look. Now, they were geared up in dark blue or black and walked around with assault rifles and gas masks, looking like soldiers at war. September 11th had changed a lot of things.

The tunnel she was in was hot and congested with throngs of people journeying in different directions. It felt like a crowded maze. Though the signs were in English, they were still confusing to her. It all became overwhelming. She needed to take a timeout and a deep breath, but she had to keep it moving. She planned on meeting Miguel outside the Port Authority. From Nadia's description, she knew what he looked like. He was to pick her up in a black Honda Accord.

Making it outside onto 8th Avenue and 42nd Street, she scanned the area for Miguel. The streets were swamped with cars, taxis, buses, and trucks all trying to get to their destinations. The street look like a clogged artery. Horns were blowing loudly, as a wall of folks crossed 8th Avenue and moved toward Times Square, where towering city buildings appeared to touch the blue sky.

Max looked around, feeling out of place. She was ready to find Miguel and leave. She didn't want to be seen like this—looking like one of the city's homeless. For a moment, her eyes darted everywhere, frantically looking for her ride to Brooklyn. Her cash was limited, and she was hungry and tired and needed a bath. She wanted to shred her shabby clothing and be alone.

Where was Miguel?

Max didn't move. She stood on the corner of 8th Avenue and 42nd Street and watched everyone and everything. New York City didn't bring about a welcoming feeling. People passed by her, even bumped into her accidentally without apology. They walked briskly and went on with their lives. But it was expected. No one knew who she was. They didn't care about her.

She noticed a few Honda Accords in the area that fit the description of the one Miguel should be driving, but they were occupied with families, females, or older men. She sighed, becoming frustrated. What if Miguel wasn't coming? What if Nadia had double-crossed her? Now that she was free, and over a thousand miles away from the prison, maybe Nadia didn't see her as a threat anymore. Max could see that happening. But she was still a threat, and she still had contacts inside the Louisiana state prison. If Nadia crossed her, then Max would put that bitch on her hit list too.

"You Max?" she heard a voice say from behind.

Max turned around and caught an eyeful of Miguel, who stood there deadpan. She locked eyes with him. He was pure eye candy. He stood five nine with an olive complexion, short dark hair, and intriguing eyes. He was wearing a black tank top that highlighted his muscular build and black cargo shorts with white Nikes. A few tattoos decorated his arms, from his biceps down to his forearms.

For the first time in twenty-plus years, Max felt something between her legs. She felt her pussy smile. "Yes, I'm Max," she replied.

Miguel had that murderous edge to him. He still looked military—Marines. Maybe he did a few tours overseas, took enemy lives, and created hell. His eyes looked like they could tell a story. "I'm parked across the street. I don't want to get a ticket," he said indifferently, walking off and leaving Max to follow him.

Max could feel his apathy toward her.

Miguel found nothing attractive about Max. He assumed that she was a dyke, with her long cornrows and her rough appearance. She was a hard-looking bitch with cold eyes.

Miguel didn't want to be there, but he felt he didn't have a choice. That she'd threatened the love of his life didn't sit too well with him. If he could, he would have broken her neck with his bare hands, but he couldn't touch her. He was smart enough to know the influence she had over Nadia, who was scared to death of Max. He hated that Nadia's life was in danger. He couldn't chance something happening to the mother of his three small children.

Nadia had told him all about Max and how things worked in Louisiana. They'd tried to move Nadia into protective custody, but the warden wouldn't allow it. PC was only entertained at the prison if you were testifying against someone or after you had testified in a high-profile trial. But what about inmates like Nadia—new and scared? Where did they fit it? It angered Miguel that his woman was a pawn in someone's plan.

Miguel climbed into the driver's seat of his Accord with the rusted bottom and aging tires. The car had seen better days. The interior had cracked leather seats and worn mats. He would have preferred if Max got into the back seat of the car, but she climbed into the passenger seat next to him and closed the door.

Without saying a word to her, Miguel drove off, navigating the vehicle into the thick city traffic. For a few blocks, there was no conversation, just plain silence. Max stared out the window, still taking in the city, observing new styles with the women and the men, and watching life happen in Manhattan.

After a few minutes of quiet time, she looked at Miguel. "When will you make it happen?"

He knew what she was talking about. He refused to look at her while driving toward the Brooklyn Bridge. He came to a red light and stopped. He stared out the windshield, eyeing the sea of red brake lights ahead of him. "Soon."

"The ten grand—I want Bugsy and Lucky dead."

Miguel quickly replied, "No, for ten grand, that's *one* murder. If you want a second person dead, then that's another ten grand. And I'm only doing this because of Nadia."

"You love her, don't you?"

Miguel didn't reply. He didn't want to talk about his relationship to this bitch extorting his woman. He despised her. She was poison to him and his relationship.

"I was just making conversation," Max said.

She was testing him, trying to outsmart him. She wanted to see where his head was at, and how loyal he was to Nadia. From her viewpoint, he seemed sharp, and he was deeply in love. He wasn't a fool, and she would not lowball him or intimidate him like she had done to Nadia. He stuck to his guns and was assertive. Max respected that. She wanted to know more about him, but he seemed reluctant to converse with her, keeping things simple and professional, if you can call it that.

"I need a name—Lucky or Bugsy—and I need some time," he said.

"I'll have a name for you soon," she said. "And you have some time."

They crossed over the Brooklyn Bridge into Downtown Brooklyn. To some extent, Max was elated to be back in Brooklyn. Her eyes were out the window again and fixed on everything. The area was inundated with residential and office buildings, heavy traffic, and a lot of pedestrians. She remembered the shopping sprees on Fulton Street and dining with Scottie at the famous Junior's Restaurant. Max loved their cheesecake. She yearned for a delicious meal and a slice of that cheesecake, but those days of luxury seemed long gone.

Moving through downtown Brooklyn via Flatbush Avenue and then Atlantic Avenue, they arrived in East New York sooner than later. Miguel parked in front of her mother's home on Blake Avenue in East New York.

"We'll talk," he said, the car idling.

"Indeed, we will," she said.

Max noticed the new neighbors, the new young faces lingering on the corner, and a few new businesses. A local bar around the corner had been turned into a community church, and new homes had been constructed. Gentrification was in full effect. Her parents' place still looked the same. The brick home surrounded by a weathered iron fence and with its own driveway was a sight for sore eyes. She was happy to be home, but there was also sadness. The place wouldn't feel the same without her father around.

She climbed out of the Accord and stood on the sidewalk for a moment. She stared at the house, hesitant to approach and walk inside. She hadn't seen her mother in so many years. She knew there would be changes, but was she ready for these changes?

Miguel drove off. Max watched the back of the car turn the corner. Another deep sigh escaped her, and she placed one foot forward and approached the front entrance. This was it, her adjustment to life on the outside after twenty-something years.

She wondered if her mother would recognize her. Who would she see? It definitely wouldn't be her little girl. Max didn't feel like that same young girl chasing a law degree and in love with a drug dealer. Time inside had hardened her, leaving nothing of the old Maxine.

S cott sat back in the high-back leather chair and eyed every soul in the room. His platinum watch peeked from his shirt cuffs, and his diamond ring sparkled brilliantly in the room. Everyone was quiet, waiting for him to speak.

First things first, he needed to smoke. Scott rolled the long cigar between his fingers, feeling out its smooth texture. It was perfect, having no lumps or soft spots. He removed a platinum cigar cutter from the inner pocket of his Armani suit jacket and snipped the end of the cigar with a quick, sharp motion. A poorly cut cigar wouldn't do for him. Scott believed in quality and taste.

Using a torch lighter, he held the cigar in his hand and placed the tip above the flame; sticking it directly in the fire would ruin the flavor. Before he placed it into his mouth, he wanted to burn the end to sort of "prime" the tobacco. He spun it around as he continued to light it to make sure there was an even burn. Once he saw an orange glow, he placed it into his mouth and puffed. He filled his mouth up with smoke and then blew it out. He did this a few times, producing a thick, white smoke that hung in the air. The flavor of the cigar lingered between his jaws.

After a few puffs, he said, "Is there any new information on this muthafucka, Deuce?"

The complete silence amongst everyone around the table—Layla, Whistler, Meyer, Bugsy, and Lucky—aggravated him.

"No one has anything to say?"

Bugsy said, "He went off the radar. No one has heard from him in weeks, Pop."

"So you're telling me this muthafucka just fell off the face of the earth—did a disappearing act like David Blaine? Deuce, a common street thug? We put over three dozen men on this man, and nothing came up."

"He's smarter than we thought," Bugsy replied.

The more Bugsy spoke, the angrier Scott became.

Scott had called a meeting to regroup, go over operations, and to strategize, since things had gotten way out of hand. Deuce had hit them where it hurt, killing three of his kids, and someone had violently beaten his daughter. The bloodshed was staggering. The man was making them all look like simpletons.

"How do we look, not being able to find one man? He's out there living and hiding, and we're looking like the gang that can't shoot straight," Scott exclaimed.

He stood up from the table with his lit cigar. His composure faded. He eyed his wife, Layla. Now that the Florida homes were completed, she was back in on operations. As far as she was concerned, she was co-owner of everything Scott had built. With three children murdered, and her only remaining daughter facing a lengthy prison sentence, she needed answers. She wanted to be in the trenches. She was ready to become a pistol-packing bitch and protect her three remaining babies at any cost.

She and Scott weren't taking any chances. Security was tight. A half dozen armed soldiers and lieutenants sat in the room adjacent to where the family met.

"We already got to his sister, and he doesn't have any family left," Meyer chimed.

"I want a ten-million-dollar bounty on his head," Scott said. "That should motivate these killers out there."

"I'll find him myself, Pop, and put a fuckin' bullet in his head. I promise you that," Meyer said with a clenched fist.

Scott looked at Meyer; he still was displeased with Meyer's previous actions and his hot temper. Meyer's recklessness had cost him money and favors. Beating down Sergeant McAuliffe put them in hot water with a few other officers, since McAuliffe was respected and liked by his peers. They wanted to take matters into their own hands and deal with Meyer, but Scott and Whistler were able to come to an agreement with them. And it wasn't cheap.

Scott had no words for Meyer. If he succeeded, then it would be a bonus for him. But he doubted that Meyer was that skilled in hunting down a man that even Whistler had trouble finding.

Whistler sat at the other end of the table quiet like a mouse. But his silence spoke loudly, especially to Scott.

Scott said, "Whistler, you have nothing to say over there? What the fuck is on your mind? I need a friend's opinion. I need some kind of information from you. I need this issue to go away and go away fast. I thought you put Maze on him. He can't find this nigga?"

All eyes were on Whistler. He sat straight-faced and was dressed similarly to Scott, wearing a dark blue Tom Ford suit.

Lucky looked at him intently. She was still sour about his aloofness toward her. For now, she kept her cool, choosing to not lash out at her former lover, a man for whom she still had a strong desire. The man she was still in love with.

"Maze got knocked on a warrant. I thought I told you about that."

Scott furrowed his brows. His jaw got tight and he had to compose himself. "If you told me, would I be asking!"

Whistler exhaled. "My bad, Scott. A lot's been going on lately that it may have slipped my mind."

"You got a lot on your mind, huh?"

Whistler didn't answer.

"Nigga, did you lose three kids? Are your three seeds six feet deep! I rely on you to stay on point as my right-hand. You need to tell me something."

"It doesn't make sense, Scott," Whistler said.

"What don't make sense?"

"Everything."

"Muthafucka, stop with the equivocation and talk to me directly!" Scott exclaimed. "Truth to power, right?"

"It all feels too personal to come from Deuce. I began feeling this way while Lucky was in the hospital."

Meyer said, "What you sayin'—Deuce ain't do this shit? I think you delusional, nigga."

"You asked for my outlook, right?"

"Nigga, fuck your outlook! It all makes sense on our end. When did this shit start happening? Right after we took over Deuce's territory. Why wouldn't he come at us hard like that? We fucked his shit up, nigga, so now he tryin' to fuck our shit up," Meyer said.

"I hear Deuce is smart, but to garner access to family and places so quickly and react in that time doesn't add up to me," Whistler explained.

"Then who you think is comin' at us like this? Huh, nigga?"

"Youngblood, you need to chill."

Meyer stood up. "Man, fuck that chill shit! And I ain't your youngblood! You think you got this shit figured out? You don't, nigga!"

Scott didn't intervene yet. He continued to stand and frown, listening to the bickering. Layla was looking to her son, believing him over Whistler.

Whistler would not be disrespected by a child, even though Meyer was Scott's son. He stood up and glared at Meyer. He was ready to knock the young boy's head off, show him how he got down back in the days. Meyer had heard the stories, but he'd never personally experienced Whistler's lethal set of skills or ever been on the other side of his rage.

"I don't see any other adversary coming at us like that, Whistler," Bugsy said.

"Y'all actually believe that Gotti, Bonnie, and Clyde were killed over a drug beef by a street thug named Deuce? A man who had no idea we existed until a few months ago?" Whistler argued.

"It's gotta be him. Who else has means and motive to touch one of our own?" Bugsy asked.

"This is the handiwork of someone who's smart but also has patience. A hood nigga like Deuce would have tried to take out the head and watch the body fall. He woulda come at Scott, not his kids. These hits were professional. No witnesses, no fuckin' warning!"

"You talkin' 'bout some mastermind—some character out a fuckin' novel," Meyer cursed.

"I'm saying to everyone in this room that these aren't business-related murders. It feels personal and deliberate. They were methodical and well planned."

"Then give us a name, Whistler," Bugsy said.

"He don't have a fuckin' name. He's full of shit," Meyer said. "Makin' shit bigger than what it is. This is drug beef, niggas. We fightin' over territory block by block. You know what it is."

Whistler's face tightened like a rubber band stretching to its limits. He clenched his fists and was three seconds from leaping over the table at Meyer. The boy was a hothead with no common sense. If it weren't for Scott, Meyer would have been dog food on the streets.

The brothers continued to bicker back and forth with Whistler, who always felt he was the smartest guy in the room. Whistler had no name for the assailants, but he knew it wasn't Deuce's doing. He needed to investigate more. There was someone in the shadows coming at them.

Their true enemy had not yet revealed himself. Deuce executing this shit just wasn't feasible. Whistler needed to make Scott and Layla believe that. But they were too emotional. They were angry and wanted bloodshed. Someone needed to die, which was understandable.

"Give me time, and I'll find a name. I'll locate the muthafuckas responsible for these attacks," Whistler assured Scott. "I'll burn them alive for ever fuckin' with the West Empire."

"We don't have time for this nigga to play Sherlock Holmes, Pop!" Meyer shouted. "We need every fuckin' nigga out there wit' a fuckin' gun—Whistler included—taking out everything that belongs to Deuce. Now this nigga wanna play detective!"

Whistler said, "You put all your eggs in one basket, and what happens when you still come up empty, Meyer? We kill Deuce, and we still have a problem out there. Cover all areas, and leave no rock unturned."

Meyer was ready to retort, but Scott intervened, saying, "Shut up, Meyer!"

Meyer scowled, especially at Whistler. He felt his father had always chosen his friend over him—his own flesh and blood. What was so special about Whistler that garnered Scott's trust and his undivided attention?

Lucky was taken aback by Whistler's theory about the murders of her sister and brothers. She sat there in silence and listened intently as he laid out his assumption that they were being set up and hunted by some mastermind. He made sense. Her attack was too deliberate. One minute she was inside her apartment getting ready for bed, and then instantly, she was swallowed up by two intruders and assaulted in the shadows. How did they get into her building? How did they get past security? How did she not see or hear them coming? Quickly, she was beaten and knocked unconscious and placed into the back of a van, and they viciously beat her. That night repeatedly played in her mind. She couldn't escape it.

Another night Lucky thought about was her arrest. The arresting cop had also mentioned something about her name and her siblings' names. Her brothers and sisters had all been named after murdered gangsters in a different era. He somewhat inadvertently had connected the dots for her, too. Lucky felt she was smart, and these clues on her siblings' murders had not only escaped her, but her father. Why hadn't Scott connected the dots? Why didn't he see there was a possibility of an enemy coming at them from afar?

Whistler was on to something. She hated to admit it. In her mind, Whistler couldn't hold a candle to her father's intelligence. She always felt that Scott was the smartest man in the room. But Whistler wasn't to be taken for granted. He was decisive, shrewd, sharp, and adept at a lot of things. If he could, then he would have started up his own organization instead of being a right-hand man for her father.

Was he loyal to her father and the organization?

Was he loyal to her and their relationship?

A deep chill ran down Lucky's spine. She always thought about that night when he didn't allow her to step foot inside his apartment. What was he hiding? She figured it was a bitch in his bed. He had become cold and distant toward her after her assault. When she needed him the most, he wasn't there. He wouldn't fuck her, or console her. In fact they hadn't fucked since the night of her attack. He looked at her with pity or disgust, like it was her fault. And right after she'd threatened to tell her father about their relationship, she was arrested with several kilos of cocaine in her car. It was all game, a game that only a mastermind could implement. Had she been caught with meth, then it would have been too obvious, because she was the meth queen.

Whistler continued to plead his assumptions. Her brothers weren't backing down. Her mother only sat there and listened. Scott spoke out, unconvinced about this unknown mastermind coming at his family so suddenly.

An outrageous thought popped into Lucky's mind. What if Whistler wasn't who he said he was? Someone was trying to destroy her family, and they were doing it from the inside. She believed it could be Whistler. Maybe he'd developed some resentment toward them after all these years. Maybe he was tired of being the second-in-command and wanted to run the entire operation himself. There was a possibility he could be behind the murders and the attack. Just the thought of Whistler setting her up to be beaten and incarcerated stirred up a whirlwind of rage and hatred inside of her.

To Lucky, it felt like he was describing himself. A mastermind.

The meeting concluded with the majority siding with the twins. Both Scott and Layla agreed that Deuce was behind their kids' murders. No one else. Scott was convinced. But now there was a change of plans.

"I want Deuce brought to me. Alive."

Maxine slid into the bath water, letting the steam consume her naked frame. She exhaled and closed her eyes, resting her back against the porcelain. She blocked out everything around her. It had been so long since she'd had a bath, she'd forgotten what it felt like to be tranquil. In prison, there was no such thing as relaxation. It was only a quick shower, then keep things moving. There was little comfort in confinement.

She had been home for a week now, and she was trying to adjust to life outside of prison. She still felt institutionalized—waking up at dawn and making her bed a certain way. When she ate, she covered her plate, as if protecting it from others.

Her reunion with her mother was comforting, but it was also awkward. The moment she stepped foot into her mother's home, it hit her how much time had passed. Her mother was happy to see her, and Maxine couldn't help but tear up. She hugged her mom tightly, and vice versa. The two women were almost afraid to let each other ago. Her mother was in tears too. Her daughter was finally home, and finally in her arms.

Her mother had aged though, her hair graying and thinning. She had sad eyes, and her body seemed fragile. She was thin, dressed in a floral housecoat. The death of Maxine's father and the incarceration of her only child weighed heavily on the woman, and it was painful. So much had been taken from her, it made her a different person. And it showed. She was alive, but she didn't seem too lively.

It broke Maxine's heart to see that her mother wasn't doing too well. She moved around slowly, and sometimes she needed a cane to get around. She had high blood pressure and diabetes. Life hadn't been kind to her. She was in her late sixties and doing more existing than living.

The house was clean, but everything looked retro and outdated. Her mother had not kept up with the times, so there were no modern amenities. She had the same TV from twenty-something years ago, if that was possible. The living room wall was inundated with pictures of family, mostly of Maxine and her father during happier times. The furniture was antique, and the place smelled like moth balls. Despite all that, for Maxine, there was no place like home.

Maxine was staying in her old room, and it was just as she'd left it so many years ago. She guessed they held on to the idea that she would be coming home soon, and keeping it the same gave them hope. The night of her arrival, it felt great to sink into her bed and stare at her surroundings. She became overwhelmed with nostalgia. Everything she looked at and everything she touched inside her room brought about some painful reminder of what she'd lost and what she'd once had. She cried over her father's death. Not attending his funeral would haunt her for the rest of her life. Prison had taken away so much, and there was no way she could get those years back.

A deep sigh escaped Maxine's lips. She lingered in the tub with her eyes closed and thought about her plan. Everything Layla had taken from her, she planned on taking right back. Revenge was her motivation—her only purpose. The thought of Layla losing everything, from her kids to her wealth, fueled Maxine's vengeance.

Miguel would be perfect with his military background. How handsome and enticing he was, with his muscular physique and dark eyes! Nadia was lucky—though being locked up so far away, she couldn't enjoy him. Thinking about him made Max slide her hand between her spread legs and penetrate herself with her index and middle fingers. She played with her clit and worked her middle, thrusting in and out. It'd been a while since she'd pleasured herself.

She sighed. Home felt welcoming. Her mother was waiting on her hand-and-foot, making grilled cheese sandwiches, homemade tomato soup, and hot cocoa for her daughter to enjoy. There was nothing better than a home-cooked meal. She'd missed her mother's cooking. Max's mother took pleasure in caring for her daughter. It gave her something to do. Max allowed it, seeing it brought her mother some joy.

Max removed herself from the bathtub and toweled off. She went into her bedroom and took her sweet time getting dressed. She was on parole, so there wasn't much for her to do right away. Her first meeting with her parole officer wasn't a friendly one. Ironically, his name was David Liberty. Her first meeting with him didn't make her feel liberated. He was rude and frank with her from the beginning.

The moment she sat across from him in his office, the vibes weren't right. David Liberty was a black male with a military background, having been in the Army. He was tall and clean shaven with cropped hair, brown eyes, and chiseled features. He looked like he worked out regularly and was dressed fittingly for his job in a white button-down shirt, black tie, and a black jacket. His credentials hung on the walls of his neat and organized office. He had a bachelor's degree in criminal justice from John Jay and ten years on the job as a parole officer. He was a stickler for law and order. Max suspected that maybe he suffered from just a touch of OCD.

Immediately, he made her take a drug test, which she passed with flying colors.

Then he broke down the rules of her parole. "First off, a job—you need to find one," he said sharply.

Max nodded.

"I see you live with your mother."

She nodded.

"Once a week, every Wednesday morning, you report to me. You stay clean, honest, and focused on me at all times, and it will keep you out of prison. Find yourself a decent job; make an honest pay for once. You stay away from old friends and old habits. You have a curfew, which is ten o' clock. You miss it, and you'll be violated. Do you understand me?"

Max nodded.

"I do random checkups on all my parolees. That means I can show up anywhere at any time, from your place of employment to your residence. If you live with family, they don't need to give me a hard time. It's your ass on the line, not theirs or mine. Do you understand me?"

Max nodded.

"I'm not the one to play with. You fuck up, and I'll violate your ass faster than you can fart. Do you understand me?"

Max did, absolutely. He would be a pain in her ass and an asshole. She knew she needed to watch her step in every way since he would be like a magnifying glass up her ass.

Parole was the last thing on Max's mind as she lingered in her bedroom, staring out the window and watching life happen on the block. There were no neighbors she recognized. They'd either moved away or were dead.

She remembered Ms. White and her assortment of baked goods she used to share with her family. Ms. White made the best cakes, cupcakes, and cookies in the city. She could have started her own bakery if she'd wanted to, but Ms. White was content with sharing her delicious goodies with her neighbors and seeing the joy on their faces when they took a bite. Max used to crave Ms. White's cakes when she was young.

Then there was Timmy and his little sister that lived across the street from her. Timmy was four years her junior, and he had the deepest crush on Max. Every day he saw her, he smiled and flirted with her. He was a playboy in training. He wasn't scared to ask her out on dates, although Max always turned him down. He was cute, and she was flattered, but Timmy was a little boy back then. She knew he was a grown man now. She wondered, if she saw him again, would she recognize him, and would he recognize her?

Then there were the Hendersons, a newlywed couple two doors down. Max thought the husband was too fine. He reminded her of Denzel Washington. He was tall, dark, and so suave. He was always dressed neatly, well groomed, and drove a black Lexus. Mr. Henderson was Max's first real crush, and she envied Mrs. Henderson for marrying such a hunk of a man. She wondered, after so many years, were they still together, or were they happily divorced? Did they have any children? Looking at the Hendersons' seemingly perfect life made Max want to start her own family back then.

The knock on the door interrupted her nostalgic moment.

"Come in," she said.

The door opened, and her mother eased herself into the room. Her mother's smile made her smile. "Hey, sweetie, can you make a run to the store for me and grab a few things?"

"Yeah, sure." Max removed herself from the window. She needed some fresh air anyway. She grabbed her shoes and a shirt and asked, "What you need, Ma?"

"I'm cooking you something special tonight." She handed Max a small list and a fifty-dollar bill.

"Ma, you did so much for me already. You don't have to do that."

"Nonsense. I want you to feel at home and welcome. They took you away from me for over twenty years. And I want you to eat good and healthy. I know they weren't feeding you properly in that place. You need to eat, and you need to enjoy your home." Her mother almost looked tearful. "And take the cart with you."

Max smiled. She felt like she'd gained twenty-five pounds in one week. With Max home, the food was going quickly, and although her mother didn't mention it, Max knew that money was tight. Fifty dollars to buy food was too much, but her mother would not take it back. Max knew she had to contribute to the household somehow, and soon. Her mother was living on her social security check and not much else. High medical bills from her husband had wiped out their savings account, and his funeral took the rest. Still, her mother's home was paid in full, so there was no mortgage to worry about, only the yearly taxes.

Maxine walked out the door and inhaled the fresh air. It was a sunny and beautiful day. The block was quiet and the traffic average. Pathmark was a few blocks from her home. The walk felt needed. Since she'd been home, she'd kept herself locked in her bedroom and thought a lot. Even from Brooklyn, Max's pull inside the prison was still strong. She had only to keep money flowing into her enforcer's commissary to keep Nadia safe.

She thought about Miguel and was tempted to call him for personal reasons, but he wasn't interested in her. Miguel had made it clear to her that she was in his life only for business and that he completely loved Nadia.

Since Max been home, she thought about sex a lot. Twenty years of not getting any made her feel like she was a volcano ready to explode. Her body felt ready to ooze with desire. Her naughty little episode in the bathtub had stirred up some long-forgotten feelings. Max needed some sexual gratification.

Pathmark was teeming with shoppers. So many people moving about effortlessly overwhelmed Max slightly. Twenty years of captivity had her fucked up for a moment. She stood at the entrance to the store and looked around with apprehension. She clenched her hands. Her feet stood rooted to the floor, she looked like a statue, feeling lost and out of place.

Adjusting to everyday life wasn't as easy as she thought it would be. Everyone had a smartphone in their hands, and with their Bluetooth headphones, appeared to be talking to themselves. There were new gadgets to help folks shop, and more cameras to watch shoppers' every move. Even security at the store looked threatening to her. The world seemed so much faster, and people seemed more rude than she remembered.

Max took a deep breath and unclenched her fists. She had to get herself together. She couldn't fold in on herself and look weak. Another exhale, and she moved. She removed a shopping cart from the selected area and traveled deeper into the store. She joined in with the other shoppers and executed her mother's list, going down aisle after aisle, collecting the items.

She spent twenty-five minutes shopping for her mother. The shopping cart was cluttered with items. Max traveled throughout the entire store and noticed the new food created, and everything cost so much more. She saw why her mother was struggling.

Max did the numbers in her head while she waited in the checkout line. She was hoping she didn't go overboard with the shopping. Her mother had given her fifty dollars, and it would be embarrassing if she didn't have enough. Pricing things silently, she figured the total cost, included taxes, would be $47.98.

The checkout clerk rang up her items, and the total for everything was $48.97. Max was close. Max was always smart. It was just too bad that her talents had been wasted in prison. She handed the young woman the fifty-dollar bill and took her change.

As Max was ready to depart with her groceries in her shopping cart, someone quickly caught her attention. She noticed a woman staring at her from three lines over. *Why is this bitch staring at me so intensely?* She could feel the tension, knowing this bitch with four kids had something against her. She grabbed her things and made for the exit, refusing to turn around. She needed no trouble. She just wanted to go home.

Max exited the store, and before she could step farther away from the supermarket, she heard someone shout out, "They fuckin' let you out!"

Max felt the drama coming her way. She didn't want to turn around, but she did anyway. The woman with the four dusty-looking children came charging out of the supermarket like she was on a mission. She was in her late thirties and looked to be on hard times; she had "welfare mama" written all over her. Her oldest child was a boy of about twelve years old. The woman recognized Max immediately, but Max couldn't figure out who she was.

"I can't believe this shit! How the fuck you outta jail?" she yelled again, creating unwanted attention outside of the supermarket.

When the woman came closer, Max finally recognized her. *Denise! Sandy's little sister.* She'd grown into a full adult now with a lot of tits and ass, and she looked more ghetto than her deceased sister ever did.

Denise held a two-year-old boy with nappy hair to her hip and cursed Max up and down crazily.

"I don't want any trouble," Max replied softly.

"Fuck that! How the fuck you get out? They ain't tell us you were gettin' the fuck out! You dat bitch dat killed my sister and you up in here buyin' milk an' shit?" Denise heatedly accosted Max. She was flanked by her children, who stared at Max confusedly.

Max tried to ignore the escalating confrontation. The last thing she needed was trouble. It'd only been a week since she'd come home. She attempted to walk away. She put her eyes to the ground and wanted to skirt past the angry troublemaker, but it wasn't happening so easily.

Although twenty years had gone by, Denise still held on to resentment and hatred. She pushed Max.

Max looked at her and said, "Look, I don't want any trouble from you. I did my time. I just want to be left alone."

"Left alone?" Denise yelled. "Fuck you, bitch!"

Denise thought Max was still Maxine; that soft, timid bitch that everyone used to fuck with and prey on, especially her sister. Denise got it into her mind she could take her sister's place and continue bullying Max.

Max clenched her fists. She saw a peaceful solution with Denise wasn't happening.

A small crowd eyed the quarrel between them.

Denise put her baby down on the ground and swung at Max. It was a broad and sloppy attack, and Max easily sidestepped and countered with her tightened fist smashing into Denise's face. It was a hard blow, which Denise didn't see coming. It dazed her, but she didn't go down.

Max struck her again. This time her knuckles crashed into Denise's nose. The two females took a huge handful of each other's clothing and attempted to wrestle the other to the ground. Max hit her again in the chest and then her side. She then went for Denise's long weave and grabbed it tightly, steering her in whatever direction she commanded. She swung Denise around by her hair and sent the ghetto mama crashing to the ground hard, some of her weave coming out in the process. Blood flowed from Denise's broken nose.

More of a crowd gathered to watch the fight between the two women.

Max angled her knee into the air, and her foot went crashing down against Denise's torso. She repeated the stomping action several times, preventing Denise from rising to her feet. She'd released that prison rage outside in public. "I told you, don't fuck with me, bitch!" Max screamed out.

Denise's kids desperately tried to aid their mama. The twelve-year-old attacked Max with his small punches, shouting, "Get off my mama!"

Max pushed him off, and he went tumbling to the ground and landed on his ass. Denise's two younger children and the baby were crying.

Some people in the crowd were filming the fight with their smartphones.

One of them yelled out, "World Star! World Star!"

It was entertainment for them. None of them had any idea that it was a twenty-year-old beef.

Seeing Denise beaten and bloody beneath her, Max finally came back to her senses. *Oh shit!* The fight would put her in violation of her parole. She quickly collected her cart and hurried away from the scene.

Max sat teary-eyed in the living room with deep worries. She didn't want to go back to prison. How would she break the news to her mother? Her jeans and shirt were neatly pressed, her sneakers were tied, and her hair had been braided neatly. Max did this for four consecutive days until she was finally convinced that Denise didn't go to the cops to press charges.

No one came looking for her. There were no hard knocks at the door, and her parole officer didn't mention the fight. Max knew she had to be more careful. She didn't want to risk her freedom and go back to jail, especially over some bullshit.

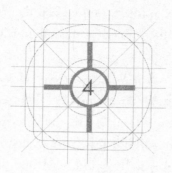

It was a balmy August night with a full moon in the sky, and the streets of Wilmington, Delaware were bustling with people and traffic. It was a party night for some folks and a business night for others. The dealers were making money hand over fist. The fiends moved about the avenues and streets in search of their next high. The new product in the city was the talk of the town. The West organization had flooded the city with high-quality merchandise, and the people couldn't get enough.

It seemed like DMC (Deuces Money Crew) was old news, and the West organization was the new power in the city. Deuce had been MIA for weeks now. The streets were talking, saying Deuce and his crew went into hiding with their tails between their legs once the bigger, badder wolves came into town. Even Detective Jones switched sides. Whatever once belonged to Deuce was now part of the West organization.

The dealers from Scott's empire sold heroin and cocaine in the streets like brokers sold stocks and bonds on Wall Street. Through word-of-mouth marketing, their product moved quickly, and the money came in with little effort. Everyone was getting rich; it felt like the 1980s again. Corruption was thick in the city, so police turned their heads from the illicit drug activity, receiving a sizable piece of the profit. Everything was at the drug dealers' and dirty cops' beck and call—money, drugs, pussy, and power. Delaware became a haven for those in the game, turning Lucky's vision into a goldmine.

N. Spruce Street was a heavy drug area where the fiends paraded up and down the street like it was their right to do so. The young dealers frequented the corners and the drug houses with little to no harassment from law enforcement. As long as the violence was down and there were no murders, everyone could live happily ever after. The lieutenants in Scott's organization moved around the city like they were kings. They had access to everything—VIP in the clubs, more money than they could count, beautiful women who would do anything for them, and the best clothes and cars.

For weeks now, the business had been running smoothly with no interference from anyone or anything. With Deuce and his crew gone, there was no more drug war.

Two young lieutenants, Martino and Crown, came to a stop in front of the row house on Spruce Street. Crown was behind the wheel of a black E-Class Benz sitting on 20-inch chrome rims. It was a beauty of a car, with tinted windows and leather seats. Martino exited the passenger seat. The man was tall and dressed in stylish jeans and a T-shirt, his jewelry gleaming like he was Mr. T. He walked toward the old row house with authority, the 9mm tucked snugly and subtly in his waistband. The block and the city were theirs.

While Crown sat in the Benz, Martino stepped toward the stash house. He was there to collect money. At the door, he was greeted by two armed soldiers standing in the foyer, there to guard and protect the product and the money. There was a verbal exchange, and Martino traveled farther into the row house to take care of business.

Crown lit a cigarette and eyed the activity on the block. Everything appeared to be normal and routine. Neighbors talked and laughed in front of their homes, and addicts loomed from darkening corners of the block, looking for their high for the night. Crown kept his gun close on his lap as he inhaled the nicotine.

Abruptly, Crown felt the barrel of a Glock 19 against his temple and the hammer cock. And the last thing he heard was, "You thought we forgot, muthafucka! Deuce is back!"

Boom!

The blast sent Crown's brains flying all over the dashboard and the deluxe interior. His body slumped in the front seat, twisted from the bullet and the payback.

The shooters weren't finished. They fired more bullets into his dead body. *Boom! Boom! Boom!*

The gunfire alerted the two soldiers standing in the foyer. They exploded from the building, guns drawn, but they were quickly met with death, as the gunfire from two Uzis riddled their bodies with bullets and sprayed their blood across the concrete.

The intense racket sent neighbors and fiends fleeing for safety in the opposite direction.

"What the fuck!" Martino exclaimed, as he pulled his pistol from his waistband. There was no doubt the stash house was under attack. He braced himself for a gunfight with the other remaining workers in the money room.

The two young workers panicked. They weren't shooters; they were just there to count money and handle the product.

Martino crouched low with his gun in hand and cautiously peeked around the corner. He saw nothing. The hallway was long and dim. He looked at the workers and asked, "Y'all niggas carrying?"

"No!" they replied, apprehension in their voices.

Martino needed to think. They were coming for the money he'd come to pick up, and the little product they had in the room. The re-up was in a few days. Once again, he carefully looked around the corner, down the hallway leading to the exit. Still, he saw nothing. He couldn't linger inside the room forever. He had to deal with the police coming and the shooters lying in wait for him to pop his head out of his hole like whack-a-mole. Time was critical.

"Muthafuckas, come get some!" he yelled out. For good measure, he fired his gun crazily, letting bullets fly down the dim hallway, not knowing what he was shooting at.

Waiting to be confronted by the enemy was the scary part. Martino didn't know how many of them there were.

Then it came rapidly. The shooters didn't intend to infiltrate the building. In fact, they had something more sinister planned.

Martino and the two workers were suddenly blinded by flames that burst from everywhere. The fire quickly grew heavier and heavier. They were trapped inside. Martino's eyes widened with fear. He staggered backward as far as his legs could take him, and then he collapsed on his behind. Beads of sweat dripped from his forehead as the fire spread and the temperature inside the room rose rapidly. It sounded like hot, crackling wind was erupting inside the chamber. Smoke engulfed the area, making it impossible to see and harder for them to breathe.

For the three souls inside, there was no escape. Quickly, the fire consumed the room, and the black smoke crippled their lungs with soot. They were swallowed up by the bright orange flames until there was nothing left. Every last man was dead.

Watching the building burn from a block away was Deuce, who sat in the passenger seat of a green Durango. He was smoking a cigarette and smiling. It was a direct attack on the West organization. Deuce didn't care about the money or product inside the building. He cared about making a statement to those trying to take away what he'd built through hard work, intimidation, and murder. Wilmington was his city.

"That's a beautiful, thing, Jimmy," Deuce said.

"It is," Jimmy replied.

"Muthafuckas think they can come at me and it would be easy—like I was going to bow down and let them have it all without a fight. They must be fuckin' crazy."

Their eyes were fixed on the row house being attacked by angry flames that wiped out its structure. The intense fire had devoured everything, and the billowing smoke stretched far into the dark sky and could be seen for miles. Sirens from fire trucks and police cars blared in the distance.

"We're done here," Deuce said. "Let's go."

Jimmy started the Durango and put it into drive. He did a quick U-turn on the block and drove off calmly, passing the first screaming fire truck arriving on the scene, followed by several police cars.

Deuce took safety and residence at an old mechanic shop on Golden Avenue. The front yard was cluttered with old cars and junk. It was a sizable building, and it was low-key. It was unused and had been closed for three years. Deuce owned the property, but it couldn't be traced back to him because of a straw buyer. The area was industrial, cluttered with a few scaffolding businesses, warehouses, junkyards, empty lots, and old buildings. The garage had a large backroom where he could conduct business and torture people.

Deuce sat at the shaky table in the windowless backroom as Jimmy produced the information and pictures he'd asked for. Jimmy was the best for gathering information and doing surveillance. Displayed on the table were several glossy 8x10 pictures of Scott and his family, and several of his lieutenants in Delaware.

Deuce took a pull from the cigarette between his lips. He picked up the photo of Scott and glared at it. "This old muthafucka still trying to run with the wolves, huh? He should have been retired from this game."

"He still wants the glory," Jimmy said.

"I'm gonna give him some glory, all right—I'm gonna put everything he loves into the fuckin' ground."

The elusive Deuce had finally resurfaced stronger and meaner than ever. He was more than ready to rebuild his empire and exact revenge. He had a new crew of killers he'd handpicked himself. They considered themselves the best at murder for hire, and their pedigree spoke for itself. His killers had put in work, some of which had even made the front page and the evening news.

Deuce had done his homework on the infamous drug kingpin who had taken over his territory. Word on the street was that Scott West was old-school, damn near fifty years old (which was exaggerated), and still in the drug game. He could have gone entirely legit a decade ago, but he kept getting his hands dirty. The man was controlling, and his children and his wife co-ran his organization. They had more money than anyone could count, and they had more legit companies than a black man could be expected to have. So why continue operating with the streets? Why come into Delaware and take over what Deuce had built with his bloody hands? This war with the Wests became personal for Deuce. They'd killed his sister and fucked with his livelihood.

Deuce had the names he needed from Jimmy. The names were a list of a motley crew—Scott, Layla, Meyer, Bugsy, Lucky, Bonnie, Clyde, and Gotti. He saw the names of Scott's children and shook his head in disbelief. "Is this nigga serious?" he uttered to his right-hand man. "He must be one dumb muthafucka."

Deuce, who was low-key, thought it was simple-minded for Scott to name all his kids after notorious gangsters. What message was he trying to send to people, to the authorities, neighbors, and the feds? "His infatuation with dead gangsters is intriguing."

"Well, I got more news for you, Deuce." Jimmy picked up three pictures of Scott's children and said, "These three are already dead."

"Say what?"

"It seems our enemy has enemies everywhere, and they're going after his family. His youngest boy was killed in Florida a few months ago in a hit-and-run. The driver was never caught. And his fraternal twins, Bonnie and Clyde, were gunned down in Harlem not too long ago."

"Wow! I see this nigga done stirred up a hornet's nest somewhere, and now they're coming out to sting his ass. Maybe all we have to do is sit back and wait."

Jimmy laughed. "Maybe."

"If the nigga can't even protect his own fuckin' family, why the fuck is he comin' after my shit? And this is the notorious muthafucka I'm supposed to watch out for? He won't see me coming at all for his head. I'm gonna sting his ass too."

"I'm ready. Let's play," Jimmy declared.

Deuce pondered his next move as he extinguished his cigarette. He was going after Scott and his organization with everything he had. The West team wouldn't see him coming. He had nothing to lose and could hide in broad daylight and disappear in the blink of an eye. The reason he was so dangerous was because he had no attachments—no wife, no main bitch, and no kids. With the murder of his sister, Deuce's enemies now had nothing to barter with. If the heat was around the corner, he could be gone in less than sixty seconds. He was always mobile and never stayed at one place for too long, and he didn't invest in large homes or real estate. Whatever he owned, it was through straw purchases, so there was nothing in his name that could link back to him and lead to a federal investigation.

Deuce felt he had no weakness, whereas Scott had too many. Scott had too many foundations—real estate in New York and in Florida, legit businesses, and most critical, he had a wife and kids. Deuce would see those foundations crumble. He wanted to see the man's empire burn to the ground.

5

Mandarin Oriental was the Cadillac of spa treatment in Manhattan. It was a world-renowned spa inside the soaring five-star luxury hotel with a restaurant and a bird's-eye view of the city. It was an oasis of relaxation and rejuvenation high above Manhattan. Mother and daughter, Layla and Lucky, both dressed in terrycloth robes, were receiving the best treatment that money could buy.

Layla sat back in the luxury massage leather chair, thoroughly enjoying the spa treatment. The pampering was relaxing and therapeutic, and having Lucky by her side enjoying the same treatment was a needed blessing. Mother-and-daughter time was rare, especially after everything that had happened lately. Their treatment didn't come cheap. At $1,200 per foot, the women received the total package from the Koreans, from soaking their feet in fresh spring water and emu oil, to letting little fish nibble away at their dead skin. Layla and Lucky sat back and sipped on champagne while the Koreans worked magic on their feet.

"They're making our feet look brand-new," Lucky said.

Layla smiled. "Like baby feet."

After everything they'd been through, it would be beyond tragic if Layla lost another child, especially the one daughter she had left. Those monsters had barely left her alive.

So far, Scott and his men weren't able to hunt down the animals responsible for the deaths of their children and Lucky's assault. Their organization was supposed to be feared and respected, but now they were looking weak and vulnerable.

Layla looked at her daughter and knew she would never be the same. The slight disfigurement to her eye made her insecure. She looked like she had been the victim of an acute stroke, with the right side of her face looking paralyzed. Lucky was still a lovely-looking woman, but she was no longer the flawless beauty she once was.

Layla downed the champagne and demanded more. There was a server close by to fulfill their needs. She asked, and they obliged. Champagne, caviar, snacks, and even hookah were all there for them to enjoy.

Lucky asked Layla out of the blue, "Do you trust Whistler?"

Layla was surprised by the sudden question. "Why did you ask that? Whistler is family, Lucky."

"He's smart, Mother. Very intelligent. And for him to be so smart, why's he been working under Daddy for so many years? I mean, he could have broken away from the organization and started his own thing."

"It's called loyalty, Lucky, something Whistler knows everything about. He and your father have been through hell and back together, and they respect each other. Plus, Whistler is smart enough to know that breaking away from the organization would create a war between them."

Lucky appeared to be in deep thought about something.

Layla quickly picked up on her daughter's serious demeanor. "Is there something that you ain't telling me?"

"I'm just talking, that's all."

More champagne came, and Layla didn't waste any time enjoying it.

The pedicure treatment felt rewarding; it was the perfect remedy for stress. There was more girl talk between the two. The day was turning out to be perfect. Perfect days felt rare after the attacks on the family. But knowing there was still a threat out there, security was close by, and Layla herself had a .380 concealed in her stylish purse.

"Move to Florida with me, Lucky," Layla suggested.

"My life is here," Lucky replied.

"I've built a beautiful home for you."

"Rent it. I'm not interested in Florida. Really, all they got down there is old people and hurricanes."

Layla sighed. "You have always been stubborn, Lucky."

"You taught me to be independent and tough. And I got a good thing going with Daddy. He don't treat me like I'm a little girl; he respects me like an equal."

Layla didn't want to talk about Scott. She had her doubts about him, about their marriage, and about his ability to protect their family. Losing three children in such a short time would be something she would never get over.

The ladies continued their day together, looking and feeling like beauty queens from the expensive spa treatments. They had dinner at the exclusive Eleven Madison Park on Madison Avenue. They were seated inside the private two balcony-level dining room overlooking the main dining room that offered a spectacular view of Madison Square Park through the floor-to-ceiling windows. The large crystal chandelier glimmered with opulence, and the diners all enjoyed five-star meals prepared by some of the finest gourmet chefs in the city.

Layla downed more champagne and feasted on a delicious meal. Despite some minor setbacks, this was a good life. She could never go back to the way she used to live—nickel-and-dime hustling in Brooklyn and trying to survive. Though their marriage was strained, hooking up with Scott was one of the best decisions she'd made. Fucking Maxine over was a chess move on her part. Besides, Maxine didn't know how to handle a man like Scott. Layla always felt she was the right woman for him.

She wanted to continue a conversation with her daughter, but Lucky was soon distracted by her cell phone. She was texting someone. Lucky did grown-people things and moved meth for her father, but she was still a teenager at heart, being eighteen years old.

"You have a new boyfriend?" Layla asked.

Lucky barely looked up at her mother and replied, "It's business."

Layla thought dinner with Lucky wasn't as much fun as the spa. While Lucky was on her smartphone, Layla's phone buzzed. She didn't know the number calling, but she didn't hesitate to answer it. Maybe it was important.

"Hello?"

"Layla, hey, it's me, Maxine."

Layla was stunned to hear Maxine's voice. "Maxine, what's up? You need something?" Layla asked, nonchalant about the call.

"I'm home!" Maxine proudly announced.

What? Home? Layla was taken aback by the sudden news. "How you home?"

"Paroled," Maxine said.

It wasn't welcome news to Layla. It was the last thing she expected to hear from Maxine. "Where are you?" she asked.

"I'm at my mother's."

"How long you been home?"

"A few weeks now."

Layla acted like she was happy to hear from Maxine. "Maxine, I can't wait to see you. Oh my God, you're home! We need to link up and catch up on lost time."

"That's what I'm calling you about. When can we talk?"

"Today. I'll come by."

"I'll be here. Parole is strict, and my movement is limited."

The call ended, leaving Layla with a bad taste in her mouth.

Lucky finally looked up from her smartphone. She noticed her mother's reaction. "Who was that on the phone?"

"Your auntie's home."

Those words meant nothing to Lucky. She hated when her mother called Maxine her auntie. How could she care for someone that she'd never met? Yes, she'd heard the stories about how Maxine took the fall for her mother, kept her mouth shut, and did the years. Maxine wasn't a snitch—hooray! Lucky wasn't even born yet. It was a long time ago, and she didn't care for her mother's dinosaur stories.

Layla couldn't wrap her head around Maxine finally being a free woman. She thought it would be a few more years before Maxine was brought before the parole board. Why hadn't Layla been contacted about it? She had connections everywhere, and yet this flew right over her head.

She was upset. Now wasn't the right time for Maxine to be out of prison, especially with things shaky between Scott and her. Layla wanted her life to be perfect when Maxine came home. She expected all of her family to be alive and residing in the sprawling, lavish Florida compound she'd built, and her marriage with Scott would be tighter than ever. She wanted to rub their relationship in Maxine's face. The pictures she had sent of her family, her wealth, and the vacations they took was only the start. She couldn't wait for Maxine to see how her life had turned out in the flesh.

But now things were different. She and her family were knee deep in one crisis after another and under siege from a maniacal mastermind. Maxine would see the tragedy unfold, and the last thing Layla wanted Maxine to see was her suffering and her pain.

Having her past up close in her inner circle on a consistent basis wasn't something Layla wanted to undertake. But she knew she had to see Maxine face to face and get this shit over with.

It was late in the evening when the black Rolls-Royce Phantom slowly turned the corner onto Blake Avenue. The streets were swamped with people gawking at the sleek chariot moving through their neighborhood. A few neighbors peeked out of their windows at the car and assumed it was a famous rapper visiting his old block to show off and give back.

Traveling behind the Rolls-Royce were a black Tahoe and a black Range Rover. Armed goons were in both trucks. All three vehicles were bulletproof.

Layla and Lucky were comforted by the rich, dark interior of the Phantom with reclining seats. Lucky stared out the window and disapproved of the area. She had other places to be than the slums of Brooklyn, but her mother was adamant about seeing Maxine.

The Rolls-Royce Phantom stopped in front of Maxine's home, a meager-looking place in Lucky's eyes.

A small crowd gathered on the block to observe the occupants of the vehicle. Many anticipated that it was a celebrity about to exit the magnificent vehicle, so they were ready to snap pictures and record with their smartphones. But when the suicide doors opened and Layla and Lucky stepped out onto the pavement, many were puzzled, asking, "Who they?"

No one had a clue who these two ladies were, both dressed to the nines and escorted by armed security. Whoever they were, they were rich, if not famous.

Layla strutted toward Maxine's home dressed in an exclusive Christian Siriano dress that accentuated her curves, and sporting a pair of diamond-studded Giuseppe Zanotti gladiator heels. Her jewelry gleamed, and her long, caramel hair was flawless. Lucky looked extraordinary too. She was younger and a lot curvier in a yellow dress by Christian Dior, and her long hair was styled over her droopy eye. Her jewelry and body outshined her flaw.

Maxine saw them coming from her bedroom window. She was shocked that Layla actually showed up, that she kept her word. She saw the extravagant caravan displayed on her block and shook her head in disapproval, knowing it was all to show and prove that Layla's life was happier and more fulfilled than hers. She chuckled at it and then pulled herself from the bedroom window and went downstairs to greet her "friend."

The door opened, and Layla was all smiles, looking like she belonged on the front page of *Glamour* magazine.

"Maxine, it's so good to see you again," Layla said joyfully, opening her arms and pulling Maxine into a warm hug.

Reluctantly, Maxine hugged her back and greeted her in a friendly way.

The show was about to start between them, each woman feigning a warm reception when, in reality, they had contempt for each other.

As they pulled away from each other, Layla looked Maxine up and down and said, "You look . . . you seem interesting, Maxine." She eyed the cornrows and worn clothing.

"And you look like a million bucks, Layla. Life must be good, huh?" Maxine countered wistfully.

"I can't complain."

"I know you can't."

"It must feel good to be back home."

"It is. How's married life?"

"Happy," Layla lied.

Maxine knew the bitch was unhappy about her kids and everything else going on, but Layla concealed her grief with money and things. She wasn't fooling Maxine, though.

Finally, Layla introduced Lucky to her friend. "This is my daughter, Lucky. Lucky, say hi to your auntie."

Lucky not only looked like a young Layla but also reminded Maxine of her mother. She had that same brash attitude as Layla.

Lucky was in no mood to be introduced to a woman she didn't know and didn't want to know. *Auntie.* She hated how her mother easily flung out that word, like it meant something to her. She looked at the dyke-looking bitch with the tore-up hair and Goodwill outfit, and she wanted to get away from her quickly. They weren't related, so she wasn't going to call Maxine her aunt. The look on Lucky's face said it all.

"She ain't my fuckin' aunt," Lucky blurted out.

Maxine chuckled at the rude comment. She took no offense to it. "A spitting image of you," she uttered.

"She can be a handful," Layla said.

"I bet she can."

Lucky frowned at Maxine. The woman was a fool for doing hard time for her mother, a lengthy incarceration that took away over half of her life.

"We're not staying long, right?" Lucky asked.

"Lucky, be quiet," Layla said.

"I got business to take care of and someplace to be, and she's your friend, not mine."

Maxine was delighted to know she was the one responsible for Lucky's brutal night with Wacka. The things that maniac and his friend did to her, she could only imagine. She wished there was a video for her to watch, something she could gloat over.

Layla and Lucky stepped farther into the home, and Lucky immediately turned her nose up at the sad décor. Too old and too cramped for her comfort; immediately she wanted to leave and go sit in the car.

"This where you live? Prison might have been an upgrade for you." Lucky chuckled. "It looks like *Sanford and Son* in here."

Maxine frowned. She didn't like how Lucky disrespected her mother's place. It was one thing to disrespect her, but when someone talked shit about her mom and her home—the home she grew up in—it rubbed her the wrong way. Lucky was only alive because Maxine didn't want her dead yet. It was a decision she was regretting. She now wished she had killed Lucky when she had the chance. But Maxine kept her cool.

"Home will always be home, no matter where I go. I'm grateful, and I'm happy to be here. How's the family?" Maxine asked calmly, looking at Layla, who didn't correct her daughter's rudeness and allowed the disrespect to continue.

"We okay."

"After everything you've been through, Layla, I can only imagine the horror. My heart goes out to you. I don't know how you sleep at nights, knowing everything you and your daughter's been through."

"Scott is handling everything. It's what my husband does best, handle things," Layla replied matter-of-factly.

"Yes, he knows how to handle things. Like how he handled my arrest and my murder trial."

"It was a long time ago."

"Yes, it was."

"I hope you're over it, Maxine," Layla said with unease. "Let bygones be bygones."

"How can I dwell on the past when my best friend is suffering in the present? To lose three children—to have them viciously taken from you in such cruel ways, is karma."

"Say what now?"

"You know, karma."

"Actually I don't know. Are you saying this is my fault?"

"Isn't that what you're thinking?"

"Why the fuck would I think that bullshit, Maxine?"

"Layla, you were always too hard on yourself. I thought you would somehow blame yourself, and as your best friend, I am here to tell you that it's not your fault. So don't go thinking this is karma," Maxine said, flipping the script.

"Hell no, it ain't my fault."

"That's what I said."

Neither Layla nor Lucky knew what had just happened.

"So how does it feel to have twenty-two long years of your life gone?"

"I'm home now, Layla. If it wasn't for you, I don't know how I would have survived in there. You looked out for me when you didn't have to."

"It's what friends do, Maxine."

Over the years, Layla had continually bragged to her kids about killing their father's first baby mama with her bare hands and making Maxine take the fall for it. Lucky knew the story well, and she respected her mother's doggedness and coldness, and she aspired to become just as coldhearted. And now looking at Maxine in person, she understood why it was so easy to have the girl take the murder rap for her. She appeared weak and stupid for her age. Lucky knew she would have done the same thing her mother had done.

As the girls continued to converse, Maxine's elderly mother entered the living room. Her mother remembered Layla. She never liked the girl and always thought she was trouble.

"Why is she here in my living room?" Maxine's mother asked harshly.

"She just came to say hello, Mom."

"I don't want that woman in my house. She ruined your life, she and that evil boyfriend of yours."

"Mom, I can handle things. Go upstairs and get some rest."

Maxine's mom glared at Layla and Lucky. Before she went upstairs, she said to Layla, "God doesn't like ugly, and you have plenty of ugly inside of you, Layla. You're a wicked person, and you reap what you sow!"

Layla frowned.

Lucky wanted to smack the old woman upside her head. No one talked to her mother like that; she didn't care how old the bitch was.

Once Maxine's mother was upstairs, Lucky said to Maxine, "You need to control that old slut."

Maxine cut her eyes at Lucky. "Little girl, you need to watch your mouth." Maxine noticed the drooping eye and some other minor imperfections on the young girl, and subtly admired the handiwork of the thugs she'd hired.

Lucky was ready to attack Maxine, but Layla kept her daughter on a tight leash. There would be no violence toward her friend.

"Layla, you and I, we need to have a talk. It's why I called you," Maxine said calmly.

Layla didn't plan on staying long, and Maxine wanted to ask her about the money and the house she'd continually promised her while she was locked down.

Maxine had it all worked out. If Layla purchased her a nice home, free from any mortgage, Maxine would immediately move her mother into it and sell her old home and give her mother the needed proceeds. Maxine only wanted to see her sick mother live out her golden years in peace and comfort, not hardship and worry. She wanted her mother to live and to travel, maybe take a needed cruise or trip to Europe.

Before Maxine could talk to Layla privately, Lucky lost her cool. Her insecurity kicked in, and she yelled at Maxine, "Bitch, why do you keep lookin' at my face?" before storming out of the house.

Maxine fumed at the lack of respect this bitch had for anyone. She made up her mind there and then. She didn't want Lucky dead, not soon anyway. She had something else planned for her. The little spoiled bitch needed to be stripped of everything. The sins of the mother would be passed down to the daughter. Maxine wanted the foul-mouthed, disrespectful little bitch to spend the rest of her life in prison with no family to visit, support, or protect her. She wanted Lucky to suffer greatly, receiving no commissary, pictures, or any communication from anyone she loved, because her family would be all dead. She wanted Lucky to rot away in prison and think about how her parents' actions led her and her siblings to their demise.

Maxine decided that her next target would be Bugsy.

Before Layla could follow Lucky out of the aging home that smelled like mothballs and old people, Maxine pulled her aside and asked for the money and house promised to her.

Layla felt disturbed by it and gave Maxine a look that could make someone's blood freeze. "Everything's mostly gone, Maxine," she said gruffly.

"Gone? You made promises to me, Layla. I gave up half my life to protect you."

"And I kept my promises by helping you survive inside. Most of the money went toward keeping you safe. Besides, things have changed, and the family has fallen on difficult times with the funerals, the properties in Florida, and this ongoing war. A lot of my money is tied up right now."

Maxine sighed. She was boiling with rage but kept her composure. She looked at Layla and just replied, "I understand."

"I do what I can, Maxine. You're my best friend, but now is not the right time."

Maxine nodded.

Layla and Lucky climbed back into the Rolls-Royce Phantom. Lucky couldn't wait to get back home and take a shower to erase the stench of the old home from her skin. The house probably had roaches and bugs. Their security detail jumped back into both SUVs, and the engines started.

Once again, the neighbors were standing outside to watch the caravan leave. They took plenty of pictures of the Rolls-Royce, a car rarely seen in their part of town.

As the vehicle pulled away from the curb, Lucky looked at her mother with inquiry and asked, "What did that bitch have to talk to you about privately?"

Layla shot a brutal look at her daughter. "It's none of your fuckin' business! You never know when to shut the fuck up, and don't know when to be seen and not fuckin' heard!"

Lucky wasn't expecting the harsh reply. Layla and Maxine seemed to talk about something personal. She wondered why her mother didn't curse out Maxine in the same fashion. Her mother didn't have to show any respect to Maxine, and she owed that bitch nothing. Who was she to them? The bitch was no one. Why did they even waste their time going to Brooklyn? Maxine did her time; now she should be happy to be back home and with her aging mother.

"I just asked a simple question, and you're all in your throwback Thursday feelings right now. Wake up. It's Friday."

Layla roared. "Didn't I tell your ass to shut the fuck up! Please and thank you!"

Lucky sat and pouted.

With Lucky finally quiet, Layla sat in silence preoccupied with a thought. Why didn't she throw Maxine some cash and the house she had promised her for years? She and Scott had more money than they could ever count.

But there was something about Maxine being back in Brooklyn that didn't sit well with Layla. It made her think about the past. She thought about how Maxine was with Scott and that she had stolen her life. She remembered Maxine and that white BMW she used to drive. It was a gift from Scottie. Maxine used to receive plenty of gifts from Scottie. She remembered the jewelry, the clothing, and how in love they seemed to be. Maxine was Scottie's first love, and Layla used to be jealous of that. It made her competitive.

Layla exhaled. She had done all she would do for Maxine. Now that she was back home, Layla felt Maxine was a definite threat to her relationship with Scott. Things were already distant between them. Though it had been over twenty years, how would Scott feel about seeing Maxine again? She didn't look the same, but Layla would not chance it. *Fuck the bitch!*

Layla downed a glass of Dom Pérignon as she lounged naked in a chaise on the large terrace, twenty-three floors up. She had a sweeping view of the illuminated city under a full moon. The top of the Empire State Building was lit up in multiple colors, glowing like a bright crayon in the sky. The view was breathtaking and picturesque, and one reason she and Scott had purchased the five-million-dollar penthouse suite on the Upper West Side.

Layla loved being naked because she felt free and had nothing to be ashamed about. At forty-something years old, her body was still shapely and incredible, thanks to personal trainers and a healthy diet. She had the money to be fit and healthy, and the resources to stay looking good at her age. Her tits were perky because of cosmetic surgery, and her stomach showed off abs because of vigorous workouts.

The sad news about her hard work to stay looking fit and healthy was, her husband took her for granted. He hadn't touched her sexually in months. She wondered if he saw something different. Was he still attracted to her? She had changed for him, but his attention seemed to be elsewhere. How many more nights could she go without having sex? She had plenty of toys and pleased herself numerous times, but there was nothing like the real thing, feeling the flesh penetrate her, thrusting in and out. Layla craved some dick, and she wanted it from her husband, but he acted like he wanted nothing to do with her.

She was too afraid to cheat because Scott was dangerous. He was a hypocrite, regularly out with his other whores, but wanting to keep her under his thumb. To Layla, it felt like Scott had thrown away the key to her pussy and wasn't trying to reopen the gate.

She poured more champagne into her glass and downed that too, and then she lit a cigarette and inhaled. She had a lot on her mind. She tried not to be stressed, but things were changing, and had changed. She removed herself from the chaise and walked toward the railing. She took another puff from the cigarette and blew smoke from her lips. Her eyes rested on the full moon above. It was such a spectacular view. The city was bustling with activity twenty-three stories below her, and the sky was clear and perfect.

She heaved another deep sigh and finished the cigarette and flicked it over the railing, not caring where it landed. She had everything she wanted and could do whatever she wanted, so why did she feel so trapped?

Her life seemed like she was in a collapsing room with no windows and no doors. There was no escape. Wherever she traveled, she had armed security with her for protection. Someone was out to get her and her family. She worried about her remaining children, and was on edge twenty-four/seven. She knew any day that call could come about another murder close to home; wickedness snatching away her children's lives.

Layla's eyes stayed fixed on the full moon above. Tired of feeling trapped, she had the urge to do something about it.

Delaware was turning into a battlefield. Bodies were piling up in Wilmington from a spate of murders. Two known drug dealers were found with fatal shots to the head in the front seat of a blue Mercedes-Benz on N. Locust Street. They were linked to the West organization. A week after that, a couple had their throats slit in the bedroom of their Quaker Hill home. Once again, the man and woman were connected to the West organization. In Baynard Village, firemen extinguished a burning car on N. Washington Street, only to find a charred body behind the steering wheel.

Deuce and his crew were coming back on their rivals. They were not only killing them off, but they were stealing kilos of cocaine and heroin from various stash houses with the help of informants, mixing it with their inferior product, and then reselling it as their own. DMC had come into the city like a thief in the night, and they were becoming angels of death and destruction. Payback was a bitch.

The local police had their hands full. Things went from quiet to chaotic in a few weeks' time. The city morgue was picking up bodies left and right. The detectives were working cases with no sleep, and the mayor was receiving the backlash for the increasing murders and violence that was crippling businesses and taking over their city. His constituents were crying out loudly, not wanting their city to become another Chicago.

Detective Jones, dressed in a wife-beater and jeans, sat on the bench in the police locker room, hunched over with his elbows pressed against his knees, his eyes glued to the floor. He was off duty and feeling despair. His holstered gun and his badge sat on the bench next to him. His locker was open with pictures of his wife and kids plastered on the inner door. He pondered as he sat still. His cell phone rang, but he ignored the call. He knew who was calling and why.

Things had been disrupted in the streets. The dealers and criminals under his protection had been swept up in war and bloodshed, and they were filled with absolute worry and alarm. News of DMC being back in town spread like wildfire, and those who had betrayed Deuce were now feeling his full wrath. Everyone was feeling the heat. Some were running scared, afraid to do business in the city. Detective Jones knew he was on Deuce's shit list. Deuce was pulling out all the stops, killing everything moving and fucking everything up.

Jones looked to his left and to his right and saw no one around. He reached into his locker and removed a small clear package containing cocaine. He sprinkled a small line between the spaces of his thumb and index finger and quickly snorted "the white girl" into his nose. He did another line, and the blast hit him nicely. He shook it off and wiped his nose clean from any white residue. With so much to deal with on the streets, drugs became his comfort. He continued to sit for a moment, thinking about his mistakes, and thinking about Deuce and his crew. He had to be cautious and think ahead. First he needed to get his family out of town and take them somewhere safe.

Jones got himself correct and put on civilian clothes. Today, he had worn his Class A's for a cop's funeral. One of theirs had been murdered last week while on duty, shot in the head by a fleeing suspect. Officer Richard Jenkins was a decent, honest cop. He was African American, had been married to his beautiful wife for fifteen years, and they had three kids together. Jones, a good friend of Jenkins', was saddened by his death.

Jones stood up and placed his holstered weapon on his right hip and tossed the badge around his neck. He closed his locker. He was ready to leave the station and head home. The station was swept up with sadness after the funeral. Officer Richard Jenkins would be missed. His killer was easily apprehended the same night, and a few boys in uniform put an ass-whipping on him that would haunt him for the rest of his life. No one killed a cop in Wilmington and got away with it.

In no mood to socialize, Jones exited the station, dodging everyone inside. He needed to get home and get his family out of town. He already had a safe place for them to stay, a three-bedroom safe house near Fredericksburg, Virginia. Not knowing what was out there, he marched toward his truck and climbed inside, his hand close to his gun, ready for the wrong person to try him. He would not hesitate to shoot first.

He started the ignition to his burgundy Cadillac Escalade and drove off. On his way home, his eyes were regularly in his mirrors, looking and observing, trying to make sure he wasn't being followed home.

Westover Hills was quiet and tranquil as usual. The affluent neighborhood was the perfect place for his family. His wife and kids deserved the best, so Jones did everything in his power to give them the best. He was affable with his children, and though he'd committed adultery on his wife with over a dozen women, he was still romantic with her.

The sun was gradually giving way to dusk and a warm evening when Jones' Escalade pulled into the driveway and he climbed out of his truck. The bedroom and living room lights were on as he approached the rear door to his nice home, indicative that his wife was probably upstairs, and the kids were most likely in the living room.

Keys in hand, gun on his hip, his badge displayed around his neck, he quietly entered the residence to greet his family. But the moment he stepped foot into the kitchen, he knew something was wrong.

They rushed him suddenly—three men from the shadows of his home. Before he could react, he felt 50 volts of electricity against the back of his neck, tightening all of his muscles at once. He instantly collapsed to the floor in intense pain. For good measure, they tasered him again and knocked him unconscious.

Detective Jones woke up in complete darkness, his body still a little rigid from the attack. Tied up with duct tape and in a cramped space with his knees bent awkwardly and his frame hunched over on its side in the fetal position, he was unable to move.

He deduced that he was in the trunk of a car. He could feel it moving. He had no idea where they were taking him. He figured it had to be Deuce and his men that attacked him in his home, though he hadn't gotten a good look at their faces.

Jones struggled and fidgeted with his restraints, but the duct tape would not loosen. They'd placed a lot of duct tape around his ankles and his wrists to keep him immobile. He thought about his family. *Oh God! Where are they? No, no, not like this.* He growled and scowled. "Fuuuuck!"

Not once did he feel the car stop or slow down, indicating to him they were on the highway. Where were they taking him? What did Deuce have planned for him? Wherever he was going, Jones knew that it would not be pleasant.

An hour or so later, he could feel the vehicle slowing down and making various turns. He was immensely concerned about his family. If they harmed his wife and kids, then he . . . *Couldn't do a damn thing about it right now.* The thought of Deuce harming his family was overwhelmingly scary. He didn't care what they did to him, but he wanted his family to be left alone.

Finally, the car stopped. Jones lay firmly bound and filled with apprehension. He heard the doors opening and closing, followed by footsteps.

The trunk opened, and several men stood over him. He glared up at them and shouted, "Y'all are fuckin' dead! You hear me? Where's my family? Where are they?"

A voice spoke out swiftly and said, "Take his ass out that fuckin' trunk."

Immediately, a pair of hands grabbed Jones and roughly pulled him out of the trunk and tossed him to the ground.

His body crashed against the dirt. *Thump!*

He looked up. The sky was dark and cluttered with stars, and the area was rural and isolated. He figured they weren't in Delaware anymore.

"You grimy muthafucka! You dare betray me," he heard Deuce say to him. The hulking gangster appeared before him with a heavy scowl and looked more menacing than ever.

Their eyes locked.

Deuce marched closer to Jones. Dressed in a black tank top that accentuated his muscled physique, dark jeans, and combat boots, he crouched near Jones and grabbed a handful of his clothing. "You let them into my fuckin' territory, when I was paying you good money to protect it. You fucked me over, huh, muthafucka!"

Jones frowned at him. "Where's my family? What did you do with them? I swear, Deuce, you touch one hair on their heads, and—"

"You'll what, nigga? Kill me? Nigga, do you look in the position to throw threats at me, muthafucka? Huh?" Deuce exclaimed.

Jones could only glare at the man.

The area, quiet and remote, was a sprawling piece of farmland in Pennsylvania, and there was no one around for miles. Two vehicles were parked nearby, and half dozen goons surrounded Jones.

Jones then noticed the deep hole in the ground. His grave had already been dug. He knew this would be his end. His fate was sealed.

"You gave her up . . . my fuckin' sister," Deuce said.

Jones didn't reply.

"My sister was the only family I had, and you gave her up to those animals. You know what they did to her?" Deuce hollered.

Jones remained silent. He was a cop, but these monsters didn't care about the badge. Deuce was determined to get payback for his sister.

"Pick him up," Deuce ordered his goons.

Two men grabbed Jones by his arms and lifted him to his feet. They dragged him to the hole in the ground. It would be his tomb.

"You know what will happen to you if you kill me, Deuce," Jones spoke aggressively.

Deuce looked at him intensely and replied, "You care about your family, don't you? You love them like I loved my sister." He nodded to one of his henchmen, who pivoted and walked toward the black Lexus IS300. The trunk opened, and he removed something from it.

When Jones swiveled his head in the direction and saw his beautiful wife in her panties and bra being removed from the trunk, he screamed out, "Get the fuck off her! Noooo!"

Immediately, Jones attempted to help her. He didn't care about his restraints or how many men surrounded him. But he wasn't going anywhere, tied the way he was.

Deuce quickly brandished a gun, aimed it at Jones' legs, and fired.

Bang! Bang!

Both bullets slammed into Jones' knees, immediately crippling him. He was then pushed into the hole, falling on his back, and the wind was knocked out of him. He could hear his wife crying. It was torture for him. She was in the hands of animals, and there wasn't anything he could do. His legs were motionless, and he was bleeding profusely.

Jones screamed out in anguish, "Please, leave her alone! Deuce, don't do this! Let her go. It's me you want, not her!"

Deuce appeared at the edge of the hole and smirked down at Jones, enjoying the cop's agony. "You did this!" he exclaimed. "You created this hell for yourself."

"While you die, we gonna have some fun with the pretty bitch. You hear me, pig? We gonna rape that bitch, take turns with your whore"— Deuce unzipped his pants and pulled out his nine-inch cock—"knock teeth out her mouth while she's suckin' my dick. You see this, you fuckin' pig? Think about this big dick goin' into your wife as you lay there and die."

Jones' face was covered with tears. Then the dirt slammed against him, going into his mouth and his eyes. More and more of the earth covered him, quickly suffocating and drowning out his pain and suffering, until he was covered by it and could no longer be seen or heard.

Deuce spat on the man's grave. He then turned and looked at Jones' wife, who was on her knees shivering and crying.

Her eyes were swamped with tears. "You monsters!" she shouted at them.

Deuce stared at her with contempt. He was lying when he'd said they would rape her. Deuce was a lot of things—drug dealer, murderer, cold-hearted muthafucka—but he wasn't a rapist. There wasn't any need to make her to suffer much longer. He placed the barrel of the .45 to her temple, murmured, "An eye for an eye," and blew her brains her out.

The dark green Durango stopped in front of the modest home on W. 17th Street in Highlands bright and early one Sunday morning. Deuce lit a cigarette and watched the porch and the front door from the passenger seat. It was a charming neighborhood with tree-lined streets, wide, paved driveways, manicured lawns, and well-off neighbors. It was the perfect area for a police sergeant to reside, far away from the urban streets he patrolled. Deuce's eyes scanned every bit of the area. These folks didn't have to worry about poverty and gang violence in their lives.

Deuce lingered in the Durango for a moment smoking his cigarette. Staying parked in front of a police sergeant's home right after murdering a cop was a daring move, but Deuce was a nigga with nothing to lose. Killing Detective Jones was necessary. Deuce respected loyalty, and Jones had none.

He took a few more pulls from the Newport, flicked it out the window, and then looked over at his driver and said, "Let's do this."

The driver nodded.

Both men exited the Durango and calmly walked toward the front door. They stood out like Muslims at a KKK rally in the suburbs. They ascended onto the porch, and Deuce knocked hard on the wooden door.

Sergeant Connelly opened the door and saw the two men. Appalled to see them at his door, he frowned and barked, "What the fuck are you doing at my house?"

"We need to talk, Sergeant," Deuce said seriously.

Sergeant Connelly knew he couldn't have a murderous drug kingpin standing outside his front door for his neighbors to see. He quickly and reluctantly invited them inside. The door slammed behind him. "Are you fuckin' crazy, Deuce? I should have you arrested!"

"You're not that stupid, Connelly," Deuce replied.

Connelly grimaced. "What is it that you want?"

"I come in peace," Deuce said.

"Not here, at my damn home!"

"Would you rather we come down to your workplace and talk business there?" Deuce asked.

Connelly suddenly noticed the small briefcase Deuce was carrying. It made him nervous. Connelly hated that he and Jones had gotten into business with him.

"Let's talk in the other room, shall we?" Deuce said.

The men entered the living room, which was tastefully decorated by Connelly's wife with a smoky brown leather sectional on the dark parquet flooring. A beautiful dark wood coffee table with an antique chess set sat atop the spread-out area rug, and a large mosaic mirror hung over the bricked-in fireplace. There was no TV or stereo system; the room was for comfort and reading.

Deuce looked around and said, "Nice place you have here."

Connelly wasn't for the formalities. He wanted to know why this gangster was inside his home. What business did Deuce have with him on a Sunday morning?

Deuce placed the briefcase on the coffee table and said, "Go ahead, open it—my gift to you."

The man with Deuce was silent. He was simply there for muscle and intimidation, although Deuce was all muscle himself and a lot more intimidating.

Connelly warily approached the bag, wishing he had his gun on him. He unzipped it and peeked inside. It was filled with bundles of cash. In fact, close to a hundred thousand dollars. "What do you want?" he asked.

"As you may know, I'm back in town, and I want us to continue business," Deuce said.

"Are you serious? Do you know the chaos you've caused out there? The mayor is on our asses for law and order, and the murders are creating unwanted attention. The media is having a field day with the bloodshed, and it's putting a bad light on my police department."

"I had to get my rivals' attention. What better way to come calling than to knock off a few heads?"

Connelly puffed. "Not like this, Deuce."

"Look, I was embarrassed and betrayed. Did you believe I was going to go down like a fool, Connelly? Let these fuckin' outsiders annex my business and territory without a fuckin' fight? They started this war, and I plan on finishing it," Deuce growled.

"Did you kill Jones?" Connelly asked him. "He and his wife suddenly went missing."

Deuce smirked. "Now, Connelly, you know I'm a businessman, and Jones . . . well, Jones was a liability. I guess he got spooked and left town."

Connelly didn't believe one word.

"Take the money, Sergeant; it would be in your best interest to do so. We've done business together for a long time now, and I know a lot about you. You and your wife like the finer things in life. You wouldn't want everyone to know how you acquired them, would you?"

"Are you threatening me?"

"It's not a threat, it's a simple proposition," Deuce replied.

"I'm not your fuckin' lackey, Deuce, I'm a fuckin' cop. Do you understand me?"

"I do, Sergeant. And you're a cop I still find useful to me. I want information, and I want infiltration on everything happening with the West organization. We're running this virus out of town. The moment they step foot back into my city, when they try to set up shop somewhere, sell anything—I don't care if it's aspirin—I want to know about it. Tell your fellow officers. You all work for me now."

Connelly knew he meant business. He had no choice but to take the money. Deuce had enough dirt on him to ruin his career, embarrass his family, and send him to prison for a long time. He was under Deuce's thumb and could do nothing about it.

Deuce and his goon exited, leaving a bad taste in Connelly's mouth.

"You have a beautiful day, Sergeant," Deuce said.

Connelly watched the men climb into the Durango and drive away. He sighed. Luckily, his wife and teenage daughters were at church.

Jimmy sat inside the old blue Ford on E. 4th Street with a close watch on a three-story decaying building. He watched as three males exited a black Tahoe and went toward the building. Security had been upgraded with several cameras, and armed goons were placed everywhere. The building was a distribution warehouse for the West organization. DMC had them paranoid.

Jimmy hooked his eyes on one of the three men. His name was Knock, a notorious lieutenant from the Bronx who worked closely with Meyer and Luna. Knock, in his early twenties, was slim, average height, and had long cornrows. He was wearing black cargo shorts, a T-shirt, and fresh Nikes. He was a rising star in the drug game and nobody to play with.

Jimmy sat in the distance and watched them operate. One phone call from him and he could have a half-dozen shooters on the scene to kill everything moving. But he saw the usefulness of keeping these men alive today. He was doing surveillance, and though it was a tedious job, it was his forte. He was a patient man and could easily lie in wait in the shadows for hours undetected to find people who didn't want to be found. And he always saw you before you saw him.

Knock was Jimmy's target. Jimmy had been following the young, temperamental hustler for a week now, studying his routine and habits. Knock was an easy person to follow and watch. He wasn't a cautious man.

Jimmy's groundwork was paying off. He'd started from the bottom and was working his way to the top. His agenda was to get intel on where Scott and his family laid their heads. He wanted to know the workings of their organization—who was who and what heads to cut off so their empire could crumble. Deuce didn't want them just gone from Delaware; he wanted them to suffer and to be obliterated from the face of the earth. This drug war had become personal, and Deuce trusted Jimmy to help him get the advantage he needed to bring down one of the most powerful men in the game.

Jimmy, a hardcore criminal, was doing detective work at its finest. Parked half a block down from the location, his attention was trained across the street as he smoked his cigarette. The Ford was twenty years old and unassuming, so no one would think twice about it sitting on the block day after day. With his high-priced Canon camera, he snapped a few pictures of the men before they walked into the building.

Now he was waiting for their exit. There was no telling how long they would be inside. He continued to smoke his cigarette and stay alert. With a loaded .45 in the passenger seat, his head rotated left and right, and his eyes were constantly in his mirrors. The last thing he needed was someone creeping up on him.

Twenty minutes later, the men walked out the building and climbed back into the Tahoe. Their ignition started, and his did right after. Jimmy watched the truck drive off, and subtly, he followed them. The only man important to him was Knock.

It was a quick drive to Browntown, where Knock got out of the vehicle and went toward a two-story house nestled in the middle of the block. The Tahoe rolled off.

Knock knocked on the door, and a young female answered. Jimmy stayed with Knock. He figured, with business done with for the day, it was now time for his target to play. He allowed for some time to pass, making sure Knock was comfortable inside with his female friend before catching him with his pants down.

Jimmy flicked his Newport out the window. He picked up the .45 and stuffed it into his waistband and climbed out of the car. The block was quiet.

Jimmy moved swiftly and in stealth. Crouched low in the dark, he went around back and picked the lock to the weather-beaten back door. For him, it was easy as one, two, three. He broke into the home with his pistol in his hand. The house was dark and sparsely furnished, and Jimmy could hear activity from the bedroom above.

Upstairs, Jimmy found the main bedroom door ajar. He peeked into the room to catch the girl on her knees and facing Knock, her mouth full of dick. Her head bobbed up and down, as she sucked and licked the young thug like he was a lollipop. Knock was enjoying the oral treat with his eyes closed as he held on to a fistful of her hair.

Jimmy quickly pushed open the door and charged into the room with his gun trained on them both. The girl suddenly shrieked, and Knock opened his eyes and frowned.

"Knock, you and I, we need to talk," Jimmy said.

"Fuck you!"

"You really wanna play it like that?" Jimmy calmly replied.

The interrogation was about to start. Jimmy needed information, and he knew ways of getting some of the toughest niggas to talk. Like the feds with their conviction rate, Jimmy had a 95% success rate.

M ax showered and quickly got dressed on a hot August morning. Miguel was on his way to pick her up. They hadn't seen each other since the day of her release. She had much to do, but she had to be careful doing it. Her parole officer was on her back, and Layla's visit had put her on high alert. The last thing she needed to do was underestimate people. She had gotten away with murder, but she couldn't get sloppy. She had to keep things methodical.

She wore shapeless sweatpants, an old T-shirt, and old sneakers. The simple outfit wasn't flattering, but she had no cash for lavish shopping sprees and expensive makeovers. All her money was tied up in her master plan. She remembered when she used to prance around Brooklyn looking so lovely, everything she wore perfectly put together. She used to take her sweet time getting dressed and would never leave her house looking unkempt. She had to wear the right clothing, with the right perfume, and the right hairstyle. It was all about her looks, and it was all for her man, Scottie. Now, looking at herself in the mirror, she hated what she'd become—raggedy and unappealing.

Upon their first meeting, Miguel didn't give her a second look. He might have even been repulsed by her. But she knew twenty years ago she would have had him kissing her feet and begging for a taste of her cookies.

She sighed. There was no time to reminisce, but there was such a thing as revenge and making things right.

The house phone rang on the bed. It was Miguel calling her. She answered, "Yeah."

"I'm outside," he said.

"I'll be down in one minute." She hung up and gathered a few things, including a small blade for her protection, before departing her bedroom.

Before going downstairs, she stopped by her mother's room and took a peek inside. The door creaked opened. Her mother was sleeping in a light blue night slip. She was doing a lot of that lately. Her skin was wrinkling more and more and blemished with spots, either from old age, the stress in her life, or maybe both. The change in her mother was palpable to Max. She had become a different woman, moving more slowly, taking a sea of pills in the morning, and she barely left the house.

Max walked into the room and lightly placed the blanket over her mother. She propped her head against a few pillows, making her comfortable, and kissed her on the forehead. "I love you," she murmured before leaving.

Max wished she could do more for her mother, but her mother continually assured her that having a home was all she needed.

Miguel sat in his old Accord feeling irritated. He had better things to do with his time than to chauffeur Max around town. He and his girl were being extorted. But after one look at Max and her condition, he wondered how that was possible. How could she harm Nadia, who was still incarcerated in Louisiana, when she was free and in New York? What connections did she have?

Over the weekend he'd taken a cheap flight to Baton Rouge to visit Nadia at LCIW. It was a long and tiring trip, but he needed to see her. He needed to touch her and kiss her. Even though it would be brief, the feel, touch, and sight of his lady would be worth it. He also wanted to tell her something face to face that he didn't want to discuss over the phone.

Miguel and Nadia held hands and sat opposite of each other in the visiting room, hugging and kissing each other briefly when the chance came. Nadia was elated. It had been months since his last visit.

Miguel leaned closer and quietly said, "This bitch, Max . . . she needs to go, Nadia. I want to take her out. What power does she have over you?"

"Miguel, don't!"

"Why not? We already got paid. Who gonna miss her? She ain't in here anymore. How she gonna get to you inside?"

"You can't do anything stupid. Please, don't go after her. She's smart, and she's ruthless."

Miguel sighed heavily. He saw the look of fear on his girl's face.

"I just want to do my time, baby, and come home to you and my babies. I can't explain it, but she still has reach. Women in here are loyal to her, and they will kill me. I tell you no lie. Besides, a deal is a deal, and she's held up her part of the deal. We need to do the same."

Miguel sighed with irritation and reluctantly agreed. He was salty because the ten grand was long gone, and there just wasn't any incentive to do a murder. He was the one at risk. Love was a muthafucka, and he would do anything to protect his lady. But now he wanted more money. He sensed that Max had no more cash to give. Nowadays you could get a hit done for five hundred dollars, sometimes less. Max had paid top dollar as an inmate. Miguel figured she received an inheritance or somehow had come into a lump sum of money, and he wanted more.

The front door opened, and Max emerged from the house.

Miguel took one look at her and frowned. "Frumpy-lookin' bitch," he muttered to himself.

She climbed into his car. There was no good morning or warm welcome, just business. "We need to find and follow someone," she said.

"Who?"

"His name is Bugsy."

She'd brought up the name before.

"So where do we start?" he said.

"I have a few locations where he might be."

Miguel was ready to get the day over with. He couldn't look at Max for too long. He looked straight ahead and drove off.

Max lit a cigarette and filled his car with smoke.

They rode in silence for a moment. The first destination was downtown Brooklyn. The agenda for today was gathering intel on Bugsy.

Layla bragged a lot in her letters, talking about her kids, her money, and the places they owned from New York to Florida. The stupid bitch even sent a few pictures of real estate to her. The letters were like a treasure map to Max, telling her more than she needed to know. She even knew all the West children's birthdays, favorite colors, and levels of education. Layla wasn't writing to Max as a friend, but as a "frenemy." Layla envied Maxine back in the day, and why not? Before her incarceration, Maxine had it all—loving, caring parents; a good home; beauty; intelligence; and a bright future. And she had Scottie, a drug dealer on the way up who doted on her, spoiled her, and supposedly had her back.

As Miguel navigated his car through the morning traffic, Max looked his way, her eyes fixed on his biceps and triceps as he steered the car. His olive complexion seemed to glisten in the sunlight coming through the windows, and his tattoos summarized who he was as a man. She wanted to place her hand in his lap, fondle his crotch, and see his dick. She was ready to put him into her mouth if given a chance.

Out of the blue, she said, "I heard Nadia had a visit this weekend."

Miguel didn't stammer with nervousness or falter with concern. He kept his cool and continued driving. He barely looked at Max when he replied, "And what's your point?"

"What sparked the visit?"

"Is it a crime to go and see my girl?"

"No, it's not. But that's a long trip to take."

"I miss her a lot."

"I miss her too," Max said dryly.

Max's knowledge about the trip surprised Miguel. He figured she had eyes watching Nadia, and a phone call was placed to her after his visit was over. Though she was in New York, the bitch still had inmates loyal to her inside the prison, just as Nadia had told him. Still, Miguel wondered how she had gotten such pull. Again, he wondered who she was connected to. Was she related to some notorious gangster he didn't know about?

She knew things about him and Nadia, now he felt it was time to learn more about her.

Downtown Brooklyn was bustling with pedestrians, shoppers, and traffic, and businesses were swamped beneath the blazing, late-summer sun. The area was the third-largest central business district in New York City. Residential and office buildings reached to the sky, gentrification being a factor since the early 2000s.

Max had half a dozen addresses to work with, and she concluded that at least one location would lead to Bugsy or someone close to him. Bugsy was her interest. She was hoping he lived in a house somewhere in the boondocks rather than some fancy high-rise apartment building with closed-circuit security and some nosy concierge.

Max knew the real Bugsy Siegel was a gangster in Las Vegas who was shot dead in his living room by an assassin's bullet through the window. She wanted Layla's son to have the same fate.

She checked out two high-end apartment buildings on Gold Street. The towering buildings had cameras everywhere. Not wanting to be caught on film, she made Miguel check things out. He was reluctant, but

Max didn't give him a choice. She gave him the apartment number and told him to be subtle. She waited in the car.

Max knew Bugsy frequented downtown Brooklyn and that he had properties. The information she had on him had come from his own mother. Layla ran her mouth in too many letters and collect calls. For a supposedly streetwise woman with a gangster husband, Layla gave away critical information about her family.

The two apartment buildings didn't turn up anything on Bugsy, but she and Miguel continued their search. They rolled through downtown, fighting against the traffic and determined not to fail. As luck would have it, they finally spotted Bugsy. He was leaving an office building on Jay Street.

Max saw him as he was walking toward a black Escalade. He was flanked by several goons and looked like some significant political figure, dressed in a well-fitting three-piece suit and polished shoes. Max smiled as she finally laid her eyes on the man in the flesh. He was handsome and sharp.

Miguel followed the Escalade inconspicuously; they couldn't chance being spotted by Bugsy's security team. Scott and Layla weren't holding anything back to protect their remaining children. The men around Bugsy would kill someone in a heartbeat.

They traveled north on Jay Street to Tilary Street, where the Escalade made a right. Miguel followed two cars behind. These men were trained to know they were being followed. The traffic was thick, so Miguel's older model Accord wouldn't stand out, even if Bugsy's people were checking their mirrors for anything suspicious.

Max memorized the plate number, in case they lost the Escalade.

Miguel was cool with his driving. He was focused on not losing the vehicle, even if it meant running through a few yellow lights to keep up. He was taking a chance, but he did what he had to do.

They followed the Escalade into a rough area of Fort Greene, Brooklyn. Someone other than Bugsy entered the housing project while the Escalade sat idling on the block.

Miguel parked half a block down, and they watched the activity from a distance. Bugsy didn't leave the automobile.

Fifteen minutes later, the man was seen leaving the housing project carrying nothing. He climbed into the vehicle, and it drove off.

Max wondered what that was all about. Was it a drug deal? Bugsy wasn't so stupid to be riding around town with drugs in the truck. From her understanding, he was an intelligent businessman.

They continued to follow the Escalade. Now they were merging onto the highway, 278 BQE, going eastbound.

Miguel sighed. "We doin' all this drivin', and you ain't givin' me any gas money. You know all this surveillance don't come cheap."

Max wasn't in the mood for his attitude. She reached into her sweatpants pockets and tossed him a ten-dollar bill.

Miguel still wasn't satisfied. "Yo, this ain't eighty-eight. Gas ain't cheap."

"It's all I have for now."

"You gonna have to do better than this. Dig in your stash or something, cuz ten bucks can't get us far at all, ma."

"What are you talking about stash? On my mother this is all I got . . . but don't worry. I got you. I'm working on something."

Miguel grudgingly took the money. They both were broke, but he felt that his needs were greater than hers. He had three kids to support, while Max was living at home with her mother. Each moment he spent with her, he wanted to wrap his hands around her neck and choke her out. Better yet, simply break her neck. The difficult situation she was putting his family into filled him with great contempt.

While doing 55mph on the BQE, now several cars behind the Escalade, Max looked at Miguel and boldly placed her hand on his knee and squeezed it gently. The unexpected touch caught Miguel off guard.

"Are you lonely, Miguel?" she asked.

Miguel, driving with composure, moved her hand off his knee. "I love Nadia!"

"I know you do."

"So don't you disrespect her at all!"

Max sighed. Two weeks of freedom and all she did was finger-fuck herself and take cold showers. She wondered whether Miguel had been loyal to Nadia since her incarceration. Nadia was doing some years in prison. Max knew everyone had their needs, especially men. Did he ever cheat on Nadia? She believed so.

"You know, you should have seen me in my teens and early twenties. I was definitely a knockout. Had men coming at me left and right."

Miguel appeared to be uninterested about her glory days. He drove, staring at the traffic ahead.

Max said, "I've been with only one man in my entire life. Can you believe that? It's been a long time for me. I didn't even mess with women inside. I refused to. I've been out of the dating scene for so long that I feel self conscious and somewhat insecure. I wouldn't know what to say to a man or how to act on a date. Do I tell them that I've done a bid, or do I lie? Do we fuck quick cause I'm a grown woman, or do I wait to get to know them better? Thoughts like that keep going through my head. Got me fucked up. It's all so overwhelming."

The speech did nothing for Miguel. He wasn't having it. He knew she was trying to get into his head, but he'd rather fuck a dog than a dyke bitch that looked like a dude to him. Not to mention, she was extorting and bullying his lady.

The day played out into the evening, with Max learning a few things about Bugsy, but the information wasn't definitive. They'd followed him throughout Brooklyn and into Manhattan. Max didn't discover much about his personal life, but she was determined to find out more about the young boy. He was only nineteen years old and already had money, power, and connections that most grown men would dream of. He was the family's golden boy. He knew how to launder money, influence the right folks, talk with charm and urging, and he knew how to move in the streets and in the business world. He was book-smart and street-smart—a lethal combination in his line of work.

Max wanted Bugsy killed. Meyer would lose his twin brother, Layla would lose her most gifted child, and Scott would lose the one son who could replace him on the throne and run the empire—maybe better than he ever had.

Miguel was tired and frustrated with Max. Spending the day with her was agonizing. He couldn't wait to take her home. He turned the corner onto Blake Street, where a few neighbors were outside enjoying the warm night. While approaching Max's house, he was ready to push her out of his car while it was still moving. He double-parked outside her home, keeping the gear shift in drive with his foot on the brakes.

Max removed herself from the car. While doing so, she noticed the Rolls-Royce Phantom whirling around the corner onto her street. It was Layla. Max wasn't expecting her. Why was Layla coming to see her? Did she suspect something? Did she know they were following Bugsy today? Was she being watched too? Max was worried. Layla could do anything, even place men outside her mother's house to keep an eye on her every movement. It was something Max hadn't thought about.

Miguel noticed the sleek luxury vehicle through his rearview mirror. It looked like a mountain of a car from his viewpoint. It was definitely there for Max, and he grew concerned. He slowly drove away from the area, spying the Phantom in his mirrors. He wanted to see who climbed out of the car, but he didn't want to stick around too long. Max was enough of a headache for him.

Max watched Miguel leave, and then she focused her attention on the Rolls-Royce. She couldn't help but feel a touch of trepidation. This game of betrayal and mistrust between her and Layla was nerve-wracking. There was no telling what would go down. Someone could emerge from out of nowhere and put a bullet into Max's head, with Layla there to simply watch the murder. She thought of her mother seeing her only daughter lying in a pool of blood with a bullet in her head near her steps. That would unquestionably send Max's mother to her grave.

Max's chest tightened. *Shit!* What could she do if it was a snare for her death? Max could only stand there and watch the suicide door to the vehicle open and observe Layla's pricey shoes step out from the back seat and touch the pavement.

Max reached into the pockets of her sweatpants and wrapped her fingers around the small blade she carried. It wasn't much, but it was something.

Once again, the neighbors stood around in awe at the luxurious vehicle parked on their block again.

Layla approached Max straight-faced. Was she coming as a friend or foe? Max would soon find out. Max stood hypnotized by her unexpected presence.

Layla didn't miss a beat. She didn't respond with a hello, but a question. "Who was that . . . the car you got out of?"

Max quickly replied, "My mother's pastor. He's counseling me."

Max knew there was no way she could have seen Miguel's face. It was a believable lie because Max's mother had always been a godly woman.

Layla's look was still poker-faced. There was no telling if she believed Max or not. She looked stunning, showing off her curves to Max and the neighbors in a red corset mini dress and clutching a gold satin bracelet bag. She was dressed for an elegant and classy event, like an extravagant ball somewhere in the city. Why the quick stop in Brooklyn? This time, she was minus Lucky and the heavy security. She had one man with her. He was tall and black and dressed in all black.

"Do you want to come inside?" Max asked.

Layla took one look at the small home and thought against it. She didn't care to run into the old and unpleasant mother again. "I'm not here to stay," she said.

"Then why are you here?"

"I'm here to give you something." Layla nodded to the man in black, who then reached into his suit jacket and removed a small, bulky package and handed it to Maxine. "In there is sixty thousand dollars," Layla informed her.

Max was somewhat taken aback. Why the cash? And why now?

"No thank-you?" Layla said with a self-righteous look.

Thank you? Max wanted to move her mother from the area and put her into a better home. Sixty thousand dollars was less than three grand for every year she had spent in prison. For her life being wasted behind bars, she was owed a lot more. Had she not gone to jail, she would have graduated from law school as planned, and she definitely would've made over three grand a year. She knew she would've been a prominent attorney in the city.

"Thank you," Max said, a forced smile on her face. The cash would help finance the next part of her revenge.

Layla picked up on Maxine's somewhat salty expression. "What? It's not enough?" Layla knew she'd contradicted herself by giving Maxine the money when she'd told herself that she'd done enough for her. But this was it; there would be no more. "Like I told you before, things are tight right now. We're having major issues. We're at war, Maxine."

Maxine smiled and said, "I understand. I'm happy to have had your help this long, Layla. This is a blessing. I just want to go on with my life and take care of my mother. She's very ill, and I need to be here to help take care of her."

"Do yourself a favor, Maxine. Get yourself a makeover wit' some of that money and buy some new clothes, for God's sake. You look like shit!

Bring yourself into the twenty-first century already." Layla walked toward the Rolls-Royce and stepped inside. She had stayed too long in the ghetto.

Maxine watched the Rolls-Royce leave. Holding sixty grand in her hand gave her some advantage. Layla had to be the dumbest bitch on earth to continue to finance her own family's demise.

The old Ford stayed parked on the street in Wilmington a week before someone finally noticed it. The car itself did not stand out, but the stench emanating from it was overwhelming and putrid. The stifling August heat amplified the foul odor coming from the car, and people complained about it.

Finally, the police were called to the block to investigate the abandoned vehicle. A marked police car arrived, and two officers went to inspect the Ford. The windows were rolled up, and there were no keys in the ignition. The smell hit the cops like a ton of bricks. With their years of experience, they recognized the smell of death and pinpointed that the odor was coming from the rear. It was coming from the trunk. They ran the plates, and the car came back as stolen.

The senior officer forced the trunk open with a crowbar, and immediately they were hit with a ghastly stench and a sight that made their eyes water and their stomachs churn. The junior cop quickly hunched over with his hand propped against the back of the car and threw up his breakfast. They had seen dead bodies before, but this headless corpse with missing fingertips was overkill.

The crime scene was soon protected by crime scene tape and crowded with several homicide detectives. Forensics was inspecting the car for fingerprints and DNA, and the residents were watching everything unfold from a short distance. Word of the cops finding a headless body had spread like wildfire. Murder wasn't anything uncommon in their part of town, but the body being headless brought more attention to it.

Unbeknownst to the cops, the body belonged to Tyrone Knead, aka Knock. Once Jimmy was finished torturing Knock for hours for information, he decided killing him was too easy. He went extreme to send out a vile message to their enemies.

Amongst those watching the crime scene from the crowd nearby were Chin and Jo-Jo, two soldiers from Meyer's crew. They suspected that it was Knock inside the trunk. He had been missing for three days now. Another one of theirs had fallen, and they knew Deuce was behind it.

The men left the area and got into a gold Lexus. They were angry and wanted revenge. Knock's murder had hit the people close to home. He was their boss, and they were bloodthirsty for payback. They carried 9mm pistols loaded with hollow-point bullets, designed for absolute destruction to flesh upon impact.

The Lexus hurried toward the Sky lounge in Cool Spring, a business owned and operated by Meyer. Meyer had a thing for clubs, and since he'd planned on being in Delaware for a while, he took over ownership of the trendy establishment when the previous owner had fallen into debt with him for over a hundred thousand dollars. It was either his life or the lounge.

The business didn't open until seven p.m., but during the day the place was a hangout spot for Meyer and his goons. It was also a drop-off and pickup point for money and drugs. Since the paperwork for the location was still under the previous owner's name, it wasn't on Deuce's radar. It was the perfect hiding place in a city turned upside down by the drug war.

Chin and Jo-Jo made it to the lounge and knocked on the steel door. The security monitor perched near the entrance picked them up, and the door opened. They walked inside and trekked toward the backrooms and then into the back office, where Meyer and Luna were talking business and going over required paperwork for the lounge.

"Knock is dead!" Chin exclaimed.

"What? What the fuck you talkin' about, nigga?" Meyer said.

"They found a headless body in the trunk of a car over on Quaker Hill," Jo-Jo said.

Luna asked, "And y'all sure it's Knock?"

"We sure it's him. I've seen that car before, and he ain't been around in three days, and Knock is always around. It's gotta be Deuce's work," Chin said.

The news was upsetting to Meyer. Right after Luna, Knock was his diehard goon. Knock was fuckin' Rambo on steroids and meth. He'd once blown a man's brains out in a crowded park and got away with it. Knock knew his shit and was a loyal nigga. It was a harsh blow to Meyer's crew.

Meyer scowled. "That muthafucka Deuce, he gotta go and go fast. I got my pops up my ass because of this clown nigga."

"What you want us to do?" Jo-Jo asked.

"Yo, I want a fuckin' hit squad on these streets twenty-four/seven," Meyer said.

"We on it," Chin said.

Jo-Jo and Chin stood in front of their commander ready to prove their worth. With Knock dead, it meant someone had to be promoted, and they both wanted the position.

Meyer wasn't in the mood to backfill Knock's position right away. He looked at the two soldiers and said, "Y'all niggas get the fuck out."

Knowing Meyer hated to repeat himself, the two thugs pivoted and left the office, leaving Meyer and Luna to contemplate their next move.

With the door closed, Meyer, with one motion of his hand, angrily cleared everything off the desk and crashing to the floor. He screamed, "Muthafucka!"

"They're not even sure if it's him," Luna said. "It's just a headless body in a trunk of a car."

"It's him." Meyer was sure of it. "Like they said, Knock is always around. Who could have gotten to Knock like that though?"

"Deuce got a nigga named Jimmy I keep hearing about."

Meyer frowned. He removed a cigarette from his full pack and lit one up. He plopped down in the chair behind the desk. Deuce had taken too much from his family already, and he was still taking from them. Meyer couldn't look weak, not to his father and definitely not to the streets.

"We need to call someone on this, Luna. I'll pay anything to have these niggas got," Meyer said.

"Call who?"

"The brothers," Meyer suggested.

"They're expensive."

"You think I give a fuck about money right now? Every day Deuce lives and breathes, I'm losing money, soldiers, and respect."

Luna nodded. He then said, "You think your father will approve?"

Meyer cut his eyes at Luna, saying he gave no fuck what his father would approve of. He needed to fix the dilemma by any means necessary. He needed to assert their authority on the streets of Wilmington. And he wanted desperately to avenge his siblings' murders.

The Greene brothers were from Chicago's North Side, and they'd grown up in the notorious Cabrini-Green projects. Their family had seen gang warfare since the late seventies. Their father was a high-ranking Vice Lord whose name was well known in the streets of Chicago, like Al

Capone's. The Greene family was bred to commit violence. It was in their blood. Every member of their family was prone to violence and murder. One of their uncles took down three rivals with his bare hands inside a nightclub in '83. Another uncle killed two cops in '91 and laughed at the murders. Their oldest brother was doing life in prison for multiple homicides, as was their father. It was rumored that their mother beat her sons with belts and bats when they were young to get them used to the street life and to toughen their souls.

In the early 2000s, the brothers enlisted in the Marines after 9/11 and were sent off to Iraq. Overseas, they were thrust into violent combat and saw their share of carnage. Some say they enjoyed their tour in Iraq too much. They hunted enemy soldiers down and tortured and killed them so gruesomely, their commanding officers were appalled and they were soon dishonorably discharged. The military deemed the brothers psychotic. Not only were they a threat to Iraq, but also to fellow soldiers.

The Marines schooled the brothers on how to kill efficiently, taught them weaponry, and once back in the States they were out of work and looking for excitement. Like sharks, they had a taste for blood. They became hired killers for drug crews and gangs in Chicago and operated under the radar. Word got out about the Greene brothers and their way of doing things, including allegedly eating their victims to hide the bodies. That was a welcome lie. It kept them employed. Their reputation soon stretched into different states, and they didn't lack for any work. But they were so sadistic and unpredictable, even the hardest criminals were sometimes apprehensive about hiring them. They didn't want the Greene brothers to linger in their cities. Yes, they took care of problems, but their behavior and appetite for chaos and bloodshed sometimes came back to bite people in their asses. These brothers were stealthy, and they were the best at killing.

"We might have another problem," Luna said.

"Like what?"

"Knock—if he was tortured, you think he gave shit up? Gave us up?"

Meyer thought about it. "I don't think so," he said.

"You wanna chance that? I mean, we're already taking losses now. If Knock talked to whoever because of what they put him through, it could be catastrophic to our organization."

Meyer knew Luna had a point. "Fuck," he muttered. He sat there thinking about what Luna said.

"We need to react now before it's too late," Luna added.

"Close down the warehouse and make the calls. We shut everything down momentarily and beef up security at every location," Meyer said.

Luna nodded, agreeing with the decision.

Meyer scowled while seated behind the desk. His fists tightened, ready to punch a hole in the wall. Yeah, he needed the Greene brothers in town. He needed them to clean house by doing what they did best—killing muthafuckas and not giving a fuck.

The penthouse terrace became Layla's favorite place to be, especially at night. She could sit out there naked for hours on the cushioned chaise underneath the canopy of the stars and bright moon, smoke her Newports, and finish a bottle of expensive wine. But tranquility didn't bring security. Though Scott had his armed goons around, she kept her .380 close by for safety. She had a lot on her mind, and she didn't need any more troubles. Although Maxine was never any trouble to her, Layla figured the sixty grand would be more than enough to help Maxine get her life back on track and help her mother out.

Did Scott know that Maxine was free? She doubted it. Twenty years together and he'd never brought up Maxine's name—out of sight, out of mind. The streets and money kept her husband busy. Layla didn't quite see Maxine as a threat to her marriage or her health anymore. She looked worn down and unkempt. The cute, young girl from the block was long gone, and in her place was a broke-down, dyke-looking bitch. Did she like pussy now? The thought crossed Layla's mind. Twenty-two years behind bars could alter someone's sexual habits, and Maxine had always been weak and easy to take advantage of.

The thought of Maxine turning gay and being raped and sodomized by some Big Bertha-looking bitch was an interesting idea for Layla. Yeah, that place had broken her, like it was designed to. It was the reason she'd never visited Maxine, besides the one time. Layla couldn't imagine prison life; it wasn't designed for her.

She and Scott did everything in their power to stay free. They were careful and smart throughout the years, and they took their time building an extensive network from the ground up, from the underworld to the business world. They'd laundered enough drug money that the feds could trace no dirty money to them. Not even a penny. It was all filtered through several expanding businesses and accounts they'd set up overseas, numerous properties they owned, smart investments, and nightclubs they'd opened. On paper, it was all legit, taxable income. They could easily account for their lavish lifestyle.

Layla downed the last of her Chardonnay, one of her favorites. She took a pull from the cigarette pressed between her full, glossy lips. Her nakedness glistened under the city lights and the moonlight. The stillness of the penthouse was sometimes frightening for Layla. She was alone. She didn't want to be alone. Her husband was elsewhere, and her living children were grown. It was times like these that she missed Gotti, Bonnie, and Clyde. Somehow, it felt like the killers made it their business to take away her youngest kids. It amplified the sadness inside her.

Maxine seemed broken from prison life, but Layla too had become broken in her own way. Her life was under attack. She had all the money in the world, but she had many enemies too, and she had a husband who had no interest in her.

Hearing someone entering her luxury dwelling made Layla turn and reach for her pistol. But she quickly relaxed, seeing it was Scott. She put her .380 back on the Euro-style glass table next to the empty wine bottle.

Scott joined her on the terrace with his lit cigar in hand, dressed handsomely in a tailored black suit and black tie. He always looked GQ and suave. He puffed on his cigar as he stood near the railing and glanced at the illuminated city for a moment, his back toward her.

Layla wondered about his sudden presence. He wasn't home to be with her. He wasn't there to make peace with her, or make love to her, and make her feel wanted. It looked like he had something on his mind.

Layla remained naked. Her body would be a treasure for other men to adore, but Scott was indifferent.

She extinguished her cigarette into the ashtray and locked eyes with her estranged husband. In her drunkenness, she smirked up at him and slowly spread her legs, showing all of her glory. She kept it tight. She had no choice.

"What's the matter? You don't like it anymore? It don't look pretty to you no more?" she said. "I remember nights when all you used to do is eat me out and fuck the shit out of me . . . when you were on that gangsta shit. What happened to you?"

"Put some clothes on," he said dryly.

Layla chuckled in disbelief and shook her head. "This muthafucka," she muttered, not believing her husband would pass up a good fuck. Tonight would have been the perfect night to make love and connect sexually on the terrace underneath the bright sky.

She wasn't putting any clothes on to make him feel comfortable. "I'm still your wife," she uttered.

"I know, and that's why I need for you to leave New York. I want you to go back to Florida."

"Go back to Florida? Why!"

"I'm not asking."

"And I'm not leaving." She closed her legs, suppressing her sexual needs. His offensive proposal made her want to cover up.

Scott grimaced. "Layla, don't make this difficult. It's for your safety."

"My safety? My safety is stayin' here in New York, not in Florida. Why would you even suggest it? You think I'm some weak bitch that needs to run off when the heat comes? You know me better than that, Scott."

"This is different. Our businesses in Florida need to continue. With you up here, how's that gonna happen?"

"We got people we pay for that."

Her Florida compound was a haunting reminder of what she had lost. Without Gotti, Bonnie, or Clyde, why would she go back there? Florida was more their home than New York. They loved it there, and they couldn't wait to permanently move to the Sunshine State. But everything done changed. The only way she would leave for Florida was if Scott and the kids came with her. Meyer and Bugsy were busy traveling back and forth from Delaware and New York trying to kill Deuce. And with Lucky's open drug case, Layla wasn't leaving the city. Her business was in New York with her remaining children, not in the South. She would leave the extravagant real estate she'd built behind. She felt the place no longer had a purpose. She had it built for her family, but now her family was torn apart by murder.

Layla remained defiant. "I'm not leaving, Scott. I'm not leaving my kids behind."

"Your kids know how to take care of themselves."

"They need to; you're not protecting them." Layla sprung up from the chaise and marched inside the penthouse.

Scott glared at his wife's plump backside as he lingered on the terrace smoking his cigar. He felt like throwing her off the terrace. No one defied him, but Layla steadily tested him. He took another drag from the cigar in his mouth and breathed out. He would make her leave somehow; the discussion wasn't over with.

He dowsed the cigar on the costly Euro-style table and walked into the penthouse. Layla was in the bedroom. He wanted to kick down the door and take her by the throat and slam her against the wall. But he decided not to continue arguing with her. He had other matters to attend to. He needed to leave.

"We'll talk later, Layla. You'll see things my way," he thundered for her to hear in the bedroom.

She didn't respond. She was too busy getting dressed. She knew he was leaving soon, and she wanted to be ready.

The door closed. He was gone.

Layla waited for a moment then exited too. Faintly disguised in a black sweat suit and a ball cap, the brim pulled down low to help hide her face, she hurriedly made it down to the building lobby just in time to see Scott and his associates exit the big glass doors and get into a black Escalade. The SUV sped off.

Layla was determined to follow the vehicle. Fortunately for her, there was an approaching yellow cab that the doorman hailed down. She climbed into the back seat, and like in the movies, she yelled out, "I want you to follow that black SUV."

The middle-aged driver wore a bright orange turban. He started the fare. Scott was already a block away, the Escalade idling at a red light. The driver moved away from the curb just as the red light transitioned to green. When the SUV drove off, Layla's taxi was four cars behind it. She had a big advantage following Scott in the yellow cab—It was camouflaged among a sea of other yellow cabs. She followed him to Central Park West, where the SUV parked in front of a neo-Italian Renaissance-style building.

Scott climbed out from the backseat. Flanked by his armed security, he approached the building and disappeared into the lobby.

Layla sat in the taxi across the street and waited, watching everything like a hawk with acute vision. She swelled up with anxiety, knowing something wasn't right. The fare continued to run, while she continued to wait. The money and time was irrelevant at the moment. She needed to find out what her husband was up to.

Fifteen minutes later, Scott resurfaced from the building, but this time he was with a female. But that wasn't the shocking part to Layla. Penelope, their former nanny, stood by her husband's side with a protruding belly. Layla was transfixed by the stomach. Her own stomach tightened with anger and jealousy. Scott was fucking their ex-nanny.

Penelope was a twenty-one-year-old immigrant from Cuba who spoke little English. She came to work for the Wests at eighteen. She was a lovely woman, a little too cute for Layla's comfort, but she was a good worker. And she was great with Gotti when he was younger. Two years earlier, when Layla had started her real estate project in Florida, Scott explained to her that Penelope was laid off because they needed someone more mature who spoke English, so there wouldn't be a language barrier if something jumped off. Now Penelope, looking seven or eight months pregnant, was snuggled against her husband on the sidewalk and smiling brightly like she was getting fucked on the regular.

The bitch's pregnancy wasn't the only thing Layla was stunned by. Penelope looked fabulous in her stylish clothes and jewelry. Her long, jet-black hair flowed down to her shoulders flawlessly. It was money well spent in the salons. Scott was spending lots of money on his pregnant mistress.

The rage consuming Layla felt like a massive nuclear bomb was inside her. She was becoming a WMD—a woman of mass destruction. She tossed the cabbie a fistful of money and jumped out of the cab, her rage fixed on Penelope and Scott, who looked so happy together.

She jogged across the street. Unable to contain her anger, her movement picked up into a full sprint toward the couple. Fists clenched, she stormed their way, and before Scott's two bodyguards, Kevin and Dwayne, could see her coming, Layla was up on them just in time to throw a punch at Penelope. Her knuckles smashed into the side of Penelope's face, and the bitch fell backwards on her ass.

"You fuckin' bitch!" Layla shouted at her.

Penelope stared up at Layla in shock and fear, her mouth full of blood. The blow was staggering; Layla had a mean right hook.

Scott shouted at his wife, "Bitch, you fuckin' crazy?"

"You fuckin' the nanny?" Layla screamed out emotionally.

Scott's two goons quickly grabbed Layla before she could do any more damage. But she tried to break free from the men's hold to go after Penelope again.

"Chill, Ms. Layla," Kevin said. "You in public."

Layla fidgeted angrily in their hold. She glared at the girl, who was still on the ground in shock and nursing her bloody mouth.

Scott quickly went to Penelope's aid, infuriating Layla even more.

"You choose that immigrant bitch over your own wife? Is it your baby she's fuckin' carrying?"

Scott yelled at his men, "Keep her away from us!"

"That's why you want me in Florida? To parade this bitch around town?"

Onlookers gawked at the minor skirmish. Scott was embarrassed by it. Concerned about the baby, he crouched near Penelope and helped her off the ground.

"Fuck you, Scott! Fuck you an' that dirty immigrant bitch!"

Layla watched in outright anger as Scott helped his pregnant mistress to the vehicle and ushered her into the back seat to get her to the hospital. Layla desperately tried to charge at him, spitting and cursing his way. Pregnant or not, she wanted Penelope gone. It was the ultimate disrespect. She couldn't hold back her tears. They trickled down her face like a waterfall. The hurt Layla felt quickly swelled inside of her like a large tumor. She loved Scott. How could he? How could he reject her and choose this non-English-speaking whore?

With Penelope safely seated inside the Escalade, Scott pivoted toward Layla. "You stupid bitch!" he shouted.

"Fuck you, nigga!" Layla felt betrayed. Her heart was beating so fast, it felt like it would burst out of her chest at any moment.

Kevin and Dwayne gripped her tightly, but she was becoming a handful for them.

Scott glared at Layla. He could kill her right then for what she did to Penelope. "You're a savage," he growled at her.

"Look who's talking."

The turning police car caught Scott's attention. His anger subsided. He didn't need any more problems.

Layla screamed, "You ready to kill me over that bitch? Huh, muthafucka? You ready to murder your fuckin' wife of twenty years? The bitch that gave birth to six of your kids and had your back on these streets?"

The police car pulled up, and both doors opened. Two uniformed officers climbed out and made their way toward the incident near Central Park. The disturbance was an anomaly.

Dwayne and Kevin released Layla.

Scott instructed his men to go to the truck. "I'll do the talking."

The cops walked up to them with caution and asked, "Is there a problem here?"

"My wife . . . she's the problem," Scott said calmly.

Layla yelled, "I'm the fuckin' problem?"

One cop attempted to grab Layla's forearm, to impede her hostile movement toward Scott, but Layla turned and punched the cop in the face.

Ultimately, she was subdued and arrested.

Scott stood there in his suit and tie and watched them handcuff his wife, who resisted arrest. He chose not to intervene. He watched them shove her into the back seat of the police car and haul her off to jail.

Penelope, still shaken up by the incident, watched the arrest play out from the Escalade. She was holding her stomach and worrying about her baby and her safety.

13

The Park Avenue suite came with world-class amenities. It offered a refreshingly modern twist on life in the sky and a breathtaking view of the city from thirty-four floors up. It featured floor-to-ceiling windows, an indoor pool and Jacuzzi, a small movie room, and top-notch furnishings. The lavish place matched the one Scott owned with Layla, but he shared this one with Penelope. He'd purchased it for her the week he found out she was pregnant with his child. He'd paid $4.8 million for it—$1.5 million less than the realtor's asking price.

"Just relax and get some rest," he told her.

"I will."

In two years, Penelope's English had improved significantly. Scott had hired some of the best speech tutors in the city to teach her the language. Penelope was smart and learned quickly. She was devoted to improving herself and advancing.

Penelope smiled Scott's way and reclined on the five-star king-size bed and propped up her feet. She had everything she needed at her beck and call. Inside the extravagant suite, she had her own butler and a small staff. A chef cooked her meals for her, and the spa came to her to provide hair and makeup, skin treatments, pedicures, and manicures. If she needed to go out, she had her own chauffeur with a Bentley.

Scott sat near his mistress. He undid his tie and let it hang loosely around his neck. He removed his jacket and tossed it on the bed. The incident with Layla didn't harm their unborn baby. The doctor had told them that Penelope was okay, and that the baby was doing great. Penelope just needed plenty of bed rest. Scott was elated by the news. Had anything happened to his baby, it wouldn't have been pretty for Layla, despite her being his wife. She had murdered his unborn baby once, and Scott wasn't going to allow a repeat of the past.

Scott fixed his eyes on Penelope's face and took in her beauty. She was seven months pregnant and looked magnificent. Everything about her was angelic. Her hair was down, and it framed her face perfectly. Her eyes were dramatic, and her full lips were seductive. The lace gown she wore with the plunging neckline attractively covered her pregnant figure. Her light skin was luminescent, and she smelled like a mix of strawberries and coconut. And she had some of the prettiest feet he'd ever seen.

"I'm sorry about Layla," he said.

"I'm fine."

"She was wrong for attacking you. I promise you, I will never let anything happen to you again. With me, you're safe and protected."

Penelope wanted to believe him, but she knew Layla was prone to violence.

Penelope's family was new to America. She fled Cuba with her mother, little brother, and uncle in a small boat to find better opportunities in the US, but her uncle drowned in the Atlantic. America was a difficult place to exist in too, especially with her and her family being undocumented. They lived in the slums of Miami, crammed together in a shabby apartment with other families who shared everything from the bathroom, to the kitchen, and food. Her mother scrubbed toilets and cleaned bathrooms to make ends meet, and Penelope and her brother also fell victim to dangerous working conditions for meager pay.

Fortunately for Penelope, she found work as a nanny through an organization that worked with illegal immigrants. For a percentage of their paychecks, this company found the immigrants better jobs and better pay. Everything was off the books. Through this organization, Penelope found reasonable nanny jobs in Miami. Within a year's time, she found work with the West family, looking after young Gotti and taking care of the household.

Scott had become smitten by the cute, young immigrant. She looked so innocent, and she somewhat reminded him of a young Maxine. Penelope carried that certain je ne sais quoi. Though she spoke little English, Scott would shrewdly flirt with her.

Years later, Penelope's wishes of opulence and fortune had come true. She used her beauty and sexuality to attain the finer things in life. Having sex with her employer was a major come-up for her. Scott showered her with the finer things in life, and in return, she pleased him sexually. Poverty became a distant memory for Penelope, and having his baby meant she would have money and support from him for a long time.

"You're beautiful," he said, expressing a genuine smile.

"*Gracias*."

Penelope gently kneaded her stomach and felt a small kick near her right side. He had been active all day. "He's startin' to kick," she told Scott. "You want to feel him?"

Scott leaned closer, and she took his hand and gently placed it against her protruding belly. Immediately, he felt some tiny movement. The feeling of life growing inside a woman never got old to him. He couldn't wait to see his son. With all the loss, devastation, and bloodshed in his life, something new, like a baby boy, was a blessing for him.

His hand lingered on her stomach. He felt another kick. His son already had a healthy kick. Then he took Penelope's hand in his and kissed the back of it.

It angered him that his wife had assaulted her. Kevin and Dwayne failed. They allowed Layla to get close enough to throw a punch at her. They should have seen her coming a mile away. What if it had been a different threat? He and his mistress probably would've been killed.

The skirmish with his wife lingered in his mind. For a moment, he looked away from Penelope and stared off into the distance. He then turned his attention back to her again and said, "I need to go."

"You're not going to spend the night with me? I can use the company, and I can relax you real good," she said.

"Tomorrow night. Tonight, I have something to take care of." He stood up and picked up his jacket from the bed. He neared his lips toward hers, and he kissed her sweetly. The aura of her was enticing. Her lips aroused him. He planted another kiss on her mouth, and then he pivoted and walked out the door, leaving the future mother of his son to lie comfortably in lavishness and fret about nothing.

The vast rolling gates to the warehouse opened, and the Escalade Scott was inside drove into the dimness of the building. The gates came rolling down, and the Escalade came to a stop inside the sprawling structure. Scott exited the vehicle with a purpose. The space was large enough to fit two semi trucks inside. Instead, it contained two dark SUVs and a dozen of his men. The warehouse was dusty with hard concrete floors and elongated shadows from long-forgotten crates and pallets. What was once used as a place for his drug distribution, Scott had transitioned into a site used for harsh interrogation and torture—a dungeon of horrors for men who snitched, opposed him, or crossed his organization.

Scott owned real estate throughout the city, so it was easy for him to shut down one drug location and set shop back up somewhere else. Being mobile in the city and across the nation was one way he remained untouched by the authorities.

He calmly buttoned his suit jacket and walked toward the minor engagement. Ahead of him, there was a circle of men surrounding something or someone. Scott approached the raucous group in a deadpan manner. The circle broke for the boss, and into view came Kevin and Dwayne. The men were firmly tied to metal chairs with their arms folded behind them, duct tape covering their mouths, and they had been severely beaten and left in only their underwear.

Scott stared at them with no remorse on his face. They were a disappointment to him, allowing Layla to follow him for blocks without being detected. Worse, she assaulted his pregnant mistress and threatened the health of his unborn son. That meant that the two men weren't doing their jobs. They were a disgrace. He needed to send a message to the others that this wasn't a time to slack off or become sloppy. They were at war with other organizations, and he could risk no one getting close to him and his family or infiltrating his empire. Everyone needed to take their jobs seriously. If they didn't, it would cost them dearly.

"You two fucked up tonight," he growled. "My woman was attacked because of y'all ineffectiveness to stop a simple bitch from attacking her."

The men muttered something incoherent underneath the duct tape.

Scott approached them closer. The mere sight of Kevin and Dwayne infuriated him. He scrunched his fists and swung at Kevin, striking him in the face so hard, his mouth almost filled with blood. He could've easily choked to death from gurgling. The duct tape allowed no escape to release the crimson fluid swirling inside his mouth.

Dwayne received the same painful treatment. His neck was about to break from the powerful blows Scott rained down on him.

They both received several minutes of an excruciating beating from Scott's bare hands, and then Scott gestured at one of his men and extended his arm. A .45 was right away placed into his hand.

Dwayne's and Kevin's eyes grew wide with fear. They desperately fidgeted in their chairs and spewed out more incoherent speech from beneath the duct tape, wanting to be heard.

But Scott didn't want to listen to their noise. He lifted the gun and placed the barrel against Dwayne's forehead. He locked eyes with his frightened soldier, giving the man a moment to accept his fate, and then—*Boom!*—Dwayne's brain instantly flew out from the back of his head. His body toppled to the concrete ground, still tied to the chair.

Kevin whimpered. He frantically fidgeted in his restraints once more and pleaded with his eyes to Scott.

Scott lifted the gun to Kevin's forehead, repeating the same action, giving him that moment of clarity to accept his fate, and then he squeezed—*Boom!* His blood splattered, and his brain matter became exposed as his body toppled to the ground.

At close range with the gunfire, the men's faces were twisted and burnt. It was a ghastly spectacle, but one that every person in the room was used to. Death was common for them. Sometimes, Scott had to get his hands dirty to show his men he was still a cold-blooded killer and they should not try him.

"Discard the bodies and dismantle and toss away the gun," Scott said to Mason, a longtime soldier.

Mason nodded.

It was business *and* personal. For a moment, Scott stared at his handiwork and felt nothing. He would do whatever it took to protect his, even if it meant making an example out of two of his own men to show the others what would happen if they fucked up.

14

Max took a long look at her rough image in the mirror. She had seen better days. Though forty-two years old, she looked fifty-five and felt it too. A strong sigh spewed from her lips. Layla was right. She needed a makeover. She needed to look like her old self again, if not close to it. Her time in prison had changed her into something and someone she despised. She was a shell of herself. Her hair was unkempt, and her wardrobe was tasteless and unappealing. She planned on using some of the sixty grand on a day at the salon and spa.

The beauty salon in her neighborhood was new. It was owned by a young female in her early twenties. Sheena was pretty and pleasant, her shop came with all the latest amenities, and she employed over a dozen male and female workers. Max deduced that the young, pretty girl had help with opening She-Girls, and that she had to be a drug dealer's girlfriend. Sheena was well put together, wearing trendy clothes, fine jewelry, and her weave was long and expensive. She pranced around her establishment and made her presence known.

Max took in everything about the girl. She saw herself twenty years earlier, looking cute and in love with a drug dealer, showing off his gifts and coming up in the hood with his money. She wished she could turn back the hands of time and do it all over again.

"I love your place," Max said to Sheena.

"Oh, thank you," she replied happily. "My man bought it."

"That was generous."

"He is. And is my girl taking care of you? You know we do it up in here. Gonna have you looking like a superstar. You're gonna catch you a baller out there when you leave my shop."

Max smiled. She'd been there and done that.

"I'm too old to catch me a baller," Max said.

"Girl, nonsense. You still in your prime, and when Tina gets done workin' on your hair, please . . . you gonna have you a nigga the minute you step out my shop. We don't play; we do it right here, girl. She-Girls is 'bout to be on the map. Watch and see." Sheena moved her hands around a lot as she talked.

Sheena knew how to work her charm on her customers. Max was sold. She couldn't remember the last time she had someone with a beautician's license work on her hair. In prison, you do what you can.

Tina examined Max's hair. As she combed it out, Max could see her reaction through the mirror. Tina was probably wondering if she'd been living under a rock for the past year.

"It's been a while," Max muttered.

"I've seen worse," Tina replied. "How do you want it?"

Tina was in her late twenties and a petite woman with black cropped hair. They said she was one of the best. She had a knack for making magic happen to any unkempt head.

"Something much different. I need a new me."

"I can definitely give you a new you."

"I want it blonde, relaxed, and cut," Max said.

"You sure you want all this cut? I mean, your hair is damn near touching ya ass. Girls pay hundreds for bundles of hair like this."

Maxine ran her fingers through her strands. "Yeah, cut it. This hair reminds me of unpleasant times."

"Have you considered keeping it natural? Your beautiful face would rock that Black Girl Magic movement. Your hair texture is a 3A. I could cut off the dead ends, add some highlights, and—"

"Let's not make this too complicated. I want a perm, cut, and color. Now if you can't do it, then sit my ass in a chair of someone who can hook a bitch up." She'd requested blonde hair for a reason.

"Consider it done."

Max sat back and let the girl get to work on her new look. Tina was adept with a pair of scissors and a comb, cutting Max's hair shorter, but stylishly, and coating her hairline, ears, and neck with a conditioner before applying the dye to her hair.

Several hours later, Max was pleased with what she saw in the mirror. The beautician had taken several years off her age with her blonde, layered hair. She looked amazing. It was a miracle how an elegant hairstyle could change a person. The treatment to her hair was costly, but it was worth it.

"So how do you like it?"

"I love it," Max exclaimed.

Tina smiled. "I knew you would."

Sheena departed her backroom office just in time to catch a look at Max's hair, and her face lit up. "Girl, you look amazing! I told you, my girls don't play when it comes to doin' hair. We the bomb up in Brooklyn. Now you can go out there an' get you that baller. They gonna be all over you, girl."

Max now felt like Maxine again. She stared at her new hairdo in awe. "Thank you," she said generously. She left Tina a very generous tip and walked out of the salon feeling and looking like a different woman.

Max had plenty of money to do whatever she wanted. Her first instinct told her to deposit the cash into a bank account. But she thought against it. It would be too much paperwork, and she didn't need any problems with the I.R.S. They would want to know where such a large amount of cash came from, especially since she had just been released from prison. Then there was her parole officer—he was an asshole and an issue. So she decided to keep the money either on her or hidden somewhere in her mother's home.

Trolling through Brooklyn, Max came across a travel agency, and it dawned on her that she could send her mother away on a nice, relaxing trip. The woman deserved it after everything she'd been through.

At the travel agency, Max had a lengthy conversation with the female agent. She wanted her mother to travel in style. She decided on a month-long cruise around the Mediterranean Sea, making several stops in Greece, Egypt, Spain, France, and Italy. Max purchased two tickets, so her mother could take a friend with her, probably Ms. Shirley. The two had been friends for over thirty-five years. Ms. Shirley was also a widow. Her husband had died from stomach cancer five years before Max's father died. The total expense for the trip, including two airline tickets and transfers, was nearly fifteen thousand dollars.

With a new hairdo, next up was a manicure and pedicure. Having the Koreans take care of her nails and feet was a welcoming feeling. Max got to sit back and relax in the leather massage recliner. She soaked her feet in the warm water and then received a French manicure.

With her hair done and nails and toes done, Max felt pretty again. She had one more thing to do before her transformation was complete, and that was to go shopping. She needed new clothes and shoes.

The cab ride to Kings Plaza mall on Flatbush Avenue was quick. She paid the fare, entered the mall, and walked around. To be inside a mall again felt like being in paradise. The stores and the choices she had were irresistible. For twenty years, she wore the same bland prison garb. Now she finally had a chance again to bring out her character.

A lot of things had changed while she was away. The fashion was different, and the people were too. Back in her time, the style icons were DKNY, Moschino, Versace, FUBU, Tommy Hilfiger, and Karl Kani, and teenagers sported one-strap overalls, crop tops, micro minis and cross-colors.

She explored the mall from top to bottom, going in and out of stores with tons of money to play with, thanks to Layla. She purchased a few eye-catching outfits from several stores and some pricey shoes too. By the end of the day, Maxine came strolling out of the mall feeling like a different woman. For the first time since her release from prison, she caught attention and brief looks from men. The red skinny jeans that highlighted her thick hips and shapely legs was only the beginning. Maxine was back in business—no longer looking forty-two, but thirty, showing off her femininity and youthfulness.

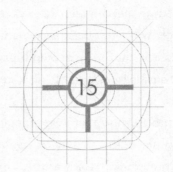

C entral Booking, AKA "the Tombs," on White Street in Lower Manhattan was where Layla sat detained for assaulting an officer. Twenty-four hours had gone by, and she hadn't heard anything from Scott or her lawyer. She was still fuming. She wanted to break the jail bars in half and go after that bitch Penelope and castrate her husband, but she could only sit in the foul-smelling cell and seethe. Surrounded by lowlifes, bum bitches, and petty criminals, she wanted to get back to her life of luxury. But she also wanted revenge. How dare her husband choose his mistress over her, after she had given him twenty years of fidelity and six kids? After she'd ridden shotgun through drug wars with bullets whizzing past her head? After they'd buried three children?

Sitting in jail, Layla kept her composure the best she could. She refused to allow the other inmates to see her cry—to see her look weak. She kept her distance from everyone, daring some bitch to try her. So be it if she caught another charge. She was from the mean streets of Brooklyn. If a bitch didn't know who she was, then she would learn the hard way.

Lance Broker came to see Layla right before her arraignment with the judge. He sat in the lawyer-client section of the courthouse bullpen behind the thick partition, looking like the million bucks he was worth. He had the gift of gab, clout throughout the judicial system, and a skilled legal team behind him. Quickly, he discussed the charges with Layla and assured her that his law firm was already handling it.

Layla scolded him for his tardiness in coming to her aid, and he tried to explain that he was busy with a trial. Layla knew it was Scott pulling strings—letting her stew in Central Booking for attacking Penelope.

The charges were read to Layla, and with Broker standing by her side looking like Perry Kevin, she pleaded, "Not guilty." Her bail was set at fifty thousand dollars. She was ready to pay it right away.

Layla contacted Lucky, who posted her bail. A day later, she walked out of "the Tombs" looking like shit.

Layla trotted down the courthouse stairs with her Lance Broker, wanting to get far away from the area. He was speaking legal technicalities to her about the charges and once again assured her that she wouldn't do another day in jail. Layla saw Lucky sitting behind the wheel of the Mercedes-Benz G-class, waiting for her.

"Where's Scott?" she asked Lance, bitterness in her voice. "He couldn't be here today? Is he with that fuckin' whore? That nasty thot? He puts me in jail to be wit' that bitch!"

Lance replied, "I don't know anything about no thot, or where Scott is at the moment, Layla. My priority is your case."

"You know what? Fuck him and fuck you!"

"Layla, listen. Let's calm down and start thinking rationally. I know you're upset, but this case will be dismissed."

"Fuck you, Lance! And when you speak to Scott, you tell him I'm gonna see that fuckin' bitch dead!" she said loudly for everyone around to hear her.

She departed ways with Lance and walked to where Lucky was parked. She hopped in the passenger seat and stared aimlessly out the windshield.

Looking at her daughter was hard. Everything was building up inside of her. Her hurt drowned her like a non-swimmer.

Lucky sat and stared at her mother with bewilderment. "What happened? Daddy's not answering his phone."

Just like that, a few tears trickled from Layla's eyes. She felt it all coming out of her like air from a balloon. She burst into tears, crying like a baby.

Lucky was taken aback by her mother's sudden emotions. "What the fuck, Mom? What's going on wit' you and Daddy?"

Layla turned to her daughter and told her everything, holding nothing back.

"I never liked that bitch anyway," she replied. She didn't want another sibling—not a half sibling, and especially from some illegal immigrant who she felt trapped her father with pussy and a sad story. "He's so fuckin' stupid!"

Hearing about her father's infidelity brought Lucky back to her own troubles with Whistler. She knew he was seeing another woman and didn't want to be bothered with her anymore.

Lucky had never seen her mother like this before. She was looking weak, and Lucky didn't like it. "Stop crying, Ma. When I see that bitch, I'm gonna handle her ass."

"Your father's protecting her," Layla said.

Lucky frowned.

Scott was always a shrewd and intelligent man. How could he not see Penelope was coming for his wealth and a come-up? Why did he put a baby inside of her? Her family was going through enough already, and they didn't need any more drama added on.

"Ma, you need to stop crying over that fuckin' nigga," Lucky exclaimed. "Stop it! Stop it! He ain't worth your tears. Scott gonna be Scott, but please, don't get weak."

Layla took a profound and needed a lungful of air and dried her tears. Her daughter was right. The tears and woe had to end right away. She pulled herself together and regained her composure. Scott and that bitch had brought her out of her character. She looked at Lucky and said, "Never allow a man to see you sweat and go crazy over him. It's embarrassing. They will not respect it."

Lucky took note, reflecting on her own situation with Whistler. She was tempted to tell her mother about the affair right there but quickly thought against it. Her mother's problems were enough for the day.

Lucky couldn't fathom why her father would choose a side-bitch over his ride-or-die wife. She had always respected her father, but today he she saw him as a fuckin' fool for cursing out his wife in front of Penelope and allowing her to sit in jail while he went to console his mistress.

Layla stared at her daughter with troubled eyes, and there was a secret behind her gaze. Layla felt like the past was coming back to haunt her. Her husband was having an affair and a baby with another woman. Was it karma biting her in the ass?

Layla released a deep breath and spoke. She had to tell Lucky the truth about her relationship with her father. "I used to be his side-bitch a long time ago," she finally admitted out loud and to herself. "I fell in love with your father when he was in love with someone else."

"It was Maxine, right?" Lucky asked.

Layla nodded.

She'd become one of Scott's mistresses back in the days. Back then, Scott was a male whore. Maxine was his main bitch, and he did everything for her. Whatever Maxine wanted, Scott bought for her. It made Layla jealous of their relationship.

Layla fell into his trap of enticement, and they fucked behind her friend's back. One day, she told him she was pregnant with his baby. Immediately, he made her get an abortion. Maxine couldn't find out about it. Maxine was his true love, not her. But when Maxine told her about Sandy's pregnancy a few months after she had her abortion, Layla became infuriated by the news. How could he allow Sandy to keep her baby when she was forced to go down to the clinic and get rid of hers? It made her go berserk. She used Maxine's incident with Sandy to justify attacking Sandy that night.

"I was the other woman, and your father was using me for sex. I wanted to change that. I wanted to flip it and make him mine," she told Lucky. "That night when I beat that bitch Sandy down, I wanted Maxine to stay and take the charge. I knew she would stay; she was weak like that. I saw it as an opportunity to get rid of the main girlfriend and another side-chick, killing two birds with one stone. And with them both gone, I stepped up and became your father's main woman. That same night Maxine got locked up, your father and I hooked up at some luxury hotel, and we fucked for hours. Yeah, he was sad to hear about Maxine and Sandy, but liquor and drugs distracted him, and that night, I gave him some of the best sex he ever had."

Lucky took it all in. She was surprised to hear her mother come clean about everything. It was definitely an earful, but she was glad her mother did what she had to do. If she hadn't, then neither Lucky nor her siblings would have existed.

"I guess karma's a bitch, right? Look at me, it's kicking my ass right now. Scott's fuckin' the nanny, and now she's pregnant. Now I'm the one who's being pushed out the door."

"Fuck karma! We fuck that bitch karma up and toss her ass in the sea, like we gonna do that bitch, Penelope. You're a survivor, Ma, and you gonna do what you need to do to stay on top. You and Daddy, y'all are meant to be. Don't let that foreign non-English speaking bitch get in between y'all two."

Layla was ready to do something about the problem. Penelope was about to become a dead Cuban, pregnant or not. She was an interference with her livelihood, and Layla was growing tired of these intrusions on her life, her well-being, and her family.

"Let's kill this bitch," she said to Lucky.

Lucky smiled. "I'm down, Ma."

16

nformation was power, and Jimmy knew that all too well. Sometimes it wasn't about muscle or firepower, but about knowing your targets—studying their movements, habits, and surroundings. Once you knew your rivals' activities and locations, then sometimes it took subtle action to wipe them out. Jimmy knew he had the advantage on his adversaries. For the past month he'd been conducting surveillance and collecting information. Sometimes he received it the hard way, making people talk who didn't want to talk, like Knock. Knock was a fierce and loyal soldier to his bosses. He would not give them up easily. He was a tough nut to crack, and Jimmy was somewhat impressed by his boldness.

Jimmy started with the garden shears to his fingers, cutting them off one at a time and inducing agonizing pain for Knock. Ten fingers later, the man was still defiant.

"Fuck you, muthafucka!" Knock cursed him.

Jimmy only smiled. In due time, they all talked. Some took longer than others, but he always got what he wanted from them.

Jimmy moved on to his next devious torture device, a blowtorch. The hot blue flames crisped, blackened, and sloughed off Knock's skin. Butt naked, Knock writhed and screamed on the table he was firmly tied down to. Knock's screams echoed throughout the concrete room, but there was no one around for miles to hear him. Jimmy worked the flames against his feet and bare legs. When he attacked Knock's genitals with the flaming device, he was ready to talk. By then, his skin looked like melting wax, and the smell of human flesh permeated the entire room.

Jimmy was ready to pass on this newfound information to Deuce and have his boss put it to good use.

Deuce loathed New York City. He thought it was crowded, rude, and hostile. He also hated New York because for a long time he was at war with New York City drug dealers. New York niggas were arrogant like the Roman Empire—invading everywhere and trying to annex everything around them. They believed niggas from out of town were supposed to bow down to them and surrender their territory to them because they were from Brooklyn, the Bronx, Harlem, or Queens. Like New York City was the only city that bred killers and get-money niggas. He felt that New York had to be stopped. They were greedy and disrespectful, and the day they invaded his territory in Delaware was the day they made the biggest mistake of their lives.

He and Jimmy sat in the Ford Taurus on Church Street in Lower Manhattan. The car was unassuming, but the men inside, not so much. The evening was flouting the daylight atmosphere of the city with a descending sun. Church Street was cluttered with cars and foot traffic.

Deuce took in the bustling ambiance. It wasn't his cup of tea. It was the far opposite of Baltimore and Wilmington. There was too much going on at one time, but he was far from intimidated by it. Business had to be taken care of, and he was the one to do it. He sat in the passenger seat puffing on his Newport and taking everything in. He took no one or nothing for granted. His eyes were transfixed on the many people moving about, the towering buildings that decorated the narrow area, and passing traffic that continuously flowed like a stream. On his lap was a loaded and unused .45 Magnum, the perfect weapon to take down a drug kingpin.

This was Deuce's moment to decapitate the king and crush the crown he wore. Jimmy always came through for him, and he'd received the perfect intel about Scott. It took some time, but it was rewarding. The more information Jimmy gathered about Scott, his crew, and his family, the more he understood why Scott would be foolish enough to come to Wilmington and try him and his crew. The West organization had serious muscle, influence, longevity, and power. Scott felt his organization was stronger and more developed in every area, and that DMC were Neanderthals. Deuce was about to show him otherwise.

Deuce rarely got his hands dirty—he had soldiers for that—but this was personal. They'd killed his sister and tried to embarrass him on his own turf. Wilmington was his gold mine, and he had everything the way he wanted it, from having the police in his pocket to the extortion of the locals. But now many people were dead because of the drug war, and business was slow. He was losing money because of the West organization.

Deuce wrapped his hand around the barrel of the .45 Magnum. He and Jimmy were very patient men. For an hour, they sat on the city block and scoped everything, watching people go in and out of LA Fitness, nestled in the middle of the city street. They knew to get to an area much earlier than their target to spot the good and bad about their surroundings. And that's exactly what they did. Knowing Scott was a health freak and that he liked to work out at a particular gym was a bonus. The one problem they had was, Scott wasn't a routine person. So every day for the past week they had been watching the place, knowing he would show up one day out of that week.

A black Range Rover with tinted windows passed their Ford and double-parked in front of the LA Fitness. The doors opened, and Scott and two of his henchmen climbed out of the vehicle. *Bingo!* Deuce finally had a real view of the man who wanted to turn his world upside down and seize his drug operation. Now, he was about to turn the tables on his rival.

Deuce gripped the pistol tighter in his hand. The sight of Scott made his blood boil. He was eager to strike, but he remained patient. He couldn't risk fucking things up by suddenly becoming impatient. He and Jimmy watched and plotted.

Deuce wondered why Scott came to this gym in the city. He thought the area was too busy and too open. Being the drug kingpin and mastermind Deuce was, he saw too much vulnerability in the area for a man with enemies.

Dressed in a black-and-white tracksuit and white Nikes, Scott traveled quickly inside the building. His two men got back in the Range Rover.

"We catch him when he leaves," Deuce said to Jimmy.

Jimmy nodded. He could easily kill Scott himself, but Deuce insisted on doing the dirty work. It was a public place, but it was their only open window.

Deuce finished his cigarette and discarded it out the window. He exhaled the smoke. The gym was on the second and third floors of a four-story building, and the area was flooded with commercial businesses, vehicular traffic, and pedestrians everywhere. There were a few passing police cars, but that didn't thwart Deuce's deadly motives. He noticed the area had several surveillance cameras in the vicinity, including three cameras near the gym's entrance.

A full hour was about to come up since Scott had gone inside, and still, there was no sign of him. Deuce didn't want to lose his target by being too patient. Maybe there was an exit they'd missed. He knew that Scott had not come this far in the game by being stupid. But his men were still seated in the Range Rover, waiting patiently.

"I'm going inside," he announced to Jimmy.

"I thought we sit and wait until he comes out."

"Fuck that! I'm going in." Deuce pushed the door open and exited the car out onto the sidewalk. Dressed in a sweat suit with a ball cap pulled low over his eyes and carrying a small duffel bag, Deuce looked like a gym member. His .45 Magnum was cleverly hidden on his person. He calmly approached the building. It was now or never.

Scott was breaking out in a serious sweat with his personal trainer. Tammy was a fitness guru, addressing all of his weak points and making them much stronger. Today, they were working on his cardio and his upper body strength with him having ten-minute breaks between. Scott was already a healthy and fit man, but he always felt he needed to improve in some areas. The streets were not forgiving, and he had to be in excellent shape if there came a time when he needed to engage in hand-to-hand combat.

He was paying good money to learn mixed martial arts from an instructor with three black belts who had won several martial arts competitions. Tammy was the best, and she was expensive, but the $200 an hour was worth it. She was a personal trainer to some celebrities too, and she was in top shape—slim waist, nice curves, killer abs, firm buttocks, and sturdy legs. And she wasn't just athletic, she was beautiful too. She had skin like night and a body like Adrienne-Joi Johnson.

Another part of the workout Scott loved was the eye candy in the place. From his personal trainer to several other beautiful ladies in the Manhattan gym, they were spread everywhere.

His workout with Tammy concluded, Scott thanked her and even flirted with her for a moment, but Tammy kept things professional between them. She had a fiancé she loved dearly, and she showed off her diamond engagement ring to Scott. Though he was a gangster, he respected her commitment.

He wiped the sweat from his face and brow and was ready to leave the gym. Before his departure, he called his goons outside to inform them he was leaving. They were to be alert and ready. He wasn't carrying a pistol, but his security was heavily armed.

Bag in hand and satisfied from his workout with Tammy, Scott walked toward the exit. He had been going to the gym for a year, but his appearances there were irregular. So far, he'd had no incidents.

He glided out the front door, and his two goons were standing outside the Range Rover parked across the street and trying to blend in.

Twilight had descended across the city, and traffic had thickened on Church Street. The people busied themselves on the street with their smartphones and conversing with each other, and the restaurants and cafés were coming alive with evening customers. It was a typical night in New York. Scott was among the crowd of people, looking ordinary, mixing in with the city folks.

As he headed toward his men parked across the street, someone immediately caught his attention from his peripheral vision. He noticed the large black male dressed in gym wear carrying a small duffel bag approaching him. Scott's first thought was that he was a customer at the gym; he was muscular and worked out. But there was something off about him. Scott had never seen him around. And his eyes, from a distance, were menacing. With over twenty years in the game, Scott knew that look of evil; he carried that same look himself.

His sixth sense kicked in, and it screamed at him—the large man was a threat to him.

He kept calm and walked toward the street. He was unarmed, but his goons weren't. The vehicle traffic and foot traffic blocked their view of him, though, and it could create a situation.

The man in the gym wear casually walked Scott's way, not going toward the gym, his eyes fixed on Scott.

Scott kept his eyes on him, his nervousness increasing, his two armed henchmen too far away to protect him from a bullet. When he saw the man reach for something, he didn't hesitate. He hunched toward the ground and took off running into the congested city traffic.

Deuce lifted the .45 Magnum in Scott's direction and blasted gunfire his way. *Boom! Boom! Boom! Boom!*

Panic and chaos ensued with screaming and a wave of people running away from the gunshots, dashing for cover, swarming into buildings, toppling tables and chairs from the sidewalk café, ducking behind cars, and hitting the pavement face down.

Deuce was on Scott, chasing after him and releasing a barrage of bullets that whizzed by Scott's head, barely missing him. Two bullets shattered the windshield of a parked car.

Scott frantically dodged through the traffic, desperately trying to escape the brazen hit on his life.

Scott's goons scrambled to reach him, their guns drawn and ready to neutralize the threat, but the scattering crowd and two passing box trucks obstructing their view temporarily hampered them. When they finally had a view of Deuce, they opened fire, and a full-blown shootout ensued.

Jimmy charged into the violent mêlée heavily armed. Deuce was on the opposite side of the street shooting at Scott, and Scott's men were shooting at Deuce.

Jimmy approached the two gunmen from a blind spot. He raised the 9mm Uzi carbine in his grip firmly and aimed their way. Distracted with Deuce, they didn't notice him. Jimmy didn't hesitate at all. *Bratatatatatatat!*

Bullets slammed into the two men, spraying their blood on the streets. Their bodies spun from the gunfire, and they went down from the hail of bullets.

Scott took off running, suddenly alone and fearing for his life.

Deuce continued shooting at him. The bullets hit everything but him.

The streets of Manhattan had quickly been turned into the OK Corral. The gunfight was intense and terrifying. Car horns blew erratically, and there was screaming and more screaming, crying, and people running and hiding.

Scott sprinted from the shooting like a track star, and Deuce lost sight of him among the sea of people fleeing the area. They'd missed their shot. Scott had gotten away.

Jimmy shouted, "We need to go!"

Deuce didn't want to leave. He had Scott dead in his sights, and the muthafucka escaped death somehow. He scowled, the smoking gun still hot in his hand.

The getaway vehicle was of no use to them; it had been blocked in by an abandoned car. The men had to flee on foot and ditch the guns. With police sirens blaring in the air, they had to blend in and get the hell out of Dodge.

※※※

The front door to the penthouse suite burst open, and Scott hurried inside. He closed the door and immediately collapsed against the floor. His legs felt like jelly. It was a long and worrisome trip home via cab ride and ridiculous traffic. He looked a mess. It was a miracle he made it home unscathed. He was breathing hard, thankful to be still alive. But two of his men were dead. How did they find him? Who were they? He had questions he knew he would get the answers to really soon.

He lay on the floor for a few minutes before he sprung up and darted into the master bedroom. He went into the drawer and removed a 9mm Ruger. Next, he checked his home, going room to room with the pistol, making sure there weren't any threats inside. The place was empty. Not even Layla was home. He was worried. If they came after him, what would stop them from going after his family?

First things first, he needed to make sure his family was okay. His cell phone had been lost in the gunfight, but he had more burners around. He knew that cops and homicide were all over the crime scene by now.

Scott had a lot to be concerned about. He wasn't just worried about the men who tried to kill him, but about tonight's mess spiraling out of control with the media, and his face being captured by the surveillance cameras. The last thing he needed was unwanted attention toward him, his family, and his organization. On paper, he was a businessman—a real estate developer, club owner—a legit millionaire. A shooting and two men murdered on a Manhattan street wasn't something he wanted to be connected to. But it was about to be headline news and a sensational story with the media. He needed to reach out to his connections throughout the city and disconnect himself from the shooting and murders and from the negativity. His lawyers would get on that right away.

His adrenaline was still pumping. His soul was on fire. Someone took a shot at him, and now it was his turn to shoot back, and he didn't plan on missing. In the midst of things, he soon noticed the hole in his track suit jacket from a bullet passing through it. They had come that close to killing him.

From then, Scott decided to triple his security around himself and his family. And everyone in his circle had to wear a bulletproof vest. He wasn't taking any chances.

He made phone calls to his children, to his wife, and then to two of his lieutenants and assassins.

17

Miguel pulled up in front of Max's place. He called her new cell and let her know that he was waiting for her outside.

"Fifteen minutes," she said.

While sitting and waiting, he lit a cigarette and chilled. The radio was on Hot 97, and Ebro, Laura Stylez, and Rosenberg were interviewing Lil Wayne on their morning show. Lil Wayne was saying some interesting things about Birdman and Cash Money. He griped about money issues and Birdman allegedly sabotaging his album release. These musicians had millions of dollars, and yet they were complaining about some catty shit. Lil Wayne had a net worth somewhere in the hundreds of millions.

Miguel knew if he had the money they had, he wouldn't be under Max's thumb, and his family wouldn't have to worry about anything for the rest of their lives. And with that money, he could easily hire someone to murder Max. It was a pleasant thought. He even smiled about her death.

It was another day, and another unwanted moment he had to spend with Max. She was a headache to him. The sooner he did his part of the job, the sooner Nadia would finally be free from that bitch. It's why he took the initiative and investigated Bugsy himself, though he knew Max would be against it. She had told him not to do any intel on Bugsy without her, but Miguel ignored her. He couldn't wait that long. He and his lady might have been indebted to Max, but he wasn't her slave. The sooner he found the perfect location to murder Bugsy, the sooner he would be done with her. And the time was now.

Miguel had taken it upon himself to track Bugsy down and follow him around town. It was a long and tedious task, but it had to be done. Bugsy was a busy man, mostly dealing with legit businesses in his father's name and moving kilos of drugs for the organization. He traveled back and forth from New York to Delaware regularly. He would meet with attorneys and businessmen one day and then the street lieutenants and his twin brother the next. He was the family's golden boy for handling the paperwork and money laundering, and he was in charge of distribution.

Scott's organization had a reliable team of people for handling large sums of cash, and Bugsy was one main guy that ran the show. Bugsy had set up offshore accounts in countries with bank secrecy laws that allowed anonymous banking. They also ran numerous shell companies for the sole purpose of laundering drug money.

For three days, Miguel had trailed Bugsy, making Bugsy's life his own. Wherever he went, Miguel went. Miguel took down notes and license plate numbers. He was playing detective. He needed to find that open window to strike. It was difficult because Bugsy had steady security around him twenty-four/seven. Wherever he went, his armed goons went too. He had little privacy in his life.

But Miguel knew there had to be something he was missing. Then, on day four, he found his opportunity. It was after midnight, and though he wanted to go home and be with his kids, his gut instincts told him to stick around and wait it out.

Bugsy was held up in a towering apartment complex on the Upper East Side. He went in alone, and his security detail retreated.

Miguel watched three men climb into the dark SUV and drive off, leaving Bugsy alone. That never happened, but that night it did.

Miguel lingered outside the building in his non-descript vehicle. He watched the lobby like a hawk, being patient and chain-smoking. He knew something was going down, but he couldn't put his finger on what it was.

An hour later, Bugsy was seen exiting the lobby and getting into a black Lincoln. Miguel figured the car to be Uber car service. Bugsy's appearance was low-key and more relaxed—a blue ball cap, jeans, and a T-shirt.

The Lincoln drove off, and Miguel followed. It headed toward FDR Drive, going northbound, and then they crossed over into the Bronx, using the Willis Avenue Bridge, and the Lincoln fused with the cars on the I-87 North.

Miguel followed them shrewdly, always remaining two or three cars behind them. I-87 took them into the north side of Mount Vernon, where the area had a suburban vibe as opposed to the south side, where its urban feel resembled the Bronx.

The drive wasn't long or far, thanks to the late hour and sparse traffic. But it was taking a toll on Miguel's gas tank. His money was dwindling, and shadowing Bugsy was taking precious time away from his kids, but this felt like it was going to be big.

The Lincoln came to a stop in front of a small, middle-class home on a tree-lined block with well-cut grass and a garden. The place was a cliché, a cookie cutter home, especially with its white picket fence. The area was quiet, and there was a park a block down.

Bugsy paid the driver and stepped out of the car. From across the street, Miguel watched him approach the front door. He knocked twice, and the white door opened up and a beautiful young woman emerged.

Miguel smiled. "Gotcha!" he uttered. He lingered on the block.

The lights to the living room came on. The living room faced the street, and it had large bay windows. Miguel could see the silhouette of the folks inside, moving back and forth inside the house. He needed to know more about the area and the house Bugsy was inside. He smoked another cigarette as he waited.

Half an hour later, the living room lights turned off, and he figured the twosome retreated into the bedroom, maybe to have sex or get some sleep. Either way, he would take advantage of the opportunity. His head swiveled, scoping out the street. Everything was still and quiet, and the neighboring houses were dark.

Miguel removed himself from the car and stealthily approached the residence, trying not to attract notice. He scaled the short fence and mapped out the house. It was old-fashioned with a short paved driveway leading into the back yard. There was one dilemma—the front and back yards both had motion lights.

The bright light turned on, and Miguel shifted from the brightness quickly and crept toward the yard. He looked up. The master bedroom overlooked the small back yard. The neighbor's dog was keen on his movements, and it barked at him.

Miguel had seen enough. The neighbor's dog was too loud, and the damn thing would raise concern with its owners. He quickly trod back to his car. He'd found his window.

Max's fifteen minutes seemed like an hour to Miguel. He was on his fourth cigarette, and now he was becoming impatient. He was tempted to drive off. Max was becoming a burden to him. To him, she was a lonely bitch who wanted to wipe the cobwebs from her pussy and get fucked. And Miguel was the handsome thug she wanted to break her drought. She wanted him badly, but Max was far from his type. Nadia was the woman he wanted to spend the rest of his life with. He planned on marrying her the day she was released from prison. Max was trying to interfere with his relationship, but it wasn't happening. Once their business was concluded, he was gone, and he wanted her to stay far away from him and Nadia.

The front door opened, and Miguel looked that way, expecting to see the same dyke-looking Max emerge from the house. And then she appeared. Miguel had to do a double-take. "What the fuck!"

Maxine sauntered toward the car looking fabulous in a pale yellow jumpsuit and a pair of heels. Her walk was mean. Her hair was different, her smile was radiant, and the outfit was kind to her curves. A glistening gold heart necklace decorated her slim neck.

She slid into the passenger seat.

Miguel was speechless, his eyes stuck on her.

Max knew he liked the transformation. The stunned look on his face told it all. She was expecting the positive response from him.

"What happened?" he asked.

"I needed to get back to being me again," she said. "You like it?"

"It's different."

She smiled. "From the ugly duckling to the pretty swan, right?"

Miguel suddenly felt odd around her. "You're beautiful . . . I never knew."

"You don't know many things about me, Miguel."

He grinned. "I guess I don't."

Maxine had seen that same look he held in his eyes with other men; she knew she finally had him. Now she was finally in charge over Miguel, and it made her gloat inside. Now she could toy with him the way she wanted to. Beauty made men weak, and Miguel was no different. He was still a man with a dick, and a dick was always weak for some pussy; it was human nature.

Before he drove off, she tossed a brown envelope on his lap. Miguel picked it up and opened it. Inside was cash. It was unexpected.

"That's ten thousand dollars," she said. "For an additional hit."

Miguel was stunned silent. Between the new money and her new look, it was a little overwhelming. Who was she?

"No thank-you?" Max said.

"Thank you."

"I told you, I'll take care of you as long as you take care of me."

Miguel secured the cash on his person. Money was becoming tighter in his household, and with him not having steady employment and raising children, he needed to make every penny. "Well, I got some good news for you," he said.

"What is it?"

"I've been following Bugsy on my own for the past five days, and I got a new location for you."

You did what? Max was upset he went off on his own and went snooping behind her back, possibly risking being caught. She was surprised he actually had some results, though. She didn't fuss but listened to him.

"He got a girl he goes to see in Mount Vernon. He goes alone, no security at all, and it's our open window," he said.

"Impressive."

"I'm ready to get this over with."

She smiled. "I bet you are."

Miguel put the car into drive, and they were off, going to look at the new location he had told her about. Once again, his eyes quietly shifted her way. He was captivated by her beauty.

Max eyed the quaint suburban home on the tree-lined street from the car parked across the street. It was early afternoon, and the neighborhood was quiet, as was the house she gawked at.

"He comes here?" she asked.

"Yeah, at night. And he comes alone. He took a cab here."

Max smiled. She needed to find out more about the girl, but it was perfect. Layla was about to get ready for another funeral, and this one would really hit home. Bugsy was a core player in the organization. The day they lost him would be the day their family and organization started unraveling, if it hadn't started already.

"Let's go," she said.

Miguel started the car, but he didn't drive away just yet. He looked at Max and asked, "You hungry?"

She returned his look and simply smiled. It was the first time he'd ever asked about her well-being. She chuckled inwardly. Yes, things had changed between them.

Max wondered just how loyal Miguel would be to Nadia now that he was captivated by her new look.

Famous for its many seafood restaurants, City Island was a small island neighboring the Bronx. There were over thirty eateries, ranging from fast food to chic establishments like the French Bistro SK and The Black Whale, a place famous for its desserts. With it being early afternoon on a fair summer day, there wasn't a crowd yet, and seating outside was available, giving diners a view of the calm sea and the many boats and yachts docked nearby. It was the perfect setting for an impromptu afternoon date, if one could call it that. To Max, she was merely having dinner with Miguel, and they were talking about business.

The Lobster Box had some of the best seafood in town. The place carried a delightful nautical atmosphere for the customers with breathtaking views of Long Island Sound.

Max sat opposite Miguel at the wood Bertram table, and the two conversed like they never had conversed before. Usually, Miguel would be aloof and standoffish toward her, but today he was a different person. He was smiling more, and he was more engaged in the conversation.

They ate their meals and took in the tranquil scenery. They both downed a few strong cocktails. Miguel also got a few laughs to escape from Max. He was humorous when he wanted to be.

For Max, the attention felt good. Her new look was worth the money, and it generated the right reaction from the right people. If she'd effortlessly turned a man like Miguel with her new look, then she could only imagine what other damage she could do. Scott came to her mind, and she wondered about him. If he saw her again like this, still looking like a goddess, curvy and sexy in so many ways after spending over twenty years behind bars, what would his reaction be toward her? Would he come groveling at her feet, begging for her forgiveness and wanting her back? She didn't want him back, that's for sure. She wanted the entire family to suffer.

"So what's your story?" Miguel asked her.

"My story?"

"Yes. Tell me about yourself. I want to know."

Max smirked at how easy it was to make Miguel putty in her hands. She was uncertain if she should tell him her business, since he and Nadia were simply pawns in her criminal scheme. "Tell me your story," she replied. "How did you and Nadia meet?"

Miguel now looked hesitant to tell her his business. He finished the cocktail and sighed. With a few drinks in his system, he felt more willing to discuss his business. He looked at Max with conviction and responded, "We've known each other since high school. It's that simple. She's my high school sweetheart. She got pregnant her senior year, and we been together ever since then."

They ordered more cocktails. Miguel continued to talk, discharging more information about himself and his relationship.

"I thought the military would be my escape from poverty, the gangs, a fucked-up life itself. I just wanted to become someone, but to join the Marines with the same demons you want to escape from only amplified the shit. I got into some heavy shit with selling military guns, and that got me a dishonorable discharge and time in lockup. But Nadia has always been there for me."

Max threw back a martini and listened. She didn't care for Nadia, she cared for him. Miguel was the man she needed, in more ways than one.

To hear him tell his story, it was intriguing. He looked like a bad ass, and he was.

"I came home with nothing, and we struggled for a long time. Nadia had my back, and she was desperate to support her family. She stole someone's identity and forged several checks for a few thousand dollars. The money got us by for a few months and kept us from being evicted. But it caught up to her, and now she's in jail because I wasn't man enough to just get a fuckin' job and take care of my family. I allowed my lady to risk her freedom for the kids and me.

"And then you came along and made it harder for us," he added. "Nadia is not a fighter. She's not from where I come from. She's a good girl that's willing to do anything for her family. She is the only reason why I'm sitting here wit' you, ready to kill. I owe that woman a lot; I owe her everything."

Max sat in apathetic silence. She felt she had a more tragic tale for him. Nadia was in prison for a crime she'd committed, but Max did twenty-two years for a murder she didn't commit.

Miguel's eyes were faint from the alcohol he consumed. He focused on Max, smiled awkwardly and said, "I showed you mine. Now you gotta show me yours."

She was still reluctant to show hers, but she felt it would not hurt anyway. "You wanna see mine?"

"I do." He smiled.

Max took a deep breath and released her pain. She told Miguel about her ex-boyfriend Scott, and how much she loved him a long time ago and that he did anything for her, and she would do anything for him. He was the only man she'd ever been with. Then she went into the real pain about her life. She spoke about Scott's infidelity with Sandy and how she felt betrayed. And then she told him about the murder Layla did and made her take the fall for it. She explained that Layla never felt an ounce of guilt for what she did to her life. Max explained Layla constantly rubbed her privileged life in her face. How could anyone do that to someone they called a friend? Max spewed to Miguel bitterly about the twenty-two years snatched from her life. She wanted to become a lawyer. She was in one of the top colleges in the city with a high GPA, and she had scholarships and loving parents who fully supported her. And all of that was taken from her in one night because of one friend and a cheating boyfriend.

"My father died while I was in prison, and I didn't find out about it until a month later because I was in solitary confinement," she said.

"Damn!"

Max explained every sordid, dysfunctional detail to Miguel about her past—Layla, Scott, Sandy, love, hate, and finally revenge.

"It's why you're going after all of them, huh?" he said.

"My life was taken from me, so I'm going to take theirs from them, one by one," Max said seriously.

Miguel saw a different side of her. She was smart, sexy, and beautiful, and an entirely different woman from the one he met that day at the Port Authority Terminal.

"I got the bill," she said.

He groaned, and she moaned. Miguel's mouth latched onto Max's hard, dark nipples, teasing them with his teeth and tongue while she rode his dick in the back seat of his Accord. Parked on a side street not too far from City Island, they fucked like there was no tomorrow. Max straddled him in the back seat, bouncing up and down against him, her breath against his, his hard erection penetrating her fully. His hands grasped her buttocks, and he pulled her closer to his sweaty frame, their exposed parts connected like Legos. The feel of her warm, wet pussy was so overwhelming for Miguel he damn near had to fight to control his release. He wanted to come inside her instantly, but his mind fought the urge.

She whispered in his ear, "It's been over twenty years."

Max's body ached for this moment badly. It felt like she was a virgin all over again. She felt her buttocks lift in the air and come back down against him by his hands, and her pussy stretched like a rubber band from his sizable width. For her, it was an unbelievable moment. Miguel was the second guy she'd been with, and she wanted it to last.

She ground her hips into his lap and pushed her body against his. Her thighs squeezed against his. "I'm gonna come!" she announced. "Oh shit! Oh shit!" She hummed and tightened her arms around him, feeling the climax quickly approaching. "Fuck me!" she cried out. The sensation coursing through her body was about to lift her through the roof.

Miguel cupped her breasts again and hungrily sucked on her nipples. It took a few more deep thrusts inside of her before she finally exploded, her body quivered against his clammy skin, and she exhaled in satisfaction.

"I'm gonna come too," Miguel yelped. He continued to thrust upwards inside of her and was soon about to approach his point of no return. His body soon stiffened underneath her, and he released quickly, shooting his sperm into the condom and shuddering from the sensation. Feeling like he was on an intense high, Miguel had never had it like that before. Max had put it on him. Though he loved Nadia, the sex with Max was powerful. Her pussy felt like it had been marinated for twenty-something years without a dick. Miguel knew he was a lucky man.

Max lifted herself from his lap and collapsed in the seat next to him. She had to compose herself. The intense orgasm lingered inside of her. "That was fun," she said simply.

"Nice," Miguel responded, expecting her to say something special.

"Yes, that was fun," she repeated nonchalantly.

It was nice to her but mind-blowing for Miguel, whose dick was still hard.

"I need to go," she said.

Miguel nodded. They dressed and climbed back into the front seat. Miguel started the car and drove off.

Max sat back and grinned, knowing she had this man pussy-whipped. Nadia who?

19

The Denali came to a stop inside the sprawling scrap yard on Stillwell Avenue in Brooklyn. The doors swung open, and Meyer and Luna hurried out of the vehicle and ran toward the large office trailer nestled inside the scrap yard. The business was temporarily closed for the day, and Scott had his men situated all through the area for his protection. The attempt on his life had stirred up the hornet's nest, and his soldiers had their stingers sharpened and ready to strike back. Meyer and Luna had heard about the attempt on Scott's life and rushed from Delaware to New York.

Meyer pushed his way through the security detail and stormed into the building scowling heavily. He stormed into his father's office. "Pop, I'm right here. Who tried to kill you? Let me know, I'm on it."

The outburst interrupted a private conversation between Scott and Whistler, who looked at Meyer and Luna with nonchalance. Scott took a pull from his cigar and stared dispassionately at his animated son who'd just burst into the room uninvited.

"It was Deuce, right? We on it, Pop. I'ma kill that muthafucka!" Meyer growled. "I've already got the Greene brothers cleaning house for us. They done took out several of Deuce's men from Delaware to Maryland. And they're vicious, Pop. I'll have them come up to New York to guard you!"

Scott removed the cigar from his lips and tapped a few ashes into the ashtray on the table nearby. He looked unruffled.

Meyer lifted his shirt, revealing the pistol tucked in his waistband. "I'm here for you, Pop. We gonna get this muthafucka! I got ya back!"

"Why aren't you in Delaware overseeing my operations?" Scott asked calmly.

"Because somebody tried to kill you! I drove here the minute I heard," Meyer said.

"You came here to protect me?" Scott said. "Nigga, you think this was the first time some niggas took a shot at me and tried to take my life? I'm a veteran in this game. In the end, I'm always gonna be the last man standing. And I got my men already on it."

"I know but—"

"You know what, Meyer? You don't know shit! I didn't call for you, and I don't need you protecting me. I need you back in Delaware handling things," Scott said sternly.

"You serious?" Meyer uttered.

"Muthafucka, do you see me laughing? Get the fuck out of here, Meyer! Go do your job, and be some good to me for once. I know how to handle the people that took a shot at me. And if you ever sanction hired killers without it being green-lighted by me again, I will personally fuck you up! Cut those lunatics off! The Greene brothers will only bring heat to our organization, you dumb fuck! And I mean, fuckin' now!"

Meyer didn't expect this outcome from his father. He wanted to be there for his pops and make him proud, but it seemed like he could never measure up.

For a moment, Meyer stood in the office looking defiant. Luna stood behind him and remained silent, knowing not to get involved in the family dispute. His job was to kill on orders and protect the family. Besides, a dispute between Meyer and Scott was nothing new to him.

Meyer pivoted and stormed out of the office. Luna followed.

Whistler said to Scott, "I think you were a little hard on him, Scott.

He was merely trying to look out for you."

Scott frowned at his friend. "Don't tell me how to raise my son, Whistler. That nigga is hard-headed and impulsive. Sometimes he does more harm than good."

"He remind you of someone?" Whistler responded.

Scott looked at him and didn't respond right away. He knew who Whistler was referring to. He puffed on his cigar and uttered, "That was a long time ago."

"Just like Dwayne and Kevin was a long time ago," Whistler said.

Scott knew Whistler would eventually find out about the murders of his two soldiers. "They fucked up," he replied.

"They were good soldiers."

"On that night, they weren't."

"Lately, you've been everywhere, Scott. It's hard to keep up with you. Penelope got you caught up. And going to the gym in such an open area—leaving your armed security in the car—what was all that about?"

He puffed on his cigar again and grimaced at Whistler. "It won't happen again," Scott said with conviction.

"No matter what, I'm always here for you, Scott, but don't make it difficult for everyone," Whistler said.

"When has it ever been easy for us?"

Whistler said his piece, feeling that Scott was becoming impulsive again. Though he and Meyer rarely saw eye to eye, he knew Meyer was loyal and dedicated to protecting the family and the organization.

Whistler exited the trailer and stepped foot into the scrap yard. There, he saw Meyer and Luna still parked on the grounds. Meyer was smoking a cigarette in the passenger seat, and he locked eyes with Whistler. Whistler read the boys' expressions, and he saw nothing good happening.

Meyer felt disrespected and hurt by his father's words. Whistler was concerned. Scott had been criticizing and spewing harsh words toward the boy lately. Whistler was hoping Scott didn't push his son too far over the edge. The last thing everyone needed was a civil war inside the organization.

Deuce missed his shot, and it angered him. How did he miss Scott? He had the man dead in his sights, and he still got away. Deuce knew he jumped the gun and reacted too quickly. Impulsiveness made him sloppy, and now he knew Scott would be gunning for him, but he was undaunted. It just meant the inevitable. The only silver lining was that two of Scott's men were killed, but they were calves, and Deuce wanted to slaughter the bull.

He and Jimmy barely made it out of the city with their freedom. The shootout brought the police from every direction. But fortunately for them, the shooting created enough panic on the city street that the two men could camouflage themselves and flee the area.

Deuce knew he had no one to blame but himself. But a missed kill didn't mean defeat. It meant next time he would get right up on his target, put the gun to his head, and blow his brains out. He would not miss a second time, and Deuce was determined to get that second chance.

Back in Delaware, Deuce found the perfect relief from his worries—drugs and pussy. After smoking several Kush blunts laced with coke, he then began drinking sizzurp. Deuce was in rare form. His eyes were bugged, his mouth and chin were twisted in opposite directions, and his heart raced. He thrust his hard dick into the young, naked stripper with vigor. He wrapped his hand around her slim neck, having her on all fours, doggy-style. He pushed down on her back and went inside of her deeply. He huffed and puffed, feeling the shaved pussy tightening around his width and feeling the young girl desperately trying to take the entire dick slamming inside of her.

Deuce was well endowed, hanging long and stretching wide. His large meat was a sideshow for the ladies. He was very proud of it and wasn't shy about putting it to good use. The girl cried out and made faces that weren't cute. It seemed like she'd taken on more than she could handle.

He spread the stripper's legs more and smacked her ass roughly, and his grip around her neck tightened. She couldn't move. He was in control. It was the sex where she moved when he wanted her to move. That night, Deuce controlled everything about the young woman. If he wanted an hour long blowjob, he would get it. Fear made her submissive, and the money made her willing.

Deuce could hear the music from the strip club blasting into the locked backroom he was in. R-Kelly and Ludacris' "Legs Shakin'" blared, as he was enjoying his little sex slave. He rammed nine inches of hard dick inside of the slim girl from the back and continued to squeeze the back of her neck.

Deuce's tight hold around her neck and the way he fucked her forcefully was taking a toll on the girl. Her body couldn't take much more of it. He smacked her ass hard, pulled her long hair, and mashed her face further against the desk, treating her like a ragdoll.

"Ouch! Ouch! Deuce, you're startin' to hurt me."

"Bitch, shut the fuck up and take this dick!" he hollered. He squeezed her neck harder as he thrust himself roughly inside of her and smacked her ass so hard, he left a small bruise on her butt cheek. His biceps and triceps flexed as he consumed the young woman in his hold.

Six three and weighing over two hundred and fifty pounds, he refused to let her go or relent on the powerful hold he had over her.

The young girl had no escape from him. She cried out, "Ouch! Ouch! You're hurtin' me! Please, stop!"

"Bitch, didn't I tell you to shut the fuck up and take this dick?"

The music coming from the strip club muffled out the girl's cry. She was on her own and desperate for him to stop or finish quickly. "Ouch! You're hurtin' me!"

Deuce was tired of her yelling. He continued to pound his big dick inside of her from the back, and as she continued to resist and scream, his anger took over. Her complaining pissed him off.

He abruptly punched her in the back of her head with a dizzying blow. She screamed, "No, get off me! Stop! Stop! Oh my God, no!"

Deuce struck her again and again, wanting her to shut up, and the third punch knocked her out cold. While punching her, he continued to squeeze the back of her neck forcefully, his fingertips sinking further into her flesh.

Finally, there was silence from her, and he could enjoy the pussy in peace. He continued to fuck her, thrusting inside of the girl's now wilted body, feeling his orgasm brewing. But he was unaware that he'd killed the girl with his punches and his firm chokehold from behind.

He came inside of the girl and felt some relief. All of his problems quickly dissipated. He pulled out of her pussy and the girl's body collapsed completely to the floor. She was unresponsive. He muttered, "Oh shit!"

What the fuck had he done? Deuce was high as fuck, but looking at the dead girl quickly sobered him up. He stared at her naked body, knowing he had gone too far. The war with his rivals had him upset, and he'd lost his temper.

He got decent and reached for his cell phone. On the other end was Jimmy. "It's me," he said. "I need you at the strip club. I got a problem that needs to be handled."

Jimmy said, "I'm on my way."

Deuce ended the call. With a dead body by his feet, he lit a cigarette and smoked. He was a cold-blooded killer, but he had a conscience and empathy. He would have never done this to this young female if shit hadn't been so crazy lately. He had fucked up. In business, taking someone's life was like taking out the trash to him—he did it without giving it a second thought. But the stripper, he honestly didn't want her dead. He felt no remorse, but still it bugged him. How was this young girl with the good pussy dead and he couldn't manage to kill Scott West? That nigga was still breathing. Looking at the corpse infuriated him. It made him feel inferior.

A few minutes later, Jimmy knocked on the door, and Deuce got up to let him in. Jimmy's face was full of questions when he saw the dead stripper.

Deuce looked at the body and back at Jimmy. "Shit got crazy."

Jimmy smirked. Deuce had lost his mind. Killing strippers wasn't at the top of his hit list.

"Yo," Deuce stated, "as far as I'm concerned, Scott West killed her. That nigga got my mind twisted. I'm gonna murder that old head. And now I prefer to do the killing in front of his entire family."

Jimmy stood silent. Deuce was making the easy complicated.

When Lucky heard the news about the attempted hit on her father, she went ape shit. Like Meyer, she was ready to get her gun and retaliate. Although he was putting her mother through some shit and she didn't like it, that was still her father, and she was Daddy's little girl. She'd immediately contacted her father. She wanted to see him, but he told her he was okay and to stay where she was. Like he told his twin boys, he told Lucky he wanted her to wear a bulletproof vest whenever she went out into public. She was against it. How would she get away with wearing a vest in the summer weather with a light outfit? Scott wouldn't relent, though. He also put armed goons inside and outside her building and instructed them to watch her twenty-four/seven.

Lucky paced around her apartment, smoking a cigarette, plotting her escape from Daddy's men. One was posted right outside her door looking like a Secret Service agent in his black suit. He stood out in the decorative hallway like a tree in the ocean. Two men were lingering in the lobby, and a fourth man sat in a black SUV right outside the building. They were always there, just watching and waiting for something that might not happen. But they were insurance if something did.

Lucky was stressed with her pending drug case, her mother's worries about the bitch her father was cheating with, and her father escaping death. The news was upsetting for her. She wondered who could have gotten that close to him. Scott moved slyly and quietly around town, and he often ran with killers that could probably take on the president's detail. Whoever they were, she knew they were smart, patient, and dangerous. Her father was a marked man, but they all were, and there was an enemy out there who hadn't yet revealed himself. She went crazy trying to put the pieces together. She didn't want to lose anyone else in her family.

The thought had never occurred to her before, but was all this, including her three young siblings' deaths, her fault? She was the one who had scouted Wilmington, knowing they would be stepping on another dealer's empire. As soon as the thought came to her mind, she pushed it right back out. She was her mother's child, and guilt wasn't top on their lists.

She smoked another cigarette and stepped out onto the balcony. She stared at the half-moon so high and sighed. The city was wrapped up in darkness and cool air.

Another thing troubled Lucky. Whistler had been avoiding her phone calls and her altogether. She questioned his loyalty to the family. There were too many what-ifs. What if he was the one responsible for her drug bust? Was it a coincidence that right after she confronted him at his apartment, she got pulled over with narcotics in her car? What if he was secretly plotting against her father? What if the drug war was with Deuce, but Whistler was behind the West kids' murders? It made sense in her eyes. He'd been the number two for so long now, maybe now he was craving for the number-one position. Maybe he wanted to wear the crown. So many thoughts. So many questions.

The funny thing, though, was Lucky still loved him and still wanted to be with him. She needed to see him alone, but with her father's men scattered all over the building, it would be difficult. However she had a plan. She needed to distract the first man outside her door.

Dressed in her nightgown, she opened the door to interact with the man. She invited him inside. At first, he resisted, preferring to stand by his post and do his job. He knew the repercussions from Scott would be severe and maybe deadly if he failed to protect Lucky.

Lucky was persistent. "Please, come inside and join me for a drink. I'm lonely. With everything that's been going on with my family, especially my father, I just need some company." She batted her eyes at the man.

He relented and stepped foot inside the apartment, and the door closed. The trap was set.

An hour later, the man lay face down unconscious on her couch. The sleeping pills she'd mixed into his drink would leave him like that for hours. She only hoped that she hadn't given him so many where he wouldn't wake up. But that was a tomorrow problem.

With him out of the way, Lucky readied herself to leave the apartment and arranged for an Uber driver. First, she had to look a certain way. She wanted to catch Whistler's attention tonight.

Leaving the apartment in red lace pasties and thong panties covered by a thin overcoat, Lucky made her way to the service elevator. Her outfit was daring, but Lucky had always been a brave woman, and tonight was no different. She took the service elevator to the ground floor and glided away from the front entrance because going through the lobby would be risky. She left the building via the rear door. A block away, she climbed into a blue Lexus and told the driver her location. He nodded.

Lucky sat back. It was definitely a risk leaving her home alone, but it was a risk she was willing to take.

Half an hour later, Lucky marched through the lobby of the towering building in midtown Manhattan, strutted into the elevator, and pushed for the 13th floor. She ascended, butterflies in her stomach. Lucky was a drug distributor, and she dealt with some dangerous men and went toe to toe with killers and police, but tonight she was a nervous little girl. She looked and felt eighteen years old.

The elevator stopped on the 13th floor, and she stepped out into the carpeted hallway. She made a left and sauntered toward Whistler's apartment. She and Whistler had to talk on so many levels, starting with their relationship. Where did she stand with him? Since her brutal beating, she had been pushed aside and forgotten. She didn't want to be forgotten by him. They had too much history together, and she felt they had chemistry too. But what if he betrayed her family? What if he wanted to wear the crown? And what if, and it was a hurtful speculation, but what if he was responsible for her siblings' deaths? Then what? Could she kill Whistler herself—choose her family over the man she had loved for years?

Lucky knew she had some hard decisions coming her way. The speculations she had about Whistler were interfering with her feelings for him. How would she find proof? Did she want to look for evidence? Once he put that big dick inside of her and thrust her onto cloud nine, would the speculation go away? Would his sins be forgiven, if there were any sins?

Lucky stood in front of the door and knocked. There was no hesitation. She wanted to see him. She wanted to talk to him and feel wanted by him, fuck his brains out, and spend the night with him tonight. She wanted to open her coat and reveal the sexy outfit she had on underneath.

And then the door opened.

Lucky was taken aback, her anticipation speedily transitioning to hurt and anger when she saw the young, voluptuous girl inside the apartment. She had the audacity to answer Whistler's door wearing one of his T-shirts.

The girl looked at Lucky bitterly and asked, "Who is you?"

"Bitch, who is you? And where's Whistler?" Lucky shouted.

The girl blocked Lucky's entry into the apartment. "Whistler is none of your fuckin' business."

Lucky couldn't control herself. Her fists tightened and she thrust them forward, striking the girl in the face, making her stumble, then pushed her way into the apartment. "I'm the bitch that's about to kick your fuckin' ass!"

The girl was down for a moment with a bloody nose. She was cursing as she leaked blood all over Whistler's pristine carpet.

Lucky needed to find Whistler. She stormed into the bedroom and saw the wrinkled sheets, the condom wrappers on the floor, and two bottles of opened champagne. The room reeked of sex. Lucky was crushed. Whistler had easily replaced her with another bitch, and she felt devastated.

The young girl stormed into the bedroom behind Lucky. "You broke my fuckin' nose, bitch!"

"I'm about to break your fuckin' face, bitch!" Lucky screamed, ready to wipe the floor with her. She was ready to charge at the girl and show her how she got down. Lucky felt she had the strength to throw the girl through the bedroom window and decorate the sidewalk with her insides.

But then Whistler came running into the bedroom dressed in a towel and placed himself between the feuding girls. He was securing his towel with one hand and holding a pistol in the other. He was shocked to see Lucky inside his apartment.

"Why are you here, Lucky?" he asked.

"Because, nigga, I fuckin' belong here, not that bitch!"

Whistler looked at the girl's bleeding nose. "You okay?"

She nodded.

He looked at Lucky like she was a monster. "You need to leave," he said to her in a calm tone.

"Or what? You gonna shoot me, Whistler? Huh?" she said with sadness. "That bitch sucks your dick better than I do, huh? What? Because I'm damaged goods, and I ain't pretty like I used to be, you gonna discard me like that?"

He sighed. "You just need to leave. Let's not make things complicated for us," he said.

Lucky stood in the center of his bedroom overcome with so many mixed emotions, she felt like she was on a merry-go-round with her feelings. Everything was turning faster, and there was no way for her to get off. She stood there looking pitiful with her droopy eye. Whistler made her feel ugly. She wanted to beat the disrespectful and loud-mouth bitch down. Seeing Whistler look out for her and ask if she was okay tore her apart. Then she composed herself as she remembered her mother's words. *"Act like a lady. Be the bigger person, and don't let these niggas see you sweat."*

He wasn't worth it. Lucky had too much going on, and Whistler would not become another problem for her. Reality set in. Their relationship was over. She looked at him stoically and calmly said, "You should have told me."

"I did, and you wouldn't listen," he replied.

She was listening now.

"You need help, Lucky, some serious help. You're emotional, and our relationship was always on thin ice," he said.

Whistler was putting everything on her as if she was an emotional and delusional child. He'd only pulled away after her attack and disfigurement. He'd never officially said to her face that they were through, that he was tired of her. He'd come up with excuses about being tired, having business out of town, and about it being late, but he'd never said it was over.

She had nothing else to say. She held her head high and refused to cry. She glared at his new bitch and walked right by them both and exited. Though she shed no tears in front of them, on the inside she was torn apart and crying like a baby. The man she loved did not love her back.

With Lucky gone, Whistler stood near the bedroom window brooding. His female company was in the bathroom nursing her bloody nose. He smoked a cigarette and watched life happen in the city from his bedroom window. He knew that his separation from Lucky wasn't going to be amicable, and chances were, she would go running to her daddy with her problems. It was the last thing Whistler wanted her to do—involve Scott. He'd fucked up, and he knew it. He needed to talk to Scott first, before the problem with Lucky spiraled out of control.

He finished the cigarette and reached for his cell phone to call his boss.

The phone rang, and Scott answered, "Speak, nigga!"

"I need to talk to you—It's important—but not over the phone," Whistler said.

"Come to the penthouse tomorrow morning, say, around ten," Scott said.

"I'll be there."

Their call ended.

Whistler wasn't a fool. He figured Lucky would run to her daddy upset and tell him everything, so Whistler figured if he spoke to Scott first, conversed man-to-man with his longtime friend, he could spin it where it didn't sound like he was a pedophile. Maybe Scott would see things his way. It wasn't like Scott was an angel himself. Whistler knew of plenty of young girls that Scott took advantage of throughout their friendship, Penelope included.

Whistler was confident that his friend would see things his way. They would talk, and he would correct the situation. They had over twenty years of friendship, and they were more like brothers than friends.

Unbeknownst to Whistler, Scott was already aware of their relationship. Lucky had already called her father, and when Whistler had called him, Scott was standing in her apartment, consoling his baby girl. He was ready to confront Whistler with two taps to the side of his dome. He felt that Whistler had no side of the story. He had taken advantage of his little girl and put his dick where it didn't belong.

Lucky called her father right after she left Whistler's apartment. The moment he answered his phone and heard Lucky choking up with emotions, he was ready to go see her. She was his only living daughter, and he couldn't lose her.

At first, Scott thought she was calling about Layla and his mistress. Lucky played dumb as if she had no clue what he was talking about.

"Lucky, where are you?" Scott had asked her.

"Daddy, I'm over at Whistler's place."

He was confused. "Why are you there? Where is your security?"

"Please, Daddy, just come get me."

"I'm on the way."

Scott arrived at Whistler's apartment ten minutes later.

Lucky got in the Escalade in tears and they headed to her place, where she spilled information out to her father like she was WikiLeaks. She knew Whistler would try to crack the news to her father first with his version. She told Scott how the thirty-nine-year-old Whistler had taken advantage of her when she was only sixteen, and she had gotten pregnant. She was careful not to say "rape," not wanting to lay it on too thick. She also told Scott that Whistler had made her get an abortion at the clinic. Lucky added the abortion part to spice up the lie, knowing what her mother had told her about her abortion twenty-some years ago would strike a chord with her father.

Scott was silent, taking everything in. The look on his face was murderous. It had transformed several times from rage, incredulousness, pity, sorrow, anger, and back to rage. He was astonished Lucky had gone to such great lengths Lucky to be with Whistler and keep their relationship a secret.

Scott's phone rang. It was Whistler. He managed to contain his rage and set up a meeting for the following day. He hung up and sat there looking at his little girl.

The tears continued to well up in Lucky's eyes. "Daddy, I still love him, but he never loved me. He used me. He fucked me, and he used me."

She also mentioned her theory to Scott, that maybe Whistler had something to do with the murders of her siblings.

"It has to be him, Daddy! He's the mastermind. He killed them all."

It was a hard pill to swallow, but Scott was listening. Whistler had always been smart and shrewd. Could he be the mastermind behind the sudden attack on their family?

The accusation created more rage in Scott, and he became so furious, he sprung up and slammed his fist into the wall, creating a crater-size hole. "I'm gonna kill him!" he shouted in a frenzy.

Lucky had never seen him so mad, but it was the reaction she expected from him.

Scott smashed pieces of furniture and shattered glass.

She let him fume for a moment, and eventually, she calmed him down, and the questions from him began. He wanted to know everything.

He looked intensely at his daughter and asked, "Why didn't you come to me with this earlier about . . . about the pregnancy?"

"I was in love, Daddy. I didn't want you to do anything to him."

The vision of his friend, a grown man, touching and fucking his daughter, made his blood boil. And the abortion made him seethe more. He treated Lucky, a fuckin' West, like a side-bitch. And right under his nose! Whistler was riding shotgun with Scott, looking him in the eye while he was dicking down his baby girl. That was a line that should never be crossed, an unspoken rule. If Scott couldn't pick up on his daughter being exploited; if he had missed all the lingering looks, passing glances, any signs of affection, then what else had he missed? Did Whistler have his children murdered?

"He was like a father-figure to me, Daddy," Lucky continued.

"A father-figure?" he shouted. "I'm your father, not that muthafucka! He was an uncle to you. He was supposed to be family!" Once again, Scott lost his temper, and he disrupted her lavish apartment with chaos, breaking and smashing more items. "I trusted him!" he roared. "I trusted that nigga with my family, with our lives and this is how he repays me? He abuses and rapes my little girl."

Lucky smirked. She had to get Whistler out of her system, and the only way she saw it happening was to see him dead. The cat-and-mouse relationship they had wasn't healthy for her. He was a risk to her and her family. She went back to her theory about how someone was murdering their family and how Whistler had put it all together at their last meeting. He had to know something. The night she was arrested, and she spoke to that cop, he'd planted something into her thinking, and it awakened her.

Lucky thought about numerous theories. Was Whistler a snitch and working with the police? Or was he working with the feds? Was there some conspiracy against her family? Who could they trust? They were a powerful dynasty with lots of money, power, and influence. And there were a lot of enemies everywhere that wanted to see her family fall and suffer, for many reasons. Could someone have corrupted and influenced Whistler to go against the man he had grown up with?

One thing bothered Scott. If Whistler was behind the conspiracy against his family, then why try to convince them it wasn't Deuce? Why not keep them in the dark? Why not make everyone believe that it was

Deuce behind it all?

There was also a small voice in Scott's mind that warned him to be mindful of his daughter. She was Layla's daughter too, and there was no telling what his wife had planted in her head. She was a female, and females were emotional. Lucky had something to gain by telling him all this. She too was a woman scorned. And Scott was no fool. Some of it just wasn't adding up. It wasn't just about a breakup with Whistler; there had to be more to the story. But there was time to figure it out later. What mattered now was Whistler had been fucking his daughter for over two years. He had violated the code. Since when was it okay to fuck your friend's daughter?

That night, father and daughter talked intensely. Lucky mentioned the riddle to him. It sounded foolish—his children being killed off in the same fashion as the old-school gangsters a long time ago. But, if true, who would be next? Lucky had done her homework. Lucky Luciano had gotten locked up, and he died of natural causes in the '60s. She figured she was safe for now. Meyer Lansky lived to a ripe old age.

"It would be Bugsy," Lucky said. "He would be next on the hit list."

Scott frowned. He could take nothing for granted. Just because it sounded foolish didn't mean the threat wasn't real. He had to take everything seriously. He had already lost too much. If what Lucky was saying was true, then they needed to call Bugsy and warn him right away.

A cigarette and a glass of vodka was how Whistler started his morning. Belvedere was breakfast, and the cigarette was to cool his nerves. He was alone, and things were quiet. The bright sun percolated through the bedroom window, indicating it would be another beautiful day. His young female company long gone, he sat at the edge of his bed brooding about his forthcoming meeting with Scott. He felt tense inside. He couldn't stop thinking about Lucky, knowing how vindictive she could be. He'd fucked up and put his dick into the wrong bitch. He knew the problem with her would not go away so quickly. There were plenty of girls over the years, some of whom he and Scott shared sexually. No girl was off limits, except for family. Whistler didn't have kids, but Scott had daughters. He should have known better than to cross that line. But Lucky had seduced him first, and he took the bait, unable to resist the sixteen-year-old beauty. It wasn't supposed to happen, their relationship, but it came about unexpectedly.

The first night with Lucky was supposed to be a one-time thing. It happened in the back seat of Whistler's SUV.

It was a warm, spring evening with light rain cascading over the city. He was chauffeuring Lucky from school to home. Scott was out of town on business, and Layla was handling new business in Florida. Whistler had become a surrogate father to Lucky, but Lucky wanted a lot more from him.

First, the conversation between them was harmless. Lucky fussed about her parents' absence, and she talked about the boys in her school, complaining she wasn't interested in them because they were young and immature. "I want a man like you, Whistler," she said.

Whistler ignored the remark. He stared out the windshield and focused on the road and taking her home. Traffic on the East Side was a nightmare. It was after six in the evening, and 3rd Avenue traffic was absolutely gridlocked. He had no choice but to wait it out and listen to Lucky talk.

Lucky's plaid miniskirt didn't cover up enough of her thighs. Her black hair was in two long pigtails, and the schoolgirl shirt she wore was tight around her upper body, making her tits protrude from her chest.

"I know you be lookin' at me, Whistler," Lucky said to him. "It's okay. I look at you all the time. I think you're fine." She leaned in closer to him and placed her hand on his leg.

Whistler glanced at her. He remained nonchalant. Lucky's touch traveled farther to his crotch. He knew he should have stopped her then, but lust was crippling him.

"How big is it?" she asked.

He didn't reply. Once again, he felt silence was his best weapon against temptation.

"I know you kill people for my father. How many people did you kill?" she asked. "The type of man I want is a nigga like you—one that can protect me and fuck me right at the same time."

He remained silent.

She had naturally positioned her left hand between his thighs and reached for the imprint of his dick through his pants. She squeezed it, and he didn't resist.

"Damn! It feels like you got a big dick, Whistler. Can I see it?" She massaged his member through his pants and could feel him becoming hard through the fabric. "I don't kiss and tell. In fact, if you were to fuck me right now, no one would ever know, not even my father."

The traffic slowed to a snail's pace on the Upper East Side, and the raindrops fell increasingly against the windshield with the wipers keeping his vision clear.

"Can I suck it?" she asked. "I know you like young pussy, Whistler. Am I not young enough for you? You don't think my pussy is tight and wet enough for you?"

"You're family," he said.

Lucky chuckled at the comment. "Family. Nigga, please! You're my father's right-hand nigga in the drug game, and you kill people for him. Don't act like we blood. Nigga, I just want some dick tonight. After that, you can go your way, and I'll go mine."

Lucky was a peculiar and very smart girl. She wasn't a stranger to her father's illegal street businesses, and she knew about her twin brothers' roles in the organization. She'd clarified to her father that she wanted in.

She continued to massage Whistler's dick through his pants, working her fingers a certain way between his legs and stimulating him into submission. She undid his zipper and removed his dick from his pants. He didn't resist—there was no fight, but there was relenting from Whistler's end as her touch excited him.

"Damn! You definitely are all man," she said. His dick was black, long, and full in her manicured hand. She tilted further into his lap and neared her full lips closer to the hard erection she'd created.

Lucky gave Whistler a blowjob while they were stuck in heavy midtown traffic in the pouring rain. Her glossy, sweet lips pressed around his big dick, causing his breathing to become ragged, and her head bobbed up and down in his lap as the downpour splashed against the car. She knew how to deep-throat too, another bonus that crippled him.

"I want you to fuck me," she said, coming up for air.

He wanted to be against it. His dick in her mouth was already immoral and could kill him. But her seduction was intense, and curiosity about what her pussy would feel like was the victor over his morals.

So Whistler found a parking garage a few blocks south, steered the SUV into the garage and out of the rain, and nestled the vehicle between two cars, among dozens of others. They situated themselves in the backseat. His jeans hung around his ankles, and Lucky's panties came down, her miniskirt rose up, and she slowly mounted his erection. The penetration was divine, and it was supposed to happen only once between them.

But it happened again a week later—same vehicle, different location. The sex was stupefying. And then came a third time and a fourth, until they couldn't get enough of each other. Before he knew it, Whistler was caught up. It was risky, but the reward was fucking phenomenal.

Two years later, his relationship with Lucky found him sitting on his bed with a lot to think about. He was uneasy and felt himself becoming unhinged.

Whistler's cell phone rang around nine, and he reached for it. It was Scott calling him.

He answered. "Hello."

"Change of location, Whistler," Scott said.

"Where are we meeting at?"

"Meet me at the warehouse in one hour. You know which one I'm talking about."

"Why the change-up suddenly?" Whistler asked, feeling apprehensive.

"We got a beat on Deuce, and we need to react quickly on this nigga."

"And that thing I needed to talk to you about . . ."

"I know. I didn't forget."

"We definitely need to talk," Whistler said.

"We'll talk. But business first. One hour." Scott hung up.

The phone call left Whistler in a bitter mood. He felt that something was off. Scott's tone was almost unsettling. He didn't want to fret, but every bone in his body was telling him to be extra cautious today.

He stood up and got dressed. Shortly, he was looking sharp in an Armani suit, a black derby decorating his head.

He left his apartment armed with two pistols, one strapped to his ankle, the other holstered under his suit jacket. Each step outside the apartment was a careful one. He entered the underground parking garage where his Escalade was parked and deactivated the alarm, and the sound echoed through the enclosed area. The time on the dashboard read 9:20; he still had some time.

Whistler took a deep breath as he lingered in the driver's seat, his mind racing with concern. He popped a few uppers into his mouth, needing the extra stimulus. The SUV's engine started, and he pulled out of the parking garage and drove toward the Brooklyn Bridge.

Twenty minutes later, his Escalade did a slow turn onto Van Brunt Street in Red Hook, and he cruised slowly toward the brick warehouse at the end of a dead-end street. A block over was docking for a water ferry service from IKEA and Pier 11 in Lower Manhattan. Whistler drove by the Holland-style factory buildings and came to a stop across the street from his location. He was fifteen minutes early and saw no one. Activity was rare on the two-way street because it was in a withdrawn area with no residences and no commercial businesses within a three-block radius.

Whistler didn't see Scott's car. He figured they were already inside. He lingered in his vehicle and tossed another upper into his mouth. His eyes stayed glued to the building. He watched the rolling gate and the side door. It all looked shut down.

Out of the blue, the side door opened, and a man exited to smoke a cigarette outside. When Whistler noticed who it was, he perked up and removed his 9mm from the holster. He watched Yayo lean against the building to smoke and make a call from his cell phone.

Seeing Yayo present was bad news for Whistler. Yayo was one of Scott's top enforcers. He was a serious muthafucka with an appetite for murder and destruction. He didn't come around unless there was a serious assignment to do for Scott—like hunt a nigga down and make a body disappear. Yayo was the Grim Reaper. Seeing him there said one thing to Whistler—this would not be a friendly meeting with his friend. It indicated to him that Lucky had already had a conversation with her father and revealed everything to him. He smelled a setup. Scott probably wanted to have him murdered brutally the moment he stepped foot into the warehouse.

Whistler put the vehicle into reverse and was ready to sneak away from the scene. So far, Yayo hadn't seen him. He was too busy with his cigarette and phone conversation. But the door opened, and another man exited the building to join Yayo outside. He was a young goon with a slim physique, average height, and long cornrows. His name was Rick.

Rick said a few words to Yayo, bummed a cigarette from him, and then his eyes stared across the street at the Escalade in reverse. Rick squinted his eyes at the vehicle, looking carefully to make out the driver.

Whistler gripped the steering wheel in one hand and his 9mm in the other. He was ready to react.

Rick was watching the SUV's movement attentively, and it didn't take him long to figure it out. He shouted, "Yo, that's Whistler. That muthafuckin' pedophile is right there!" He snatched the gun from his waistband and charged at the Escalade with his arm outstretched and let loose a hail of bullets as Whistler drove off.

Bak-Bak-Bak-Bak-Bak-Bak!

Whistler hunkered down into the seat, holding on to the steering wheel firmly, and frantically peeled away in reverse from the threat as the passenger glass shattered around him. He accelerated to 60mph in reverse. The truck swerved, but he kept it in control. He could hear the bullets pounding into his vehicle, shattering another window and exploding shards of glass all around him. He didn't panic. Panic would kill him. Instead, he blew through the intersection speedily while Rick chased after him, emptying his entire gun clip.

Whistler did another block in reverse, losing the shooter and escaping death. Quickly, he spun the truck around and made his escape. All Rick and Yayo saw was the back of the Escalade fading away from two blocks down.

The gunfire sent Scott and others flying out the building. Everyone was armed. It sounded like the Fourth of July on the street.

"What the fuck is going on?" Scott asked.

"We just missed Whistler," Rick said.

"What the fuck you talkin' about? He was here?" Scott asked.

"Yeah, sittin' in his truck and watching us from across the street. I was on dat nigga. I emptied my clip at his truck, but he got away," Rick said.

Scott was furious. Rick's impulsiveness was uncalled for. Scott wanted Whistler inside the building, where he was to be taken care of, but now that all changed because of one man's recklessness.

Believing he did the right thing, Rick looked proudly at Scott. He was confident Scott would praise his effort.

Scott stared at him intently and said, "You missed the nigga, huh?"

"Yeah, but I ain't gonna miss him again, fo' sure!"

Scott wanted no attention to the warehouse, and multiple gunshots definitely would bring it. And now Whistler was on to him and would be looking for revenge.

Without pause, Scott lifted the Desert Eagle to the side of Rick's head, the triangle barrel thrust against his skull, and he pulled the trigger—*Bang!*

Rick's body immediately collapsed to the pavement, right by Scott's feet, and gun smoke billowed from the .50-cal.

"Fuckin' idiot!" Scott said. "Take the body and dump it somewhere. It's time to leave."

Scott's men removed the body from the pavement, carried it back into the warehouse, and tossed it into the trunk of a car. It would be taken care of immediately.

Scott pivoted and marched into the warehouse. He gave instructions to shut the place down—clean up and clear out quickly. He knew that no one was safe. Whistler was a lot more deadly and ruthless than any of his killers, and he was smart and perceptive too. The only killer that Scott felt could measure up to Whistler was Yayo.

"Fuuuuuck!" Scott screamed madly, knowing the position Rick had just put him in.

Whistler was aware now, and that meant trouble for his organization and his family. Whistler knew all of Scott's tricks, hideaways, and secrets. Twenty years of friendship and doing business together now brought vulnerabilities and concerns to Scott. Scott had to increase his security and alert everyone about Whistler, including Lucky, his only remaining daughter. He figured Whistler would go after her too. Scott would send a hit squad after him, but he had his doubts that it would resolve his problem.

Scott was about to retreat from the building, and then his cell phone rang. He was shocked to see who was calling. He answered right away, scowling.

Whistler drove his bullet-riddled truck to the edge of Brooklyn, fifteen miles south of where they'd just tried to take his life. Parked near the Coney Island boardwalk, he had a view of the Verrazano Bridge. The morning was crazy. He was upset and angry. He barely got away by the skin of his teeth. A bullet had grazed his head, and there was minor blood, but it was nothing that couldn't be easily taken care of with a cloth, some rubbing alcohol, and a small bandage. Whistler needed time to collect himself and think. Lucky had fucked everything up, and now he had to go off the grid and change his entire life. He already had a go-bag packed with stacks of money, fake IDs and passports, and guns. He also had various places to hide and remain low-key. He would regroup from this incident and survive. Because that's what he'd been doing all his life.

He made a phone call. It took two rings until Scott answered. Whistler immediately said to him, "Are we really going to go down this road?"

"You're a dead man!" Scott shouted.

"How long have we known each other, Scott? Let's talk."

"You're a fuckin' dead man!" Scott reiterated.

"She came on to me a long time ago, and I resisted—"

Scott screamed, "You're a fuckin' dead man when I find you!" He hung up.

Whistler saw there was no reasoning with him. He knew that Scott would do everything in his power to make his demise happen, and

Whistler would do whatever it took to avoid it. He felt he had a slight advantage. He had no kids, no family, so there was no one Scott could torture and hold hostage for his surrender. But Scott had plenty to lose, from his family to his business to his pregnant mistress, Penelope. He'd made a home for himself a long time ago, whereas Whistler had no home, just locations to lay his head. He could walk away from everything in a heartbeat. There was enough liquid cash, real estate throughout the US, and overseas accounts in a different countries for him to depend on.

Whistler torched the SUV somewhere far. It was too hot, and the bullet holes and broken windows stood out. He needed a different means of transportation. Using his street tactics, he broke into a car and hot-wired it, breaking the steering lock and connecting the ignition wire to the battery cable. It started, and he sped off. It was something he'd learned to do when he was fourteen.

He traveled to New Jersey and took up temporary residence inside a modest two-bedroom home in South Orange. It was a home he owned under an alias, so it couldn't be connected to him. The house was furnished with just the bare necessities—bed, table and a few chairs, and a TV. For now, he felt safe there.

He got rid of his cell phone and depended on a burner phone, since it wasn't easily traced, was easy to discard, and wouldn't leave a trail back to him. He sat shirtless on a twin bed in the unfurnished bedroom and dialed a number he thought he would never dial again. He doubted she would pick up because it was an unknown number he was calling from, but she did.

Lucky answered, "Who the fuck is this?"

"Call off your father, before everything gets really ugly," he said to her. "Tell him it was all a lie."

Lucky didn't falter with regret upon hearing Whistler's voice. "You made your fuckin' bed, so now you die in it."

"You think it will be that easy?"

"You're scared. It's why you're calling me. But I have no more love for you, nigga. I gave you everything. I loved you, nigga, and you shit on me for a new bitch when I needed you most. Burn in hell, you bitch-ass, snitch-ass, pervert!"

It wasn't true. He loved her too, but their relationship could never be. It was a fantasy. They could never become a family.

She screamed at him, "When my father kills you—and he will kill you—I'm gonna pour a forty-ounce of malt liquor on your unmarked and shallow grave and piss on it, because that's all you fuckin' deserve. Go to hell, Whistler!"

The call went dead.

Whistler realized there was no getting through to her, either. She was a young, jilted, evil bitch; unreasonable and arrogant just like her father. He'd made the biggest mistake of his life fucking her.

But did they forget that he was a stone-cold killer too, and he was ready for any killers that Scott sent after him?

Whistler went into the closet of the bedroom and switched on the lights. He looked at his small arsenal of weapons. He removed several guns from the closet and placed them on the bed. In his possession were two sawed-off shotguns, an Uzi, several handguns, and his favorite, a Heckler & Koch G36C. The weapon was a very efficient killing machine. If they wanted a war with him, then he would give them the fight of their lives.

24

The Uber driver stopped in front of the Mount Vernon home around 11 p.m. Bugsy gave the driver a healthy tip and climbed out of the vehicle. He took a deep breath and looked around the suburban neighborhood with middle-class homes. The block was so silent, he could hear his own heartbeat. Bugsy made sure he was careful with his trips to his girlfriend, switching up transportation and not having a routine. And when he spoke to her, he used a burner phone, and he remembered her number by heart.

The driver took off, and he walked toward the front door.

The front yard was all open lawn, without shrubberies or trees for anyone to hide behind, no flower garden or obstacles, and it provided a clear view from the sidewalk to the front door. Bugsy hadn't come alone, though. Concealed on him was a .45 handgun in his jacket, loaded with a few hollow points. He didn't take the warning from his father lightly, but it would not prevent him from seeing Alicia. She was the only thing that felt normal in his life. She was a breath of fresh air and a ray of sunshine.

Bugsy was beside himself with anger and grief at the hospital the night Lucky was beaten. As he lingered in the hallway, Alicia, one of the nurses on the evening shift, noticed his pain. She went up to him to console him, and at first, he was standoffish. But it didn't scare her away. She had a friendly spirit, and she was soft-spoken. Her beauty was natural, and her smile was bright. She calmed him.

Low key, the two had coffee at a diner a few blocks away from the hospital. Their conversation flowed like a stream, and it was polite. She was young and ambitious, but she was innocent to his world of chaos, death, drugs, and destruction. Bugsy felt drawn to her.

When she asked about his career and ambition, for a moment, he wrestled with himself about whether or not he should tell her the truth. She was honest with him, so he didn't want to lie to her.

"I'm in the family business," he said.

"And what's your family business?"

He looked at her calmly and replied, "Drugs, money laundering, illegal and legal businesses—we're into a lot of heavy shit."

He felt it was stupid at first, exposing himself to a woman he hardly knew. Why did he do it? Why did he violate a family rule—never reveal yourself to anyone that wasn't family?

At first, he thought she would get up from the booth and walk away, but she didn't. Her reply was shocking.

"You've got kind eyes," she said.

"Kind eyes?" He wondered whether she was looking into the right man's eyes.

"Yes."

"I'm not the best person, Alicia."

"And who is?"

Though he wasn't vile and malicious like his twin brother, Bugsy still was a killer, and he had blood on his hands too. She didn't judge him. It seemed like she understood him.

They continued to talk. There was no way Bugsy would let her go. It felt like she knew him. His honesty didn't scare her away, and he was impressed by it.

But he kept Alicia away from his family. He didn't want an innocent person like her to get mixed up in the drama that was spiraling out of control. He loved his family, especially his father, but he feared his family's stench getting all over her. Bugsy felt relaxed with her in her home, talking to her about anything. He could kick off his shoes, have great sex with her, and not worry about his life being in danger.

The house was dark, indicative that Alicia was still at work. She had transferred to a new hospital in Mount Vernon two months earlier, which made traveling to see her easier, and she worked the evening shift. Bugsy was happy all around. He didn't like the long hours she worked and the long commute from Mount Vernon to her former Staten Island hospital. He always feared she would fall asleep at the wheel, and he couldn't lose her. Usually, after her shift was over, he would travel at night to come see her. He rarely spent the night, knowing he had to travel back to the city and conduct business. But the nights he stayed over, it was harder for him to leave.

Bugsy slid the key into the locks and entered the place. It was quiet and dark. He turned on the living room lights and looked around.

Alicia was a meticulous person. She liked things clean and in order; she hated clutter. Her wood floors were polished, her classy furniture was positioned a certain way throughout the house and well maintained, and the place smelled refreshing with a flowery fragrance. Alicia had made her house into a home for Bugsy.

He kicked off his shoes and raided her fridge, making himself a quick sandwich and grabbing a beer. He then called Alicia's cell phone and asked what time would she be home. She told him her shift would be over at one a.m.

He smiled. "I miss you."

"I miss you too."

In the living room, he put his gun on the table and sat on the couch, picking up the remote to the 50-inch flat-screen TV and powering it on. CNN came into view. Alicia always liked to keep up with politics and current events. *Anderson Cooper 360* was showing. He sat back and watched the show for a moment.

He was drained and exhausted. Tonight, he only wanted to lay and cozy up with Alicia in her comfortable bed. He didn't want sex this evening. He wanted to hold her and just chill, get a good night's sleep.

Bugsy spent a half-hour watching *Anderson Cooper*. Still hungry, he picked himself off the couch to go back and get a snack. As he turned toward the window, he noticed a quick flash of light beam through the bay window and a red dot dancing around him. Abruptly four bullets pierced the window and slammed into his chest, knocking him off his feet and sending the plate he held crashing to the floor, shards of white porcelain scattering everywhere.

He looked like Neo from *The Matrix*, plugged into various machines that were monitoring his vital signs. His pulse was weak, his blood pressure was all over the place, and his body temperature had to fall. His breathing was so thin, he needed a machine to breathe. Wacka had been in a coma for eleven weeks, and once awake, he could barely speak and he couldn't move. His body felt like it was encased in a hard block of ice. The doctors did what they could, but it was an uphill battle for his survival and his recovery.

When he'd arrived at the hospital with multiple gunshot wounds, they operated on him immediately. His lungs were filled with fluid, and his brain was on the fast track of shutting down. He was alleged to be brain-dead, but he held on. He was supposed to die that night, but his body fought somehow, and he survived.

Wacka had been in ICU at the Holy Cross Hospital in Silver Spring, Maryland for months. At first, his coma felt like a long dream. When he woke up, he was hysterical, and he couldn't remember much, but it all came back to him gradually. He could hardly speak. All he could do was just lay there and be tended to twenty-four/seven.

After getting shot several times at his mother's apartment, he'd leaped from the bedroom window, crashed into the ground, and hobbled away from the danger as bullets zipped by him. Bleeding profusely, Wacka stumbled to his car and took off. He fought the impulse to pass out and give up. They'd killed his mother and his friends. They'd attacked his home, and revenge was inevitable.

Somehow, Wacka made it to his baby mama's place in Maryland. When he arrived, he collapsed at her front door. He'd lost a lot of blood and was in bad shape.

The shooting made headlines and the evening news. And there was an all-points bulletin for him because he was a person of interest in the gangland shooting at the Frederick Douglass Garden Apartments.

There, at his baby mama's home, he cleaned his hands from any gun residue and left his .50-cal. with Tarsha, his son's mother. That long detour and those precautions almost cost him his life. The doctors removed the bullets, but his body was racked with problems, and he was still touch-and-go even after being awake from his coma.

Once he was fully conscious, as with every gunshot victim, the police were called. It didn't take them long to visit Wacka in the hospital and bombard him with questions about his injuries. Two detectives visited him, and they had his hands tested for gun powder residue and confiscated his clothing to see if he had any weapons or drugs on him. Both came up negative. But he wasn't out of the frying pan yet. They soon went after the person closest to him, his baby mama. They questioned her relentlessly, trying to get her to name the person that shot him. Where was he when he was shot?

Tarsha told the detective she found him banging on her front door and dying. Being from the streets herself, she was aggressive toward the police and no pushover.

Fortunately for Wacka, they didn't tie him to the DC shooting—not yet anyway. In the files, he was a gunshot victim in Maryland with no ID. There was no reason to suspect he was a killer, so the Silver Spring detectives lost interest in him.

Tarsha remained by his bedside faithfully. She knew about his menacing nature, the people he'd killed—and he probably deserved the bullets pumped into his flesh—but he was still her baby's father.

She looked at Wacka in his fucked up condition and wondered if his life was spared for good or evil.

B ugsy lay sprawled across the wood floor. At first, it was hard for him to breathe. It felt like a Mack truck had slammed into him at full speed. He felt ran over and compressed to the floor. The impact from the four bullets had lifted him off his feet and sent him crashing to the floor.

He sat up suddenly and breathed like he'd never breathed before. It felt like hot coals were burning into his chest. He was winded and in shock. He grabbed his chest in a panic, and felt the thick Kevlar that saved his life. Nothing went through—no penetration, thank God. *Shit! What the fuck just happened? Someone just tried to kill me.*

Two things immediately came to his mind. Why did he leave the blinds open? Second, he was thankful he'd taken his father's advice and worn a vest. If not, he would have been dead. He was tempted to take it off inside the house to relax and watch TV, believing he was safe and no one would find him in Mount Vernon, but thankfully he was too lazy. They'd tracked him down—and they probably believed he was dead.

Soon after he picked himself up from the floor, he heard tires screeching in the night. Bugsy remained crouched low and stayed hidden from the window. He hurried for his gun and snatched it from off the coffee table. He cocked it back, and he remained crouched, not taking any more chances.

With his gun in hand, and the Kevlar still on, Bugsy remained quiet and watchful of everything as he moved slowly to the door. Oddly, everything was silent—nothing moved. Did the neighbors hear the gunshots? Did they not listen to the disturbance of breaking glass and tires screeching in the dark? No one was coming to his rescue. He had to handle and protect himself.

Cautiously, he opened the front door and aimed into the night; he looked everywhere and saw nothing. He had to leave. Unfortunately for him, he had no vehicle. He figured it would be safer to travel Uber or taxicab into Mount Vernon than risk having his own car tagged and tracked, creating a difficult situation for him. He knew that he needed to make a phone call to have his people come get him.

Half an hour later, a black Tahoe arrived, and four soldiers approached the house. Aware of what had just happened, they were heavily armed. They ushered Bugsy toward and into the vehicle, and he was secured like a commander-in-chief in hostile territory.

He called Alicia and told her not to come home. He told her to check into a hotel, and he'd pay the expenses. Bugsy was sparse with the information, not wanting her to panic, but not telling her what was going on made her panic more. She agreed to check into a hotel. He would go see her, but not tonight. He had to compose himself.

He vowed to find the people who tried to take his life. They'd violated his girl's home and turned her residence into a battleground. He had two of his goons sit on the house to make sure it didn't get looted and that no unwanted company came snooping around.

Riding in the back seat of the Tahoe, Bugsy finally removed the vest from his body and examined the damage carefully. They'd struck him center mass. He definitely would have been dead.

"Muthafuckas!" he uttered with disdain. He knew whoever tried to kill him was professional. It was a quick, tight shot. *A sniper*, Bugsy thought, *but from where and how far?* He saw nothing strange when he had arrived at the house. He'd been looking for any anomalies, but there were none. Was the killer that good to camouflage himself? Was he held up in a neighbor's home, holding a family hostage and stalking Alicia's house? Bugsy had so many questions.

First thing tomorrow, he would have someone board up the broken window and immediately have it fixed. He would have his men clean everything up. There would be no police involvement. He and his family would be the judge, jury, and executioner of the perpetrator or perpetrators.

Day after day, Tarsha sat by Wacka's side, stewing. Most days it wasn't looking good for him. His body and mind were still in treacherous territory, but the doctors continued to do all they could for him.

She wanted to believe that God had kept him alive. Wacka had cheated death. He became conscious and spoke coherently, but his voice was raspy and coarse. He had lost nearly forty pounds and was freakishly thin, and his right leg, with several metal pins fastened through it, was hoisted in a sling. He had shattered his ankle and knee when he jumped out the window.

Tarsha was upset that when the nurses would administer pain medication and Wacka showed various levels of consciousness, all he would repeat was, "Maxine . . . Maxine . . ." He'd uttered the name quite a few times. Tarsha didn't know who Maxine was.

"Who the fuck is Maxine?" she asked.

Wacka was still groggy in the head, but it all came clear to him. She wasn't a friend; she was the reason his mother and friends were dead.

"I want her dead," he said faintly to Tarsha.

"What did she do? She did this to you, right?" she asked.

He frowned a little, his body aching badly. He looked and felt a mess.

Tarsha closed the door to the room and moved the chair closer to his bedside. It was time to talk. She stared keenly at him, wanting to know everything.

Bit by bit, Wacka explained the situation to her—he had done a few murders for Maxine for some money, and the murders were of children.

Tarsha was taken aback. "Children?" she uttered with surprise. "Explain yourself."

Wacka told her about the hit-and-run on Gotti in Florida and then about the vicious killings of Bonnie and Clyde in New York City.

Tarsha could feel the hairs on her head rising like she had been hit by electricity. "How did they find you?" she asked.

"Only one person could have told them—Maxine."

Wacka had pissed off some dangerous and influential people. They'd killed his mother and his friends.

"Do they know about me and your son?"

"I don't think so," he said.

"You need to think clearly," she spewed, feeling her and their son's life might be in danger too.

"I'm goin' after every last one of them," he proclaimed with his raspy voice.

"You're in no condition to do anything right now."

Wacka hated that he was weak and disabled. He desperately wanted to yank the wires from his body and get up from the bed.

"I need you to get in touch with Shiniquia," he said.

"Shiniquia?" Tarsha squarely looked him in the eyes and told him, "She's dead."

"What the fuck you talkin' 'bout?"

"She was murdered in prison—stabbed to death by several inmates."

The news was another crushing blow to Wacka. How many more people would he lose? What he heard sent his body into a freefall of pain and relapse, and his vital signs went haywire. The machines hummed loudly. He was out of control. He convulsed in the bed.

Tarsha, frightened by it all, leaped from her chair and ran to notify the nurses what was happening. "I need some help! I need a fuckin' doctor!" she screamed frantically.

A team of nurses and physicians came charging into the room to aid Wacka. He had flat-lined, his body going into cardiac arrest due to added stress. They brought in a crash cart to revive him once more. They went to work on Wacka's fragile body with multiple medical instruments, including a defibrillator.

A nurse steered Tarsha out of the room, as a team of people quickly operated on Wacka. The door closed and Tarsha was left in the hallway wondering if she would see Wacka alive again. She had no clear view of him anymore, as his bed was surrounded by white lab coats, nurses, and machines.

Fifteen minutes later, she received some news from the doctor. Wacka had slipped back into a coma.

This was news that Miguel wanted to deliver to Maxine personally. It could have been easily done by phone, but he wanted to see her face to face and let her know, "Mission accomplished!" He wanted to see her for other reasons too. The first time with Max in the back seat of his car was fantastic. He never thought he could have pussy so good. Nadia was his girl, and the mother of his children, but Max became his infatuation. He couldn't stop thinking about that day in City Island.

He parked on her street and called her cell phone. When she answered, he replied, "I'm outside. We need to talk."

"I'll be out in ten minutes."

He lit a cigarette and waited.

Killing Bugsy was easier than he thought it would be. He set up inside an elderly couple's home that lived right across the street from the girlfriend. Early that night, Miguel masked up, put on black latex gloves to avoid leaving any fingerprints behind, and broke into the home. He held the old couple at gunpoint and tied them up downstairs. Then he removed a sniper's rifle from a Blackhawk Long Gun Drag Bag, positioned himself at the front window in the living room, killed all the lights inside the house, and waited. He'd waited for hours before Bugsy finally arrived at the house via cab. Miguel watched his every movement outside the home. He had him in plain sight via night scope and could have taken him out right there, but Max wanted it done inside the house, near the window—shot dead like the legendary Bugsy Siegel. So he held off from the shot and waited for the right moment.

The moment came half an hour later. Bugsy got up from the couch, and Miguel used a laser pointer to grab his attention. When he was in the line of fire, Miguel squeezed off four shots and watched him go down. He then fled the home and made his escape, assuming the man was dead, with four bullets in his chest.

The front door opened, and Maxine stepped out of the house. Once again, Miguel was blown away by her beauty and her outfit. She strutted toward the car wearing an outfit fitting for the late summer month—a pink and white Adidas open-back dress with a pink Kangol and a pair of high-top Adidas. She looked old-school and so cute. She climbed into the car and waited for the news from him.

"You look beautiful," he quickly said.

"Thank you," she replied nonchalantly.

"It's done. He's dead."

Maxine was elated. "You're worth every penny. Tell me. I want the details."

Miguel told her about the neighbors he'd held hostage and the rifle he'd used. Then he added, "He took four in the chest by the window."

"In the chest?"

Miguel nodded. "Yes, in the chest."

"I told you I wanted him shot in the head," she whined.

"It was a difficult task already. I did the best I could. Be happy he's dead."

"I wanted a closed casket funeral for him. I wanted that bitch to see her son's face twisted."

"He's dead, Max. That's torture enough for any mother."

They argued about the hit, but Miguel was able to deescalate the drama. He had become sweet on her and didn't want to upset her.

Layla raided the private bar in the lavish hotel suite she was staying in and poured herself a drink. She dropped her behind into the plush chair and threw back the scotch. She enjoyed the taste of the alcohol and then lit a cigarette. Since her release from central booking, she'd checked into the Waldorf Astoria hotel in Manhattan. The price of her stay was very high, but money wasn't an issue for her. She needed time away from her own place, and she wanted the best. The sprawling suite was bedecked with a glass chandelier, and the living room had a bio-fuel fireplace and an enormous 80-inch TV. The master bedroom had a bedside control panel that gave control of all features of the suite, including the draperies, lighting, and temperature. The bathroom had an enormous sunken marble tub with a large window overlooking Park Avenue.

Layla had been plagued with one issue after another. With so much on her mind, she wanted to disappear for a moment. She heard about the attempted hit on her husband's life, but she didn't run to see him. She didn't feel the urge to comfort him and be that wife by his side, saying it would be okay and she would be there for him. No! Thinking about Penelope, his mistress, and how he had treated her blocked any wifely duties on her end.

Instead, she indulged herself with everything the luxury hotel offered—room service, spa service, facials, the gym, and simply being lazy and drinking in the comfort of her room. But with all that, she was still depressed, bitter, and angry. The luxuries that the hotel offered weren't the cure to her hostility toward her husband and Penelope.

She felt a strong urge to do something sinister. She wanted Penelope gone—nothing ambiguous about it. The Cuban bitch was a problem, and if she stayed alive and had that baby, Layla felt that the problem would grow out of hand. She needed to cut the rotten root from the tree before it spread. The only family tree that mattered was hers.

She knew her two sons, Meyer and Bugsy, well. Bugsy, smart and focused, was a daddy's boy and wanted to be just like Scott. She knew that she could request nothing from him, especially to do the unthinkable and have a pregnant Penelope killed. But Meyer was different. He was a mama's boy, and he was a stone-cold killer. What he'd done in DC, killing off Shiniquia's family so brutally, made her a proud mother. If she wanted something done, he rarely asked questions. He did what he was told because he loved his mother unconditionally. And he loved a challenge. Both sons would kill for her, but she knew Meyer wouldn't hesitate to kill a pregnant woman—a woman he once knew.

She poured herself another drink and lit another cigarette. She inhaled the nicotine and pranced around the hotel room in a luxurious red cashmere robe. She walked toward the window and stared out to watch the city transition from afternoon to evening. Standing there, she made the phone call to Meyer.

He answered, "Yeah, Ma, what's up?"

"Meyer, I need to see you," she said.

"I'm in Delaware. Is it important?"

"It's crucial."

He sighed. "A'ight. Tomorrow I'll be in the city."

She smiled. "Wonderful. I'm staying at the Waldorf Astoria." She gave him the room number, and their call ended just like that.

Layla knew he would come. Her pussy got wet just thinking about Penelope's demise.

The next day, Meyer showed up at the lavish suite as promised. He didn't come alone. He brought Luna. The man was becoming his shadow. Layla didn't want him around. She only wanted Meyer's ears to hear this, and no one else's.

"Tell him to leave," she said about Luna.

Meyer looked reluctant, but he did what his mother said. "Yo, go wait for me in the car. I'll be all right," he said to Luna.

The man nodded and left.

Meyer stepped farther into the suite. He looked around and was impressed. "This some nice shit," he muttered.

"You know me, son—I deal with nothing but the best."

"Yeah, you do."

"Have a seat."

"Nah, I'm good," he said. "I got places to be, Ma."

Meyer was dressed like some hoodlum from a rap video, wearing a black tank top highlighting his young, muscular physique and tattoos, black cargo shorts, expensive Jordans, and a large platinum chain around his neck with a large diamond gun medallion. A Yankees baseball cap sat askew on top of his head.

Layla was shocked that he got by the clerks and security dressed like that. But Meyer had his ways, and he easily intimidated people.

"What you call me here for, Ma?" he asked, ready to get down to business.

"I take it you heard about the drama between your father and me?"

"Yeah, and that's y'all business, not mine." He waved it off like he didn't care.

"Well, I have a problem."

"What? You need me to take care of someone?"

She smiled. "You read my mind."

"Who we talkin' about?"

"I want his fuckin' mistress dead, and you're the only one I can trust to handle it."

Meyer was somewhat taken aback by her request. "Yo, you mean Penelope?"

"Yes."

Meyer shook his head and chuckled at his mother's request. He looked his mother squarely in her eyes and said unequivocally, "Nah, I can't do that. It ain't happening."

"What you mean, no? I want that bitch dead, and I want you to make that happen," she said.

"I said no! You know I'll do anything for you, Ma, but that—it ain't happening. And you better not try anything on your own. Just let it be."

"Have you lost your muthafuckin' mind?" she shouted.

"No, but you're losing yours, Ma. If Pop gets a whiff of this, you know what he's gonna do? Just let it be, Ma."

Layla needed another drink. Not in a million years did she think her son would go against her. "So you sidin' wit' that bitch, huh?" she exclaimed.

"It ain't like that, Ma. I love you, but I know this shit ain't gonna end right for anyone."

Layla didn't know that Bugsy and Meyer had always been sweet on Penelope. They both liked her. They both had known of their father's affair with the young girl for some time. It was a secret they'd kept from their mother for a long time. Penelope was cool peoples. She would feed them Cuban food, and she was pregnant with their family. There was no way Meyer would take either life. He also knew that if he listened to his mother and killed Penelope, his father would no doubt come after him with full vengeance and maybe take his life. Besides, his father was a man, and he did what men do—fuck some good pussy. To him, it didn't mean that his father stopped loving his mother.

"Get the fuck outta my suite, Meyer," Layla growled.

"Ma, look, I always got your back—"

"Get the fuck outta here, nigga! You ain't shit to me!" she screamed. "Leave!"

Meyer was upset. "So, you gonna do this to me, your own son?"

"You ain't shit, nigga!"

"Well, fuck you too, bitch!"

Layla was furious. It felt like all the men in her life were turning against her. Had they all lost their minds over this immigrant mistress? Did they want a piece of her too?

"You trippin', Ma, fo' real. You need to calm the fuck down!"

"Don't tell me to fuckin' calm down! Scott's my husband, not hers!"

Layla didn't want to hear anything else Meyer had to say. She wanted him gone from the room.

Meyer said, "Fuck you! And don't do anything stupid!" He angrily pivoted and marched away from his mother and the room.

Layla slammed the door behind him. She heaved in anger. She would not quit on having Penelope killed. She hadn't gotten this far in life by giving up. If Meyer wasn't man enough to do the job, then she was determined to find someone who would.

Layla and Scott had recruited over three dozen new goons into the organization to protect the family. In fact, five new goons she knew of were parked outside the Astoria at the moment for her protection. It was a risky idea, but Layla was desperate to do the job. Maybe it was better to hire someone new, who wasn't as connected to the family and her husband.

She consumed another drink and lit another cigarette. Once again she lingered by the window overlooking Park Avenue and simply watched people's lives pass on by. She was overwhelmed with stress and disappointed with her kids. Meyer especially broke her heart, but she refused to dwell on it. Something had to be done about Penelope.

After extinguishing the cigarette, Layla got dressed and left the room. She traveled down to the lobby in her "red bottoms" and sauntered through the atrium and through the front entrance with her cell phone in hand, looking for her security detail. Wherever she went, they went. Scott made that very clear to everyone.

It didn't take long for two men to approach her. Mrs. West was what they called her. They believed she was leaving the premises, and they were to accompany her. Her life was their life.

"Where to?" the older man asked.

But Layla wasn't interested in him. The second one was younger and looked easier to persuade. He looked no older than twenty, but he also looked like an angry pit bull that wasn't afraid to show its bite.

She looked at him and said, "I need you to come up to my room."

He looked flabbergasted. "You need me?"

"Did I fuckin' stutter?"

"I'll be right up," he said. The young goon had two bodies on him, yet he found himself fearful of the woman, knowing her status.

Layla turned and marched back to the hotel and went back to the coziness of her suite.

Moments later, there was a knock at the door. Layla opened the door and allowed him inside.

"What's your name, *nigga*?" she asked him, emphasizing the word "nigga" to him clearly.

"Trans," he said.

"Trans, you're new to our world, aren't you?"

"Yeah."

"And you know my husband?"

"Yeah."

Layla was stern with him; he needed to know that she was a boss bitch and that he answered to her.

"I got a job for you."

"What kind of job?"

"Murder. And I know, for a nigga like you, that ain't no thang."

"It ain't," he replied coolly.

"That's what I like to hear."

Layla walked farther into the suite, and Trans followed.

She put a small picture of Penelope in his hand, a pretty picture of her. Trans' eyes lingered on the image, and Layla took notice.

"That picture gets your dick hard, nigga?" she asked him with an attitude.

"Nah!"

"Good. Because I want her dead by week's end," she said. "You understand?"

Trans nodded, looking deadpan.

Layla provided a little more detail about Penelope, and to give him some incentive, she removed five grand from a small bag and placed it into his hand. "That's for your troubles," she told him.

He didn't smile or anything but carried that same deadpan gaze. He kept the money, and she sent him on his way.

With that out of the way, Layla went to the private bar and poured herself another drink. Lately, she'd been drinking more to alleviate her pain, but it wasn't working too well.

Layla slid into the warm, soothing bath. She wanted to relax and feel some peace. Nearby, she had a bottle of Dom Pérignon, and her long-stemmed glass was filled almost to the rim. Layla's naked body felt like it was getting a thousand massages from head to toe. A sigh of relaxation escaped from her lips as she was submerged from the neck down in the bubbly water. She took a sip of champagne and closed her eyes.

She'd spent about ten minutes in her watery paradise when she was suddenly interrupted by an intruder in the hotel bathroom. She heard the door open and opened her eyes to find Scott towering over her, dressed in his first-rate three-piece suit and clutching a lit cigar in his hand. He glared at her, invading her space. She stared back.

He tossed the knot of money at her, but she refused to catch it, and it landed in the tub and sank to the bottom. It was the five grand she'd given to Trans.

He moved closer to Layla while she lounged helplessly in the tub. All she could do was watch his movement. She watched him take a seat at the edge of the sunken marble tub, his eyes ice-cold toward her. She could hear others in the next room moving about, most likely his thugs and goons that were there for his protection. Suddenly she felt like she needed some protection of her own.

"You're a piece of work, you know that?" he said, locking eyes with her.

Layla remained silent. She had nothing to say to him. She wanted to get out of the tub and wrap a robe around herself, but the water by some means became a barrier for her. She didn't move. She sat there and returned her own hardened gaze.

"You think I wouldn't find out? I own these niggas, so when you go behind my back to pay a nigga to execute Penelope, did you actually believe he would have the balls to go through with it?"

"I don't know what you talkin' about," she replied, playing stupid.

"Don't fuck with me, Layla! You're lucky I don't drown your ass in that fuckin' tub right now," he said with a tight jaw. "But listen to me clearly, as I'm gonna say this to you once and in clear English. If anything happens to Penelope—I don't care what it is—I'm gonna blame you and I'm gonna come after you. And it will personally be me, no one else, with my own two hands."

Layla stayed silent. The corners of her mouth turned downward in an intense scowl at her husband.

Scott scooted closer to her, his eyes burning into her. "Don't fuckin' push me, bitch. You don't wanna be on my bad side."

"So that's it, Scott? Huh? Her life is worth more than mine? I'm the mother of your six kids, been there for you since day one, and you choose that bitch over me?"

Coldly, he replied, "If something happens to her, then something will happen to you." He quietly lifted himself from the edge of the tub and exited without looking back at her.

Once Scott was gone, she could no longer control her emotions. A few tears trickled down her face, and she huffed and puffed with rage. She lingered inside the tub, feeling hurt and betrayed by her husband all over again.

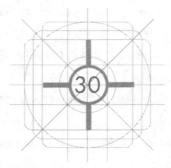

I t was the third cigarette Layla smoked within an hour, and she downed another drink. Lucky hated to see her mother in such a sad state. She watched Layla sit in her living room in silence and mope over her father's actions. The two ladies had had a detailed conversation that night. Layla felt her daughter was the only person she could trust and talk to. The men in her life were all against her, while Lucky understood her pain.

Layla became transparent in front of her daughter. Though she was a gangster bitch, she still had feelings, she had needs, and she still loved her husband. Both women were highly perturbed by the men in their lives, with Lucky thinking about her troubles with Whistler. But Layla felt disrespected. She'd paid a man to do something, and he went running back to Scott. How dare her underling betray her?

Layla felt she should've gone to Lucky first to take the mistress out. She would have done it without hesitation. She told Lucky about Meyer, and that Scott had threatened her.

At first, Lucky was annoyed with Meyer's action and angry about Scott's threats. Her brother could have gotten the murder done on the low without Scott knowing. Luna would have easily done it for Meyer. The two men were inseparable, and it seemed like Luna was becoming more of a brother to Meyer than Bugsy.

Second, it was a bitter pill to swallow to hear that her father threatened to kill Layla over some bitch. Lucky knew that her mother could exaggerate sometimes and was known for going over the top with things, but the tears in her mother's eyes flowed non-stop. And although her mother had said to never let a man see you sweat, and don't cry over a nigga, she was contradicting herself tonight.

Lucky knew that her father would lay down his life for his family, but she thought Penelope was clouding his judgment. She had always hated Penelope and probably hated her even more than her mother did.

Lucky remembered when her male classmates used to come to the house to study, which was really a make-out session. The boys used to gawk at Penelope. They were stuck on her beauty and hung onto every word she spoke in her Spanish accent. Even her brothers were gaga over the bitch, but Lucky saw right through her.

Corey was Lucky's crush before Whistler came into the picture. She remembered Corey so vividly. He was tall, lean, and in excellent shape. He was light-skinned with hazel eyes, had short, dark hair, and waves that spun like a top. Lucky wanted him to be her first, but he wanted no parts of Lucky, even though she was a beautiful young girl. He used her to get to Penelope. She would catch Penelope brushing up against him when she thought no one was looking. And the seductive smile she aimed at Corey pissed her off. Whenever Lucky confronted Penelope about it, she would say, "Me no understand. No speak English."

Lucky believed the bitch understood every word spoken in the house. She knew for a fact that the bitch was manipulative and dangerous, and now she had her father caught up in her web of deceit and sex. It made her furious to know her father put his seed into that bitch.

With the night still young, the two women talked and drank, until Layla finally fell asleep. She took comfort on Lucky's plush couch, an empty bottle of vodka near her reach. Her father had her mother stressed out and transitioning from wine and champagne to vodka and Scotch.

Lucky felt the urge to do something about the trouble. She was gradually watching her family fall apart. Three of her siblings were dead, her father and mother were at each other's throats, Meyer was becoming estranged from everyone, and there had been an attempt on Scott's life. So much was happening, but the king of the family had his head so far in the clouds with pussy, he couldn't see he was about to crash and burn soon. If something wasn't done immediately, they would lose everything that everybody had worked so hard for.

Early the next morning, Lucky left her mother passed out on her couch and left her building. She climbed into her Benz truck and drove to the scrap yard her father owned in Coney Island, Brooklyn. It was one of her father's headquarters, a place where he liked to hang out and take care of business. She steered her Benz truck into the cluttered area of junked cars and machines and left it parked in the center of the property. Seeing his Escalade parked in the yard told her that her father was there also.

Lucky swung open the driver's door, and her "red bottoms" quickly hit the dusty, rocky pavement. As she marched toward the trailer, her father's bodyguards watched her every movement.

One of them said to her, "He's busy right now."

"I don't give a fuck what he's doing," she answered. "I need to see him." She pushed her way through the men and charged into the trailer.

Inside, Scott was holding court with some men, all of them dressed in dark suits.

Lucky glared at her father seated at the head of the table in his high-back chair, cigar in his hand like always. "I need to speak to you in private."

Scott looked at his daughter coolly and said, "Gentlemen, excuse us for a moment. Let me have a moment with my daughter."

Each man lifted himself from his chair and departed from the room, and the door closed behind the last man.

Lucky stood across the room from her father, who stayed seated in his chair, eyeing her daughter stoically.

"Why are you fuckin' choosin' that low-brow bitch over my mother? What the fuck is wrong with you?"

"Watch your mouth," Scott warned her.

"Fuck that! You need to get rid of that foul immigrant bitch! She ain't shit. Just kill that bitch and her baby, and go back to Ma."

"Lucky, I'm warning you. Watch your tone," he said sternly.

Lucky refused to listen to her father's warning. "Fuck that bitch!" she yelled. "If you don't get rid of that bitch, I'll do it myself and cut that bastard out of her fuckin' stomach!"

Scott swiftly moved like he was the Flash, launching himself out of the chair and charging toward his daughter with such quickness. The back of his hand came across Lucky's face with such tremendous force, he knocked her clear across the room.

He stood over her, ready to strike her again.

Blood trickled from Lucky's lips as she was on the floor. She was in shock. Though the slap hurt, Lucky didn't flinch. She glared up at him, seething. "Go ahead, nigga. Hit me again."

Scott stepped back from his daughter. She was pushing him to a dangerous point.

In eighteen years, with all the temper tantrums, missed curfews, backtalk, and promiscuity with the boys, Scott had never put his hands on his daughter.

Lucky stood to her feet like she was a soldier, her face coiled into a deep scowl toward her father. She stood near him with hard-staring eyes that didn't blink, and she shed no tears. He had crossed that line. Now she knew where she stood with him. Scott stared back, and there was dead silence between them.

Lucky backpedaled toward the door, and before she left the building, she said to him, "I'm done with you! You put your hands on me for that bitch. I see you now. I see you."

Scott remained quiet.

Lucky stormed toward her car.

The goons outside were curious about the commotion inside. They knew that father and daughter had a falling-out.

Lucky climbed into her vehicle and slammed the door shut. The engine started, and she shifted the Benz into drive and sped away from the area. Immediately, she got on the phone with her mother and told her everything.

"He's fuckin' dead to me!" Lucky screamed into the phone.

I t was time for Layla to play chess instead of checkers, and for her to think about a future without her husband by her side—a future where she might even be at war with him. It was time for her to holler checkmate. Scott would never anticipate her next move. He wanted to play daddy with Penelope, then so be it. But the day he put his hands on Lucky to honor his mistress' name was the day he dug his own grave.

The drive to Garden City, Long Island was a quick one due to the light traffic on the LIE on a Sunday morning. Alone, Layla steered her pearl-white Range Rover through the suburban streets of Garden City and parked in the parking lot of a storage facility on N. Franklin Street, a commercial street flooded with numerous businesses.

Dressed in blue jeans, white sneakers, and a white ball cap with her long hair flowing from the back, Layla climbed out of the truck and strutted toward the facility. She tossed a smile at the three employees present and greeted them with a polite, "Good morning," and went about her business. She traveled farther into the facility, walking by numerous storage lockers, and stopped in front of one of the larger units. It was secured with three padlocks and a security system. It was the only storage unit with cameras on it twenty-four/seven and its own alarm. Briefly, she checked her surroundings before she undid the locks and punched in several numbers into the keypad to disarm it. With that done, she lifted the rolling gate, stepped into the unit, and closed the gate back down behind her. The light came on, interrupting the darkness of the unit, and in front of her was a pallet covered with a blue tarp.

Layla removed the tarp to reveal an abundance of cash stacked on the pallet. She knew how much it was—fifty million dollars. It simply sat in the unit untouched and unknown to everyone, except for two people: her and Scott. It was supposed to be for emergencies only.

Six years earlier, Layla had implemented an "out" plan. If their empire crumbled or came under fire from the feds, they would need money and a new identity. It was likely that all their legit assets would be frozen and their properties seized. Layla had seen the nightmare happen far too often to many individuals in their line of work. She'd seen kingpins fall into ruin and despair because they had no escape plan and no access to their capital because of federal seizures of their accounts and anything in their name. She'd seen lawyer's fees in the millions, where the clients were still found guilty and sentenced to lengthy prison terms. Their lives could be turned upside down overnight, and then what?

It was a nightmare that Layla was prepared for. She wasn't going out like that. She would not be scrambling for cash and paying lawyers with borrowed money, and desperately searching for a way to protect her empire and provide for her family. So instead of laundering all of his illegal money, and putting everything into legit businesses that most likely would be scrutinized and audited by the feds and IRS, she'd convinced Scott to set some aside and keep it stored away for a rainy day. They had enough cash to live through a hundred rainy days.

The money was safe in this storage unit. They owned the building and the company through a straw purchase. They wanted no paperwork linking them to the building via forensic accountants. The staff was on standby twenty-four/seven, and the entire area was outfitted with closed-circuit security. The unit was air conditioned, and the bundles of cash had been shrink-wrapped to protect it from the elements while sitting on the pallets.

Layla took a deep breath, her eyes fixed on the mountain of cash. The kids weren't even aware of it, and she was sure that Scott had forgotten about the money or thought she wouldn't tamper with it. Scott's net worth was over three hundred million of legit cash and tens of millions in assets. So why would he worry about the fifty million hidden and secured in one location for years?

She lingered at the storage unit for one hour until two 18-wheeler trucks pulled into the parking lot. The drivers descended from their big rigs and met with Layla. They knew who she and her husband were and how violent and dangerous their organization was. She gave them specific instructions, making it clear to the drivers and two other men that there were to be no errors while dealing with and moving the money.

Five million was strategically placed into each of the steel barrels and loaded onto the trucks, twenty-five million apiece on each rig. Layla made sure not to put all of her eggs into one basket. It took a while to load both trucks with the money for the thirty-five-hour drive to Florida. The tractor-trailer drivers were paid twenty-five thousand dollars each, and the rigs would be followed by a car. Layla wasn't taking any chances.

Deuce sat in the back seat of the Durango, with Jimmy and a lieutenant named Neal seated up front. They were in the Wilmington neighborhood of Cool Spring on N. Van Buren Street, a one-way residential block decorated with long-standing attached homes with steps leading to the front porches. The area was quiet. Deuce kept his eyes fixed on one particular house as he smoked a cigarette. They sat parked across the street and three houses down from the location, trying to remain inconspicuous.

"How did you find out about this place?" Deuce asked Jimmy.

"Now, Deuce, you know me. I find out about everything. They can't hide anything from me. I'm Jimmy, nigga, and I got eyes everywhere."

"My nigga!" Deuce had a hard time concealing his excitement.

Deuce took a pull from his Newport. The place they were watching was one of Scott's drop-offs for significant amounts of money. It was the main stash house in the city. From there, the money would travel north to New York City. There could be from hundreds of thousands to a few million inside the house.

The home was unassuming, well taken care of, and quiet. The front porch was barren of any outdoor furniture, and no goons were lingering outside. The West organization purposely kept the exterior thug-free, but they did have several small cameras placed on the location to watch everything coming and going. The front and back doors were reinforced with steel, the blinds were always drawn, and in the backyard were two pit bulls.

Deuce and Jimmy knew that though it looked simple on the outside, the interior was nothing to play with—guns, armed men, security safes, and mostly everything reinforced. But they didn't plan on breaking in. They wanted to watch the operations of the location; the more information they had, the better.

"I wanna know everything about this muthafucka," Deuce said. "Even the color of his piss. He fucks wit' me, we gonna fuck wit' him."

They'd waited over an hour, and everything was quiet. Their plan was simply to watch and learn. It wasn't easy tracking down the stash house. It took bloodshed, violent intimidation, and torture for people to talk. It also took surveillance and the help of crooked cops.

"We follow the money, and we get our hands on this muthafucka and everything he's close to," Deuce said.

Jimmy nodded. "No doubt."

"Sergeant Connelly is definitely on the money. I think fear motivates that pig more than money does."

Jimmy laughed. "I thought pigs don't sweat."

"Well, this pig does. He knows the consequences now if he decides to go against me. But y'all niggas stay on this," Deuce said. "I gotta be somewhere soon."

Jimmy nodded.

Deuce pulled out his cell phone and made a phone call. Into the phone, he said, "Come get me. You know where." He hung up.

Deuce finished his cigarette and flicked it out the window. "What about this nigga's twin sons? We on them niggas too?"

"Meyer is an unpredictable muthafucka. He's everywhere. But word is, somebody tried to take Bugsy's ass out last week."

"Fo' real?"

"Yeah. Muthafucka had on Kevlar though. Smart man."

Deuce chuckled. "That's why you always aim for these niggas' heads. Ain't no vest protectin' your fuckin' skull."

"Right, right."

"And that bitch?"

"Lucky? She's been quiet so far."

Deuce said, "I would love to get the entire family in one room and just have my way with them. Ooh, the fun I would have."

Jimmy chuckled. "I can only imagine."

"I love his wife, though. Layla a fine bitch for her age. The fun my dick would have with her . . ."

"I hear she's a piece of work."

"That's fine with me. You know I like these bitches feisty because I can get feisty right back."

Jimmy smiled. His boss did. He'd cleaned up his last mess with the stripper. Deuce killed her with his bare hands, asphyxiating her. It was an easy mess to clean up.

"When I get my second shot at this nigga, it's all head shots. I'm not missing," Deuce proclaimed.

"I got my peoples on it. He'll turn up again."

They continued to watch the house with little activity happening. Deuce lit another cigarette.

Fifteen minutes later, Deuce's cell phone buzzed. He answered, the conversation was quick, and he hung up. "I'm out. Let me know what happens," he said to Jimmy and Neal.

"Will do," Jimmy replied.

Deuce exited the vehicle and walked opposite from the house they were watching. A block away, he got into the passenger seat of a silver Lexus GS, and it drove off.

The Sunday evening brought about an extensive orange glow across the Brooklyn sky, as the sun was trying to shine the last of its ocher limbs over the urban rooftops. The streets were calm, and the people were out and about as a crisp chill sliced through the area. For many, it was a regular fall day in Brooklyn, with the World Series approaching and several NFL games showing on millions of TV screens across the nation.

But Sunday wasn't just an average day for Layla. Earlier in the morning, she had transported fifty million dollars via semi trucks to Florida. It was more money than the majority of the nation would ever see in their lifetime.

Layla couldn't help being nervous. If anything went wrong with the transport—if word somehow got back to Scott of what she had done, she was a dead woman. Scott would become more than furious. So everything had to go right. She was smart enough to place GPS trackers inside the steel drums, so she could watch the money's movement from state to state.

She stopped her Range Rover in front of the Brooklyn home. This time, she came alone. There wasn't a caravan of black SUVs or armed soldiers protecting her. She wanted to see and speak to Maxine alone. She wasn't glamorous like her usual self, wearing a burgundy jumpsuit, colorful Nikes, no makeup, and her hair pulled back into a ponytail. Things were different at the moment.

She climbed out of the Range and walked toward the front door. She exhaled quickly and knocked. She glanced around her surroundings. The block was typical and quiet. A few neighbors eyed her from where they lingered, but there was nothing to worry about.

The front door opened, and Maxine loomed. Immediately, Layla was taken aback by her refreshing appearance. The makeover was remarkable. Layla wasn't expecting this much of a change from her friend. Maxine had lightened and cut her long hair into short layers, which brought out her chestnut brown eyes. Her thick eyebrows were arched, and her lips were covered with a nude lip gloss. Twenty years later, Maxine was even more beautiful.

"Layla, hey."

"Can I come in? Can we talk?" Layla asked humbly.

Maxine had to hold in her anticipation, figuring Layla was there to speak about her dead son, Bugsy. The fact she was alone was almost surprising. But it was about time. She'd been calling Layla for days but hadn't received a return phone call yet.

"Yeah, sure. Come inside." Maxine stepped aside for Layla to enter the house.

"Where's your mother?"

"I sent her on a cruise with her friend."

Layla didn't care for Maxine's mother. She thought the old woman was a bitch.

"Is everything okay, Layla?"

"I need a friend right now."

"Of course, I'm here for you always," Maxine said. "What's going on?"

"Come with me," Layla blurted out.

"Come with you? To where?"

"To Florida for a few weeks."

"Florida? Why?"

"So we can catch up on lost time. So we can talk."

"To just catch up on lost time and talk? Why do we need to go to Florida to talk and to catch up on lost time? Did something happen? Is everything okay with the family?"

"The family's fine."

"That's good to hear," Maxine said, trying to hold back her shock. Bugsy was dead. Why was Layla not admitting that? Suddenly, Max felt very threatened. Had Layla finally figured it out? Was her life now in danger? What game was she playing and why? She couldn't dwell on it right now. Layla was standing right in front of her face, and she had to continue with her façade.

"I just don't want to be alone right now, Maxine. You stood strong for me, and I respect that."

"I'm on parole. I just can't up and leave the state like that. I have to check in weekly."

"Don't worry about your parole; I can take care of it."

Maxine was skeptical. Was it all a ruse to set her up for something violent and murderous to come? Miguel told her that Bugsy was a ghost, took four to the chest. Even if he had survived and was laying up in ICU, Layla would have told her unless Miguel had lied to her.? Maxine didn't know what was going on, but it was all suspect.

"Come to Florida with me, and I'll have my connections with law enforcement handle your parole officer. What's his name?"

"David Liberty."

"I'll make the nigga an offer he won't refuse."

Maxine was still uncertain. She could be walking into something dangerous. Florida could be her last stop. But Layla was adamant and wasn't taking no for an answer.

"Okay, I'll go."

Layla smiled. "Pack light. I'll take you shopping once we're there."

Maxine was floored when the Escalade drove onto the tarmac of the Long Island airport and stopped in front of the idling Learjet 60. Long and lean, it looked like a bullet with wings. The stunted stairs were down, and the pilots and worker were nearby, waiting to assist them with any luggage from the vehicle to the plane. The back door opened, and the ladies were ushered out and greeted with respect. Since Maxine was with Layla, the staff treated her like she was a boss bitch too.

"Good evening, Mrs. West," the pilot greeted them. "She's gassed up and ready for flight right away."

"Good. I'm ready to leave as soon as possible," Layla said.

The pilots were white and middle-aged. They dressed in bright white shirts with gold wings pinned above their pockets.

Maxine remained in awe. She was about to board a private plane for the first time. She went from prison to first class, and though she still felt some nervousness about the trip to Florida, she couldn't help feeling excited.

The ladies boarded the Learjet. It was a mid-sized cabin with a 15-inch aisle to provide additional space for comfort and maneuverability throughout the cabin. The seats were white leather with removable armrest caps and panels and berthing capabilities. The interior was also equipped with a 24-inch flat-screen monitor and Wi-Fi connection.

The pilots boarded the plane and positioned themselves into the cockpit and were ready to raise their bird into the sky.

Maxine sat across from Layla, who played the part of a veteran flyer—nothing was new to her. She remained nonchalant, busying herself with her smartphone for a moment as she waited for the plane to taxi and take off.

As the jet taxied on the tarmac, Maxine fixed her eyes out the window. They had their own flight attendant—a man dressed nicely in a white shirt, blue tie, and black pants. Smiling widely, he poured bubbly champagne into two glasses and served them to the ladies.

"Whatever you want, don't be afraid to ask," Layla said.

Maxine downed the champagne and asked for more.

The take-off went well. The nose of the plane levitated, and the jet soared into the air smoothly, cutting through the sky like the wind itself. It was a beautiful fall day, and the plane ascended thousands of feet into the sky and soon leveled off.

Maxine still kept her eyes out the window, staring at an all-blue sky of nothingness for miles and miles. It was her first time on a private plane, and it felt extraordinary. She could get used to something like this.

"Just relax and enjoy the flight," Layla said to her. "We'll be in Florida in no time."

Maxine wanted to relax, but in the back of her mind, she didn't trust Layla. But she enjoyed the flight. Twenty thousand feet in the air, she was treated to more champagne, caviar, and lobster. It was opulence at its finest.

A few hours later, the plane descended into a private airport near Miami. From the plane, the ladies right away got onboard a luxury helicopter, the Sikorsky S-76. The bird lifted quickly into the sky, tilting in the air, and headed west toward the Florida Keys. Offering a bird's-eye view of everything for miles, the helicopter moved swiftly in the air, flying at speeds up to two hundred miles per hour. It was an invigorating trip from Miami to Key West, bypassing hours of traffic and saving hours of time. For queens like Layla, it was one grand way to travel.

The turquoise ocean, extending endlessly on both sides of the Keys, seemed so calm and gentle as the sun's rays made it glisten like a giant diamond.

The helicopter descended toward a huge piece of property below. In Maxine's eyes, everything looked exquisite and sprawling. She saw the roofs of extravagant homes and more land than the eye could see. The property had its own heliport. It was unbelievable. Maxine was getting a firsthand look at how Scott and Layla were living.

Inside, Layla showed off the prime estate that sat on an expanse of pristine and picturesque land.

Maxine was blown away by the extravagance. Every square inch was detailed and handsomely built. The rooms were furnished tastefully with furniture that cost more than her mother's house, and the exterior was amazing with its rambling greenery, tennis court, basketball court, a small lake, and large marble fountain at the threshold of the property.

Maxine knew Layla must have spent a small fortune to get it all built to her liking. Each home on the estate was grand and had its own unique design. But it was the primary home that stood out the most. Layla took over an hour to show Maxine almost everything.

That evening, as they sat and talked in the stylishly decorated great room with the antique African statues and priceless paintings by Claude Monet and Vincent van Gogh, they downed more champagne.

Maxine still felt apprehensive, but she let her guard down a little and enjoyed the moment with Layla. It felt like old times between them. And Maxine wasn't sure if that was a good thing.

"I miss us," Layla said out of the blue.

Maxine didn't quite know how to respond to the statement. Remembering how things used to be between them so many years ago, it wasn't the best friendship. It was more like a use-and-get-used type of association, where Layla did the using.

They talked about their old neighborhood and friends and people that came and went. But the one thing Layla didn't bring up was Sandy.

After a few drinks, Layla's face quickly looked troubled by her present issues. She said to Maxine, "Scott's fuckin' some next bitch."

Maxine wanted to hear more about it. She tried to appear shocked and sad for Layla, but it was a façade. She felt Layla deserved a lot more than a broken heart from her husband.

Layla spoke about Penelope—the *mi speaks no English* bitch pregnant by her husband.

"I'm sorry to hear about this," Maxine said.

"You don't need to be sorry. I guess it was coming to me, right?" Layla said, almost sounding apologetic. She downed another glass of champagne, her sixth within a half hour. She stared Maxine in her eyes and that hard street look she forever carried softened. "I gotta be honest wit' you—I was fuckin' Scott while y'all two were together. I wasn't a good friend to you. I let you take the fall, and I got all this while you were locked down. But you the real gangster. You kept quiet, and you did your time like a true fuckin' *G*."

Maxine swallowed hard and remained expressionless.

"I was always jealous of you, Maxine. I mean, you had beauty, an education, parents, and most of all, you had Scott."

"It was a long time ago," Maxine replied quietly. "And it's good to be home."

Like the old days, no outburst of rage or anger spewed from Maxine's lips. She sat there and listened peacefully.

Hours later, they both fell asleep in the living room right before dawn was about to crack open the sky.

It was early afternoon when Maxine was awakened from her sleep by some sound coming from outside. She opened her eyes to find Layla no longer in the room. The sun was shining brightly, and the champagne was wearing off.

For a moment, she lay there. She heard Layla moving around the house, and then she heard a door slam and the faint sounds of truck engines. Curious, Maxine went to the window and saw Layla exit the mansion and walk across the compound just as two 18-wheelers were arriving.

Two men climbed out of their cabs and greeted Layla.

Maxine stood discreetly near the window to observe what was going on. Layla and the drivers talked briefly, and then the unloading started. Several pallets containing steel drums were loaded off the trailers and hauled toward the three-car garage of the home Layla had told her was Lucky's. The men were very careful with whatever was in the drums. Maxine first assumed it was drugs, but then she thought Layla wouldn't be stupid enough to have that amount of narcotics on her newly built property. But she knew there had to be something vital inside the drums.

When the men completed the task, Layla handed them something that appeared to be a payment concealed in a thick envelope. They were happy to receive it. A half-hour after the trucks had arrived, they were leaving the property.

Layla strutted back to the mansion, looking around the area with paranoia. Maxine wondered what type of cloak-and-dagger MI-6 mission she was on. Something important was in that three-car garage, and it made Maxine curious.

Seeing Layla enter the house, she removed herself from the window and pretended like she had just woken up.

Layla entered the great room with a smile and greeted Maxine, "Good morning, sleepy head."

"Good morning," Maxine replied.

"I made plans for the helicopter to pick us up and take us into Miami," Layla said. "Let's have a girls' day out, you and me."

M axine's day with Layla went smoothly. They went shopping, had drinks near the beach, and got manicures and pedicures from one of the top nail salons in the city. They enjoyed South Beach like two toddlers roaming free on the playground. They spent hours together, and not once did Layla mention the trucks that arrived on her property. It wasn't Maxine's business, but she couldn't shake the thought, wondering what might be in those drums. She'd counted at least ten drums unloaded from the trailers.

Also, not once did Layla mention Bugsy. If something did happen to him, she was nonchalant about it. Maxine knew she couldn't bring up the issue about Bugsy because it would create suspicion, so she continued to smile and put on a show for Layla.

The one distraction Layla had during their time in the city was her smartphone, which rang constantly. She was always on the phone. Mostly it was Lucky calling.

Layla desperately wanted Lucky to come down to Florida, and Lucky promised she would. But her attorney had advised her it would be better to stay in the state of New York, since her drug case was still pending. It wouldn't look right if she took a trip to Florida. The prosecutors would believe that she was running. Besides, she had an important hearing that could get her charges dropped. Somehow, the five kilos she allegedly had been caught riding dirty with suddenly went missing from evidence. The missing kilos sent the case into a tailspin, and Lucky's lawyer was certain she wouldn't see a day in jail.

Layla told Lucky to keep her posted on the hearing and that she had made moves to build a loyal team, but she needed to politick with her daughter first. It was important.

Then the conversation shifted to Maxine being in Florida with her.

"Are you out your mind?" Lucky barked.

"I know what I'm doin'."

"I don't trust her, and you shouldn't either," Lucky said.

"I'm okay. We're just catching up on lost time."

"It's stupid. She shouldn't be there," Lucky exclaimed.

Layla assured her daughter she had everything under control and guaranteed Lucky that Maxine wasn't a threat—that she was still the same docile, pretty, naïve girl from twenty years ago. And, besides, she was lonely and needed someone to talk to.

Each day Maxine stayed in Florida, she regularly heard Layla gripe about Penelope, but there wasn't any whining about her two sons. Did he die? Was he in the fuckin' hospital?

Maxine's skepticism about Bugsy was confirmed when she witnessed Layla and Bugsy FaceTime. She asked Bugsy when he and his brother were coming down to Florida to check out the new homes she'd built for them. Being busy, he made no promises to his mother.

Layla was unaware about the failed hit on her son. Scott and Meyer knew, but Lucky and Layla were kept in the dark purposely. A lot was going on inside the family, and the men agreed they didn't want the women to do additional worrying.

Maxine was burning up inside. She saw the man alive and well on the phone with Layla. She felt Miguel had lied to her after taking her money and some pussy for himself. He probably believed she was stupid.

Suddenly, her mood changed, and she needed to get back home and have a word with Miguel.

"I need to go," she said to Layla.

"Go? Go where?"

"Back home."

"But it's only been two days," Layla said.

"I just need to go. I have things to take care of. And I'm still on parole."

"I told you I had that taken care of."

For all Max knew, Layla was probably setting her up for a parole violation to have her sent back to jail. It would be the easiest way to get rid of her. There was no way Layla could convince her to stay any longer.

"I need to go!"

The following morning, Max was on the next flight back to New York City. She was still curious about what was placed inside the garage that day. Maybe next time she would find out, but right now she had other plans.

35

Miguel ran around the apartment chasing his three-year-old. When he finally caught up with her, he tickled her playfully, and they both laughed while rolling around on the floor. His four-year-old son joined in on the fun, while his six-year-old daughter watched TV on the couch. Miguel had bought each one of them a gift with the money he'd received from Max, and they'd talked to Nadia on the phone via collect call.

Spending quality time with his kids was priceless, and talking to Nadia from prison was comforting. In so many cautious words, he told Nadia that everything would be okay, that he had taken care of "that thing" for their friend.

It was getting late, and Miguel was ready to put his kids to bed. It had been an eventful day—the movies, fast food, shopping, and the park.

As he was tucking his youngest into bed, his cell phone rang. It was Max calling. He answered.

"Hey, I need to see you," she said.

"Now?" he asked.

"Yes, now. It's important. I need to discuss some business."

"Max, it's late, and I got my kids. I'll come by tomorrow morning."

"Come by tonight. I'll make it worth your while."

Thinking with his dick and knowing how good her pussy was, he sighed heavily and replied, "A'ight, give me an hour."

"Don't have me waiting long."

"I won't," he said and hung up.

Miguel had a dilemma—three kids and no babysitter. He thought about doing the unthinkable. Knowing his children were heavy sleepers, he woke up his six-year-old girl and told her to watch the others, and that he'd be right back. He reminded her to call his cell phone immediately if there was any problem.

"Goodbye, Daddy," she said.

"Daddy will be right back, sweetheart." He kissed his daughter on the forehead and exited the apartment, making sure everything was locked.

He climbed into his old Accord and headed off to see Max. His dick was already growing hard just thinking about his rendezvous with her tonight.

It wasn't long before he pulled up in front of her home and called her cell phone. "I'm outside," he said when she answered.

"Five minutes," she said.

It was a cloudy night, with the clouds blanketing the sky and covering the moon, and a fall breeze was gusting through the quiet Brooklyn Street. It was after midnight.

The front door opened, and Max stepped out onto the steps looking sexy in a green tank flare dress, a pair of embellished thong sandals, and carrying a purse. She smiled his way, and he smiled back. The anticipation was growing inside of him. Never in a million years did he think he would be infatuated by Max.

Max got into the car and said, "Drive from in front of my house."

"I can't go far. I have my kids tonight, and they're home alone."

His problems didn't fall on her. She didn't care. "Drive away. We don't have all night."

Miguel shifted the gears into drive and moved forward. While doing so, he glanced at her long legs crossed over each other in the front seat.

They gleamed like they had been rubbed down with baby oil. The view stimulated him. He wondered if she had on any panties under the dress she wore.

"Make a left," she instructed.

They had small talk inside the car, but Max seemed focused on something else.

They were now five blocks away from her home and still traveling. "How far away?" he asked her.

"It's not that far."

They drove down Fountain Avenue and parked under the freeway bridge, a secluded area with thick shrubbery and open areas of land near the water—no homes or businesses for a mile. He killed the engine.

Max looked at him deadpan and asked again for the details on the Bugsy hit. Why she wanted to hear it again boggled him, but maybe the details turned her on. Once again, he told her about the break-in across the street and holding the old couple hostage, tying them up, and how he waited and waited until Bugsy finally arrived. He told Max about the rifle he used, and that he shot him in the chest and saw him go down.

"I have another job for you," she said.

He nodded. "I know. I still owe you for the ten you got on credit. Are you ready for me to kill Lucky or someone else? Honestly, I hope you add someone to the list, 'cause I could really use the money for my kids."

"Well it's your payday 'cause I want to add Meyer, the remaining twin. I want you to kill him and Lucky together. I'm tired of the games, all games, and want to get this over with."

"You and me both. The sooner the better."

"Half now and half later," she said.

"I can't do that, Max. I need the entire payment now," he said. "I'm taking all the risks here. Besides, I'm worth it, with one down, two to go."

A moment of pause came from Max. The look in his eyes was truthful, but she knew he was fucking playing her. He used her just as Layla had done. Anger fizzled inside of her.

Calmly, she replied, "Okay. Tomorrow I'll have it all for you."

He smiled. "You look breathtaking tonight."

A quick smile developed on her face. "Thank you."

"You said you were going to make this trip here tonight worth my time, remember?"

"I did, right?"

"Yeah." He looked at Max hungrily, wanting to fulfill his needs at once. He was like a drug fiend aching for his next high. "Let's fuck in the backseat," he suggested.

Max agreed.

Miguel climbed over the front seats and situated himself in the middle of the rear seats. Max lifted her legs to hurdle the seats, and he saw she didn't have on any panties, which turned him on even more.

He sat back and allowed Max to straddle him slowly. It was a treat he was ready to snack on.

"You like fuckin' me, Miguel?" she whispered into his ear.

"You know I do."

Max gyrated her hips in a circular motion into his lap, feeling his erection growing underneath her. Her arms were wrapped around him, and her breath was against his neck.

Miguel desperately wanted to unzip his pants and slide his penis inside of her. She snuggled her thighs against his waist, fully facing him. She looked into his eyes and felt her sexual power over him. She was in control. She ran the show.

He couldn't take it anymore. He wanted to penetrate her. His dick was about to tear from his pants and slam inside of her. He was that hard.

Max placed her lips to his ear and continued to tease him. Then, in a quiet whisper, she said, "You lied to me."

"What?" He was confused. "I lied about what?"

Unfortunately for Miguel, he would never know the answer.

Swiftly and abruptly, the sharp blade pierced the side of his neck, and he jolted from the pain, his eyes open wide in shock and panic.

Max plunged the blade deeper into his flesh, and he twitched violently against her. It was scary how she kept her cool and continued to straddle him while watching him die right before her eyes. He couldn't talk, and he couldn't breathe. He gurgled and spat out blood. His body became numb, and soon he was dead.

Max lingered atop of him for a moment with the knife protruding from the side of his neck, as his body lay slumped in the backseat. Blood trickled, but it didn't spray everywhere.

She took a deep breath and removed herself from the body. She felt no remorse. She cared nothing about his three kids. Rage toward Nadia simmered inside her. The only thing Max cared about was herself, and her revenge.

Carefully, she wiped the car clean of her fingerprints and placed dead hair that she'd collected from the hair salon in his hand and in the back and front seat. It wasn't anything too crazy, just little strands of hair here and there. After that was done, she closed the car door and walked home.

36

The sniper's bullets came crashing through the car window out of nowhere, and two rounds barely missed Scott. The attack sent everyone in the area into immediate action and panic mode. The two bullets meant for Scott pierced the skull and neck of one of his bodyguards, and he dropped dead, his blood pooling on the ground.

Scott took cover behind a parked box truck, as his goons scrambled to protect him and return gunfire. The warehouse Scott was coming out of was out of the way near the harbor, a location that not too many people knew about. But somehow the sniper after him had found it.

Another three shots from the sniper screamed at him, but they boomed into the box truck.

Scott remained crouched low. "Shit! Muthafucka!" Scott yelled. He found himself helpless, while four of his goons went on the defensive.

"Kill this nigga!" he yelled.

Rat-a-tat-tat-tat-tat-tat-tat-tat-tat!

Bak! Bak! Bak!

His men's machine guns and handguns exploded, but they were shooting blindly, since they didn't know the exact location of the sniper.

When the smoke cleared, one man was dead.

Hurriedly, they escorted Scott into the black Escalade and sped off. It was the second attempt on Scott's life, and though he escaped unscathed once again, he was furious.

Hours later, Scott held court with many of his lieutenants and soldiers. The Long Island building and the entire area was heavily guarded by men armed to the teeth. Scott wasn't taking any more chances with his life. The loss of one man was tragic, but they knew the risk when he'd hired them into his organization. The man's family would be well taken care of.

Bugsy stood by his father's side. He too was angry, and he wanted revenge. But Bugsy warned his father to think evenly and not to do anything irrational and stupid. Lately, his father had not been making wise choices with his businesses, his movement around town, and his love life.

"We need to get ahead of this thing smart and subtle," Bugsy said.

"I am ahead of it," Scott growled. He looked deeply at every man in the room and said, "The fuckin' price just went up on Deuce and his crew. Fifteen million dollars for Deuce alone, and for every man dead in his crew, I'll pay up to a quarter of million."

A whistle was heard from someone in the crowd. It was a lot of money. It would create havoc in the streets not just in Delaware, but in the DMV area too.

So far, the West organization had come no closer to finding Deuce. They'd caught and murdered many soldiers and associates of his crew throughout the DMV area, but he continuously brought in more reinforcements and was becoming harder to deal with. And since Scott wasn't going anywhere, the two forces were frantically trying to kill each other off.

It was now about ego and pride. Neither man would give up, despite the heavy loss of life on both sides and the money both organizations were losing.

Bugsy remained nonchalant around his father. They were spending a lot of cash on this war, and too much heat had developed around his father since the first attempt on his life. His political connections were watching him closely, and Bugsy had heard from a reliable source that the feds might be investigating them too.

"I want blood to continue to run on the streets, and I want that muthafucka's head on my fuckin' desk," Scott said. "Y'all niggas are dismissed. Get the fuck out and go do y'all jobs."

They pivoted and marched out of the room, leaving Scott alone with his son. When the door closed, Bugsy said to his father, "You need to keep a very low profile, and you should leave town."

"You tellin' me I should run?"

"Nah, Pop. It's not running, it's falling back and regrouping. This is the second attempt on your life, and there was my incident in Mount Vernon. This shit is not a coincidence. We need to ask ourselves, how is this muthafucka getting so close to you and me? Who's the snitch in our organization? Who's working both sides of the fence?"

"That's what I need you to find out for me, Bugsy. I need you on your A game with this one," Scott said.

"I will, Pop. But we need you to chill for a moment, lay low, and we get Deuce another way. You're the face of this organization, and you need to be protected. The best way I see that happening is for you to leave the city for a moment. Deuce is smart, and we've been coming at him incorrectly. He's not just some ignorant thug. He's a patient, calculating man like myself. But everyone has a weakness, and we need to find his. But we need to change up everything in our organization, starting from the ground up."

Bugsy had his father thinking rationally now. Scott knew his son was right. They had to go about things a different way with their inner circle to not scare off their political and business connections. Scott would leave the city for a moment, giving him the perfect alibi—he was out of town.

K illing Miguel came too easy for Max. She'd plunged that knife into his neck without giving it a second thought. It was all done because he had lied to her. He failed to do what she had paid him to do. Max felt disrespected. She had been done wrong so many times. She had nothing, yet everyone was still trying to take from her. But seeing Miguel's blood spill and witnessing his life drain gave her this adrenaline rush. The power and control was alluring and fulfilling. But now she had one problem— she needed another hit man.

And then it dawned on her—why not her? She'd already gotten her hands dirty, and that kill felt good—made her feel alive. A taste for blood was stirring up inside of her. Her innocence had long ago been destroyed. Twenty years in prison and the violence she endured was her cocoon of imprisonment, and now that she was free, she was ready to spread her razor sharp wings and cut down everything in her path.

There was so much to do, so where to start? Back in Florida, she told herself. Layla was hiding something on the compound that was very important to her. Max was determined to find out what it was.

She called Layla and arranged a trip, and a few days after she killed Miguel, she was back on a plane flying to Florida. Besides, she needed to get out of town after the murder and give herself some space from the city. And her stern parole officer, come to find out, Layla had handled by blackmailing him. The people she hired had found some dirt on him, which gave Layla the leverage she needed to help Maxine out. He wasn't as squeaky clean as he appeared to be, cheating on his wife with a man, and he had a shady background that could cost him his job. He was warned to leave Maxine alone. If he didn't, and she was violated and sent back to jail, then his secrets would come out and ruin him and maybe even put him in jail too.

Layla had her money and her resources, so she got whatever she needed. Max was thankful, but it was because of Layla she was on parole.

Her flight landed at Miami International Airport early that afternoon, and a black Mercedes-Benz with a well-dressed chauffeur picked her up from the terminal and took her to the nearest heliport, where she boarded a helicopter that lifted her away into the air and hurried her toward the West's estate miles away.

The helicopter landed at the lavish estate after a quick ride, and Layla was there to greet Maxine with open arms and a kiss. She was happy that her friend had changed her mind and returned to Florida.

Max displayed her crooked smile and greeted Layla humbly.

Their night together was simple; they drank more champagne and talked. Once again, Layla griped about her husband's mistress. They watched '80s movies on the giant 90-inch TV in the vast living room, and it felt like an adult slumber party. The night was getting late, and the fifteen-hundred-dollar champagne was emptying fast. Max was stretched comfortably across the $32,000 authentic hand-knotted Persian rug in her long T-shirt and cotton slippers. When she got up to stand, she "accidentally" tipped over the champagne bottle and spilled it across the carpet.

Layla waved off the spilled champagne on the expensive rug like it was nothing. "I'll buy a new one."

"In that case, let me spill some more," Max joked.

Layla laughed. It was a good night, one that Max wished had happened twenty-two years earlier. Delete the twenty-two years taken from her life, then maybe she and Layla would still be the best of friends. Maybe.

"We need another bottle," Layla said.

Tonight, she wanted to get shit-faced. She wanted to drink with Max and forget about her troubles.

Their night was going good, and then the front door opened.

Layla was floored to see Scott walking into their home. Suddenly, everything stopped, and she gawked at him like he was some apparition.

"Scott! Ohmygod!" she uttered in disbelief. "Why are you here?"

Scott stood in front of her dressed sharply in his three-piece suit. He was shocked to see that Maxine was free from prison and in his home with his wife. Layla had never mentioned that she was home. What scheme was his wife brewing?

Scott couldn't take his eyes off Maxine. After all these years, she was still a stunning woman.

"What's going on here?" he asked.

"As you can see, we have company," Layla said.

"When did you get out?" he asked Maxine.

"A few months ago," she said.

Maxine didn't expect to see him, but there he was, her former boyfriend, the man who took her virginity, and the man who'd told her to take the fall for Layla. He was still handsome, but more distinguished and rich. There was a tone of power and arrogance about him. She'd always wondered what she would do when she saw him again. What she would say to him? How would she react? Now her chance came, and she was just silent. And though they didn't speak, there was intense eye contact.

Layla immediately picked up on it. She interrupted the moment by asking Scott, "What's goin' on in New York? Where are my kids?"

"They're fine," he responded curtly.

"I don't believe you. You show up out the blue in the night. What is really goin' on, Scott?" Layla stood between Scott and Maxine, breaking up their moment.

"You wanted me here. Now I'm here. I need a fuckin' shower. It's been a long day," he said, walking away.

Layla stood there stunned with everything suddenly happening. She didn't know what to expect from Scott. But she wasn't a fool. Her intuition told her he came to Florida for a reason, and it wasn't to see her. Something had happened. He wasn't telling her what it was. Her concern was with her kids, especially Lucky.

"It's getting late. I'll go to bed," Max said.

With Scott home, Layla didn't want Maxine anywhere inside the house. The look Scott gave Maxine was unsettling, and Layla didn't trust him or Maxine. Was it a coincidence that Scott showed up while Maxine was visiting? Layla wasn't sure, but her husband had something up his sleeve.

"You're not stayin' here," Layla said.

"Where do I sleep?"

Layla went to get a set of keys and tossed them to Maxine. "Here, they're the keys to Meyer's house. He's not using it anytime soon. Feel free to enjoy it."

Max didn't argue with her. She took the keys. She knew the reason Layla wanted her gone from the main residence. Scott's unexpected arrival was a game-changer.

"Good night," Max said.

Layla didn't respond. She quickly pivoted and marched toward the master bedroom to continue her conversation with Scott.

Max left the house and walked across the compound and entered the house that Layla had built for Meyer. The interior was stunning, and the décor was riveting. It was breathtaking, with the crystal chandelier above the room, a spiral staircase leading to the four bedrooms above, marble flooring below, an opulent fireplace, and a skylight in the living room.

Max toured the home, and it was paradise, but she was there for other reasons. Being alone in the house allowed her to investigate what Layla was hiding in Lucky's garage. It was late, and she knew Layla would be too preoccupied with Scott to care what she was doing. She threw on some sweats and a T-shirt, and like Bruce Lee in *Enter the Dragon*, she crept outside to look around the complex.

During their drinking time together, Layla had loosely mentioned things to her she probably didn't mean to. She had mentioned that each alarm code was the date of birth of each child. Max went to the three-car garage at Lucky's house and punched in the code. It deactivated the alarm system. Max couldn't believe her luck.

Carefully she lifted the garage door and slid inside. She then shut the garage door to remain unnoticed. Inside the garage, she saw the steel drums. She counted ten drums, and they were all stacked neatly on the pallet. The drums were the only thing inside the garage besides a decked-out workshop area. Curiosity got the cat, and she opened one of the drums carefully with some tools from the workshop area. The lid came off, and what she discovered inside blew her mind. Bundles of shrink-wrapped money were stuffed into the drum. She figured it had to be in the millions. And with nine more drums, she thought there had to be maybe tens of millions inside the drums.

Max was floored and overwhelmed. "Oh shit," she muttered.

Max had the urge to take some for herself, but it was too risky. With that large amount of cash, Layla most likely had some security measures in place. Then it dawned on her. *Shit! Security cameras could be watching me right now.* Max looked around for cameras inside the garage and didn't see any. But just because they weren't visible didn't mean they weren't there.

She placed everything the way she found it, grudgingly placing the large bundle of cash back into the drum, and exited. If Layla knew she was ever there, it would create problems for her. She needed to stick to the plan and stay focused. But that greed to take money from Layla had been planted inside of her, and she wanted to take it all.

Scott stepped out of the shower, toweled off, wrapped the towel around his nakedness, and went into the adjacent bedroom to find Layla sitting there and waiting for him to finish. He was surprised to see her seated on their king-size bed like a statue, her full attention fixed on him. It didn't bother him. He remained nonchalant.

"What is it that you want?" he asked her.

"What's goin' on? Why are you back in Florida? After what you told me in New York, go be wit' your fuckin' whore. I don't want you here," she hissed, her face twisted into a frown.

He chuckled at her comment. "You're cute!"

"Fuck you!"

"Is that what you want from me, Layla? A good fuck?" He moved closer to her and stared at her strongly. "I haven't fucked you in quite a while."

He stood close to her, his body fit and lean, his abs showing, and his chest protruding. "You miss me?" he asked.

She frowned. "I hate you!"

He laughed and dropped the towel to the floor, revealing himself to his wife.

She didn't budge. She didn't care for the dick anymore, although it was imposing and lengthy.

"This is what you want from me, right? Some dick."

She jumped up and pushed him away. "Tell that bitch to go fuck you, because I'm tired of your shit. I'm tired of you treatin' me like I'm not your wife. You have the audacity to threaten my life for that bitch!"

Scott kept his cool. He knew Layla would be a headache tonight, and he was in no mood for her shit. He didn't want the pussy that badly.

They argued briefly.

"You know what? I'll be in the other room. Go fuck yourself." He marched off.

Layla stood there dumbfounded. She did her best to hold everything together. With Scott home, it thrust her emotions into turmoil again. How often would he have to disrespect and embarrass her for her to get the hint? She wanted him, but he couldn't have his cake and eat it too. She didn't want to share her husband, especially with Penelope. Her chest heaved in and out from anger and frustration. She struggled to regain her composure. The nerve of him, taunting her with sex because he was horny. There were numerous times when she threw herself at him and he rebuffed her advances like she was gum stuck on his shoe.

She went to bed angry, but she couldn't sleep. Scott was heavily on her mind. It was ironic that she didn't want to be alone in Florida, and now she had Scott and Maxine with her.

Hours went by, and it was nearing dawn, and Layla still lay awake. She did her best to fight the urge, but she couldn't take it anymore. She removed herself from the bed and left the master bedroom and found herself in the room where Scott was sleeping naked. She was naked too, and she crawled in bed with him and planted kisses against his bare chest.

Scott took his wife into his masculine arms and stared at her smugly, his eyes saying, *I knew you would come sooner or later.* They kissed passionately, and he tossed Layla onto her back and spread her legs forcefully before thrusting himself inside of her, his width stretching her walls, his length roaming deep.

She pushed him off her and straddled him, squeezing him between her thighs and gyrating her pelvis, wanting to give him something powerful and unique to remind him how good it was. She moaned and groaned softly. She missed the feeling. Oh, how good he felt. His hands squeezed her breasts, as he rotated his hips between her thick legs, letting his dick caress her clit. He pulled her to him and snaked his tongue between her moist lips and slid it around inside her mouth.

"Ooooh! Ooooh! Oh shit! Scott . . . Scott . . . fuck me!" she moaned faintly.

He flipped her on her back. The dick was taking her places she hadn't been for a while. She closed her eyes, and her manicured nails traveled down the length of his back. Her legs were upward and pushed back toward her shoulder, as she took his big dick in the twisted missionary position.

"I'm gonna come!" she announced, huffing and puffing.

And soon she came.

But it was only the beginning. Scott wasn't done with her yet. There was round two and three, and an hour later, Layla felt depleted. Scott done fucked all the sex out of her, but she wasn't complaining. For a moment, she felt happy.

The next morning Scott was up early, walking around the bedroom naked and holding a conversation with Penelope on his cell phone while his wife was lying on the bed a few feet away. She wasn't sleeping. Her eyes were open with her back turned to him, and she heard everything he was saying. Just like that, he made her feel dirty and used. Why did she fuck him? Why did she give in so easily? She knew he wasn't leaving his mistress. She was upset, but she lay there quiet. She wanted to jump up kicking and screaming at him, but why give Penelope the satisfaction of hearing them argue? So she remained silent and pretended to be asleep.

Lucky climbed out of the Mercedes-Benz and stared up at her mother's new real estate development. It was magnificent. She was blown away by the houses on the property, passing through the large Victorian-style black-and-gold toned cast iron entrance and seeing the large marble fountain at the threshold.

Lucky wasn't in Florida for a vacation. She had a bone to pick with her mother. Her lawyers had worked everything out via litigation, and when the chance came, she hopped on a private jet and flew to Florida.

She ascended the stairs looking fabulous in a short black beach dress and a pair of strappy heels. The staff removed her bags from the car, and she marched into the large mansion on a mission to set her mother straight.

Immediately, Lucky was rude toward Max, the word *bitch* spewing from her mouth a half dozen times. Max kept her cool and allowed the disrespect, wishing Wacka and his goons had done more disfigurement to her face.

"Ma, we need to talk now . . . in private," Lucky said, like she was the one with authority.

She and Layla retreated into another room. Lucky closed the door, and right away she spoke her mind. "Are you crazy? Why is that bitch back here? And then you have Daddy here too? Ma, tell me you're not that stupid."

Layla scowled at her daughter's harsh choice of words. "First of all, I know what I'm doing. And, besides, your father isn't worried about her. He's too obsessed with tryin' to repair this marriage and keeping Penelope happy. He wants the best of both worlds."

"Are you fucking crazy?"

"You know nothing about marriage," Layla said. "I've been with your father for over twenty-somethin' years—longer than you've been alive—and to simply let him go is not that easy. But just because I can't let him go, it doesn't mean I still can't let him pay for his shit."

Layla mentioned to Lucky the money she'd taken from her father—fifty million dollars in hardcore cash. She told her not only about it, but she also took her to the garage and showed it to her. Lucky was in awe. Layla explained what the money was for, and how long she'd been hiding it.

Lucky told her, "Ma, you need to move this money."

"I'm already planning to do so."

Lucky saw that her mother, though still in love with her father, wasn't a complete fool.

Layla told Lucky that if her father didn't dump Penelope right after she gave birth to that bastard boy or girl and bring his black ass back home for good, then she would divorce him, start her own organization, and use the money to hire her own goons with allegiance to her and not Scott.

Lucky liked the plan, except for it being still contingent on her father's move.

Thanksgiving!

The entire West family traveled down to Florida for a holiday, and Max was included in the festivities. Bit by bit, she was implementing her plan of getting in close with the family, knowing the in-and-outs of their organization, and having Layla trust her fully. She continued feigning innocence and hiding any hatred toward the family. No one was any wiser about her role in the gangland murders of their family members, and Max wanted to keep it like that. She'd started killing off the children; now she wanted to rob them blind.

Meyer and Bugsy came down together, so Max stayed in the main house with Layla and Scott. Layla wasn't ready to have anyone stay in the homes of her slain children. Meyer brought Lollipop with him, and Bugsy brought Alicia. Lucky was alone. She didn't mind. She didn't miss Whistler. He was old news. But she had something to celebrate for the holidays—her drug case had been dropped. Her lawyers did a wonderful job with filing motions, and eventually getting the case dropped. That burden of doing time in prison had been lifted from her.

Thanksgiving was supposed to be a special time of the year, a time for the family to come together and feast. The cooks and the staff prepared a wonderful meal for the house, from a giant turkey that could feed an entire village to numerous side dishes like macaroni and cheese, collard greens, shrimp, and caviar.

It was the first time that Layla introduced Maxine to her twin boys, Bugsy and Meyer. She introduced Maxine as "Auntie Maxine," which disgusted Lucky.

Bugsy was the only one who smiled and greeted her with a hug and a kiss on her cheek. He was pleased to finally meet Max. He'd heard what she had done for his mother twenty-three years ago, spending time in prison for a crime she didn't commit. She didn't snitch. She kept her mouth shut. In Bugsy's eyes, she deserved some respect for it.

Maxine was thrown off by Bugsy's hospitality. It made her question her revenge against the children. She had waged war against the children who were blameless. Funny thing though. Looking at the smart, charming, and handsome Bugsy with his educated and sweet girlfriend, Alicia, Max was actually glad he was still alive.

Meyer was a different story. He stood aloof and cold toward Max and didn't smile or greet her warmly. He wasn't rude and vulgar toward her like Lucky, but his eyes revealed that he didn't care for her. He didn't even shake her hand. And his date, Lollipop, was just as dismissive toward her. Max noticed that the twins' attitudes were reflected in their dates.

Thanksgiving dinner went smoothly. Everyone feasted on the large meal prepared by the staff. There was no argument and no offensive distractions, although there was tension at the table, particularly toward Maxine and Scott.

After dinner, Meyer pulled his mother to the side, and though she was still sour about his defiance, Meyer had her ear. Away from everyone, he voiced his disgust about Maxine. He thought it was foolish to have her under the same roof as his father. He didn't like her, and he didn't trust her. But Layla didn't want to hear it, saying they had more pressing issues to deal with than to worry about Maxine. She assured him that Max was harmless.

"She's an institutionalized fool. A scared rabbit afraid of her own shadow. I know Maxine. She would rather gnaw off her own foot than to fuck wit' me over Scott."

Lucky still wasn't speaking to her father. She hated how Scott treated her mother like shit and had slapped the shit out of her over his whore—a bitch who was just a couple years older than her. During dinner when Scott tried to talk to his daughter, she ignored him. But her childish actions didn't faze him. He smirked, figuring she was still a kid.

It was another steamy night for Layla with her husband. She straddled him on the king-size bed and felt his firm erection fill her pussy completely as he thrust upwards into her. Layla didn't want it to end. She kissed him lovingly, her body forgiving him. Her mind wasn't as forgiving; it still felt marred by his unfaithfulness.

She panted in his ear and gave into him entirely, feeling her body about to orgasm against him. "I love you," she said, breathing heavily into his ear.

Thanksgiving with the family was long gone. Meyer and Bugsy were back in New York and Delaware handling business, and Lucky was out and about, putting her life and business back together after her arrest and Whistler's betrayal.

With Penelope nearing her due date, it was becoming more difficult for Scott to have sex with her the way he wanted to. So he stopped having sex with her completely and spent more of his time in Florida, having sex with his wife. Layla was more eager to please him.

But Scott was also thinking about Maxine. When the chance came, he would steal looks her way, watching her closely and knowing something was different about her. Although she still appeared sweet and naïve, her eyes had hardened. He was aware that her stint in prison had changed her. Now Maxine looked to be a mixture of Penelope and Layla—a perfect combination in his eyes.

For Florida, it was a chilly night. The wind from the ocean blew steadily, and the full moon played peek-a-boo, weaving in and out of the clouds. The Maybach pulled onto the compound and stopped in front of the sprawling mansion. Scott was returning to Florida from another New York trip. He stepped out of the Maybach but hesitated to proceed. Instead, he told the driver to leave, and he pivoted and walked toward the home he knew she would be in. He wondered, though, why Layla would keep her there around him, tempting him like this. Regardless, he wanted Maxine tonight, and he was determined to have her.

He walked into the quiet home. It was dark, and it was late. He undid his suit jacket and trekked up the spiral stairway and headed toward the main bedroom. The door was ajar, and he peeked inside and saw that Maxine was asleep. He grinned. For a short moment, he stood at the door in the darkened hallway and watched her. She looked fresh and alluring. He couldn't look at her any longer without touching.

He walked into the room and placed himself against Maxine, and his sudden presence startled her. She jumped up and was ready to attack him, not knowing the face for a moment.

"Chill, baby. It's me."

"What are you doing in my bedroom?" she exclaimed.

"Your room? That's cute," he said with quiet laughter. "I came to see you."

There he was, face to face with her, and smiling like everything was okay between them. Max wanted to punch him in the face, but she didn't.

Smiling, he reached for her and grabbed her wrist. He wanted to pull her closer, but she resisted.

"You look beautiful . . . more beautiful than I remember you," he said.

She remained quiet.

"I missed you so much," he said.

She stared at him deadpan. If he missed her, then why didn't he come to visit her? Why did he coerce her to take the fall for Layla?

"You're not going to say anything?"

"What is there to say?" she said.

"You and Layla are the best of friends again, I see."

"We're just catching up."

"I find it ironic to see you here."

"Well, I'm here. Do you want me to leave?"

"No, I wanna catch up too, on lost time."

She chuckled. "Lost time? I did hard time."

"Yeah, lost time," he said with a lecherous grin, his eyes intense and piercing.

Max felt vulnerable around him in her T-shirt and panties. She wanted to cover up and walk away, but she didn't. She found herself rooted on the bed right next to him, and his touch against her skin had paralyzed her.

"Let me make things up to you," he said.

"And how are you gonna make it up to me?"

"I'll show you," he replied with confidence.

"You wanna fuck me tonight?" she said.

"You know I want you."

Max wanted to take as much away from Layla as possible, and what better way than to fuck her husband, the same man Layla took from her? After all, he was hers before he'd married Layla. It was perfect. She could have Scott eating out the palm of her hands. Prison had taught her a lot, and she was putting her knowledge to good use.

She leaned back on the bed, indicating to him she was his for the night. She wanted him inside of her.

Scott hovered over her lustfully, removing her panties and stripping away his clothing. Her legs spread, and he eagerly slammed himself inside of her, feeling all of her womanhood grip him. He grunted from the intense feeling she gave him, already feeling her pussy milking his dick to come.

Maxine forgot what he felt like, how big his dick was, and how vigorously he used to fuck her. The man hadn't lost his touch.

They had explosive sex. When it was all said and done, it was Scott who had to rethink all his moves.

"Damn!" he muttered.

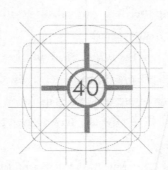

Layla noticed that Scott had been spending more time in Florida. She wasn't complaining, assuming that he'd finally come to his senses and cut off Penelope. He must have realized she was his ride-or-die wife and that she would do anything for him. Lately, she'd been floating on cloud nine, feeling like her husband was back in her life. But once again, their sex was lacking. But what else Layla noticed and gloated about was the constant bickering between Scott and Maxine. They couldn't be in the same room with each other without squabbling. Layla saw they despised each other, and she loved it. She believed that Maxine hated Scott for everything he'd done to her and had been more forgiving toward her. With Christmas right around the corner, Layla felt cheery about having her husband back in her life, Penelope out of the picture, and Scott and Maxine hating each other. It was her early Christmas gift.

Lucky was against everything going on, but Layla told her that she and her father were working on mending their relationship. Lucky warned her not to trust him, that he was still a dog. And she forever warned her mother to get rid of Maxine. To her, it didn't make sense. If she was working on her marriage with Scott, then why have the former girlfriend around? Lucky felt that her mother was setting herself up for disaster.

✶✶✶

Max felt in charge. Everything was going smoothly between her and Scott. It was her plan to pretend they didn't like each other when they got around Layla, but behind closed doors, they would passionately fuck each other's brains out. She sucked his dick like a porn star and threw her pussy at him like an animal unleashed from its cage. Scott ate her pussy out like it was dessert and fucked her as if she would be his last fuck. But now, wanting to rewrite the program, she had to change things up.

It was after midnight, and she was expecting Scott to come by tonight for his usual dosage of sex and good loving.

He was on time, walking into the house with anticipation of having another great night of sex with her. She sat in the living room, dressed in sweats and a T-shirt. When he came to her, she pulled away from him, her look hardened and unfriendly.

"What's wrong with you?" he asked.

"Not tonight," she said. "I'm not in the mood."

He laughed, thinking she was joking. He wanted her badly tonight, but she continued to resist, making him angry.

"What the fuck is your problem, Maxine?" he barked.

"Everything is my problem—this entire setup with us, this sneaking around. I was meant to be your woman, your wife, not your mistress. But you left me to rot in jail while you got my friend pregnant and married her. You gave her six kids, a luxurious life to live, and what do I have to show for myself? Huh? What do I have? You know what I have? A father who died while I was in prison. I couldn't even attend his funeral. And I have a mother with one foot in the grave and a fuckin' federal record. I have nothing, Scott, but you want me. You need to really show that you want me, that you really love me like you say you do. I don't want you part-time anymore."

She knew her threats were a gamble, but she saw her opening and knew it was time to go for it.

Hearing Maxine break it down, all the foul shit done to her, Scott felt some remorse. She didn't deserve it. She had a bright future ahead of her, and it was all snatched away. She had always been smart and ambitious, and she came from a good family. There was always something about Maxine that Scott loved. She had that innocence about her he still saw, even after her time in prison. There was a slight change, but that simplicity in her character drew him in deeper. And the way she fucked him had him obsessed. It was time to correct things. And, besides, he was never in love with Layla.

The shock on Layla's face when she saw Scott and Maxine walk through the front door together was clear as day. The two looked too comfortable around each other, and Maxine had a smirk on her face that immediately rubbed Layla the wrong way.

Scott looked at Layla intently, his eyes already showing her that whatever he had to say wouldn't be good.

"You need to sit down," he said to Layla.

"Fuck that! I don't need a fuckin' seat. What is this shit about?"

"I'm divorcing you," he said.

Layla was dumbstruck.

"I never really loved you, Layla. I just tolerated you all this time."

Those words cut her deeply. And there was Maxine, standing beside him with that annoying smirk. Layla wanted to rip it off her face.

"And I never loved Penelope; she was just a good time . . . some young pussy I got caught up in. Y'all bitches were just placeholders. I thought I could be happy with y'all, but I wasn't."

To hear the love of her life, a nigga she'd been fucking with since she was eighteen, tell her she was just a placeholder for the next bitch, and that bitch being Maxine, made her furious. A fuse ignited inside of her, and she charged toward Maxine, ready to crush her with her bare hands, but Scott quickly intervened, coming between them. He grabbed Layla, holding her back.

"I'ma fuck that bitch up!" Layla shouted. "I trusted you! I brought you in my home and looked out for you all this time, gave you money, and you do this to me?"

"He wasn't yours to have in the first place," Max shouted back.

"Bitch, he will always be mine. You couldn't handle him twenty years ago, and you can't handle him now," Layla screamed. "That's why he sent your ass to rot in prison, bitch! Let me go! Let me go!"

Layla desperately wanted to sink her teeth into Maxine. Her eyes flared with rage, and she was almost foaming at the mouth. There was no way Maxine was leaving her home without an ass-whipping. But Scott held her tight, preventing it from happening.

"Get the fuck off me! I'ma kill that bitch!" Layla screamed.

"Let her go," Max said calmly.

Scott glanced at Maxine, knowing she couldn't be serious.

"Let her go," Max repeated in the same calm tone.

Scott released his hold on Layla, and she went charging after Maxine like a discharged bullet, ready to tear her nemesis apart. But it was Layla who caught the shock of her life. She was quickly struck with a left hook by Max—a hard, dizzying blow. But Layla kept coming, and the two women grappled at each other's clothing and hair.

Max was the more aggressive one, repeatedly punching Layla in the face while having a fistful of her hair. Layla shouted obscenities at Maxine, as she felt herself losing the battle. Max's grip on Layla's hair tightened, as she controlled her movement, and then in a swift motion, she brought Layla's face down sharply on her bent knee and broke her nose. Layla hollered from the pain, blood flowing down her face.

With blood gushing from her nose and clearly embarrassed, Layla angrily shouted, "Get the fuck out my house! Both of y'all! Get out!"

Scott had heard and seen enough. He saw red with Layla, and the audacity of her trying to kick him out of his own house. "Your house?" he replied. He smacked Layla out of the blue and grabbed her roughly by her clothing and dragged her to the door.

She fought, kicking and screaming, but Scott was adamant in throwing out the trash. He tossed her out the door by her hair, and the car keys and her purse followed. Layla yelled and cursed at him.

Maxine just stood there and watched it all. Everything was working out perfectly.

That same night, Scott and Max made love in the main house. But she refused to fuck him in the master bedroom. In contrast to the earlier scuffle with Layla, she continued to play innocent and harmless, and she had Scott eating out of the palm of her hand. Her character and her pussy worked like voodoo on him.

41

It all felt like it was coming to an end for Layla, but she'd planned for this day. She called each of her kids and told them what had happened, and not one of them was shocked.

Lucky said, "I told you so," but Layla didn't want to hear it. She wanted revenge on Scott and Maxine.

While eating breakfast with Scott in the kitchen and acting like she was on her honeymoon with him, Maxine casually asked him, "Why would you keep so much money on the compound?"

Confused by her statement, he asked, "What money? What the fuck are you talkin' about?"

"In the three-car garage, the house built for Lucky. There's tons of money in steel drums placed on pallets in the garage, maybe millions."

Immediately Scott removed himself from the kitchen and hurried to the location. Max followed him. He opened the garage and saw only empty pallets, but he noticed the disturbance in the garage, and the skid marks the pallets had made. Right away, he got on his cell phone and planned to fly to New York City to confirm his suspicion.

Several hours later, Scott and Maxine were back in New York. At once he had the chauffeur drive them to the storage unit in Garden City, Long Island. It'd been a while since he visited the place. He hurried toward the storage unit, with Maxine following right behind him, and immediately he knew something was wrong. When he opened it up, there was nothing. The fifty million dollars was all gone.

"That sneaky fuckin' bitch!"

Max felt betrayed too. She wanted a piece of the money, but instead, she got Scott. Maybe he was a much bigger prize.

Scott was enraged. He called Layla's cell phone, but it went straight to her voice mail. He left her an angry, threatening message. He didn't care that she was his wife and the mother of his kids; he was ready to put the bitch six feet under. His composure gone, he thrust his fist into the gate and put a dent in it. "I'm gonna kill that bitch!" he shouted.

"Baby, calm down," Maxine said.

Scott continued to fume. He was close to putting a contract on his wife's life. Fifty million dollars was no drop in the bucket, and he'd killed men and women for a lot less than that. There was no way he could allow Layla to disrespect him like that.

Max was in his ear, calming him down. "There's another way, baby. No bloodshed. We can come at her subtly and make sure she has nothing left. And I'll help you. I'm here for you."

"What you got planned?" he asked.

She smiled. "Something easier, a way to get your money back. But first, you have to do something for me."

"And what's that?"

At Maxine's behest, Scott ended his relationship with Penelope. He would not stick around for the remainder of her pregnancy. He stood there coldly in her living room on a Sunday afternoon and frankly told a very pregnant Penelope that their relationship was over, and he was with someone else who he would soon marry.

Penelope was confused and appeared devastated by the sudden news. "Did I do somethin' wrong, Poppi?" she asked him.

"You can keep the apartment, and my child will be well taken care of. You don't need to worry about anything."

In tears, Penelope tried to hug him and kiss him, but he pushed her off and away from him.

"Keep it simple, and don't touch me."

"Now I can't touch you? I'm carryin' your baby," she cried out.

"And like I said, you and my child will be taken care of. But you and I, we're done."

He turned and marched out of the apartment, and the door slammed behind him.

Once he was gone, Penelope stood up and wiped away her crocodile tears. She was glad he was gone. She giggled. "Good riddance."

Scott was a strategic come-up for her, and getting pregnant was the icing on the cake. She didn't have to worry about cleaning toilets, cleaning homes, cooking anyone's meals, or tending to anyone's children. The way she was living now was paradise.

She rubbed her belly, feeling her baby kicking and moving, and she smiled. The baby wasn't even Scott's. She was pregnant by his son, Meyer. The two had been carrying on a hush-hush relationship for years, and no one was any wiser.

Everyone believed Meyer was sweet on the stripper, Lollipop, but the truth was, his heart belonged to Penelope. It burned him up inside when his old man went after what he believed was his woman. But Meyer kept quiet about it and allowed the affair to happen. He couldn't let his feelings be known. It was one reason he was so angry and violent in the streets. He felt insulted by his father in so many ways, but there wasn't anything he could do to Scott. He was the boss, the big man in charge of everything, and his father.

When Layla had called him to do the hit on Penelope, it tore him up inside. There was no way he would let that happen. He told everyone in the organization they better not lay a finger on her, especially if his father didn't sanction the hit. And if he did, Meyer would have gotten involved. But everyone believed he was concerned about Penelope for two reasons: she belonged to his father and she was carrying his sibling. They didn't understand Penelope meant everything to Meyer.

With Scott out of her life, Penelope felt she could finally move on with her own life. She wanted to come clean about everything. She wanted Meyer in her life. She loved him dearly, and she knew he loved her back.

Happy about her future, she picked up the phone and dialed Meyer. When she heard Meyer's voice on the other end, she immediately told him everything that had transpired with his father.

"I want to tell him about us," she said.

"No, you can't do that," he said quickly.

"Why not? He's not with me anymore, he doesn't want me, and besides, this is your baby, and I love you, Meyer."

"Penelope, that wouldn't be wise. Just fall back and keep your mouth shut."

"No! I'm tired, Meyer. I'm tired of hiding our relationship and being in people's shadow. When I have this baby, I want you in the delivery room with me, not him."

Penelope despised Scott. He had taken advantage of her when she worked for him, using his powerful position to throw himself on her and take what he wanted. It was borderline rape and sexual harassment.

She had chemistry with Meyer. While everyone saw him as a violent, murderous monster, she saw a man who could make her laugh and didn't judge her, unlike Scott, who used her for sex.

"Penelope, listen to me clearly, you do this, and it will be a mistake. I'll be at your place in a few hours so we can talk in person. But don't do anything stupid or irrational. You might fuck around and get us all killed," he said. "You don't know my fuckin' father."

After he hung up, she sighed heavily. She was adamant in telling Scott.

"Shit, you gonna make me come, ma," Meyer said to Lollipop, right after he hung up with Penelope.

The promiscuous stripper was curved over in the front seat of his Beamer, her face thrust in his lap, his dick jammed in her mouth. She licked and sucked his dick like it was a lollipop, hence the name, while he was reclined in the driver's seat, enjoying his treat.

"Who was that?" she asked him, momentarily stopping her freaky blowjob on him.

"Just something I gotta take care of soon. And who told you to fuckin' stop? You 'bout to make me come," he said.

Lollipop went back to work on his dick, sliding her lips up and down, up and down. She made him huff and puff, as her moving lips against his erection were about to make him explode.

"Oh shit! Oh shit! Aaaaahhh shit! Damn it, ma," he grunted and groaned as he exploded a heavy load of semen into her mouth, and she swallowed it effortlessly.

His body deflated like a balloon. He had never felt so relaxed.

Lollipop raised up into the upright position in the passenger seat and wiped her mouth. "You had fun?"

"Yeah," he said, fixing his pants.

Meyer knew he needed to get to Penelope soon and have that talk with her.

It was late Sunday night when Meyer finally arrived at Penelope's luxury apartment near Central Park. He rode the elevator to the sixth floor and headed to the place, feeling apprehensive. She was the one girl he cared about, and he didn't want to see anything happen to her. And the things she used to tell him about Cuba blew his mind.

He rang her bell and waited. A nervous moment went by, when she didn't answer her door, so Meyer took it upon himself to enter the apartment with the spare key she'd given him. He stepped inside, and the place was dark. He immediately called out to her, "Penelope, it's me. I'm here. Where you at?"

He received no answer. He turned on the living room lights and saw nothing out of place. "Penelope," he called out again, but there was no answer.

Maybe she went into labor, he said to himself. But the problem with that was, she would have called him right away if she had.

He pulled out his pistol and combed through the apartment cautiously. He reached the bedroom and pushed open the door, and was greeted with stillness.

"Penelope," he continued to call out, now feeling uneasy. He walked in the bedroom slowly and noticed the bed was neatly made and her overnight bag for when she went into labor was packed and placed near the walk-in closet. There was a light creeping from the closet with the door ajar.

Meyer approached with added caution, gun in hand. He was ready to react if it wasn't Penelope. He opened the closet door slowly, aiming his pistol into the closet. But what he saw crippled him with angst and made the gun fall from his hand. He was gripped with shock.

"Penelope!" he shouted madly, seeing her naked body hanging from a white bed sheet that served as a noose. Her body was already in a state of rigor mortis.

Meyer quickly rushed to her aid, fearing for his unborn baby. He cried out in pain. This wasn't happening to him. He knew she wouldn't kill herself, but it was made to look like a suicide. He knew only one man could be responsible for this sudden tragedy—his father.

Like a bat flying out of hell with its wings on fire, Meyer raced toward the warehouse in New Jersey, a new location where Scott had been hiding out in and conducting business from at the height of the war with Deuce. His black Beamer flew through the Holland Tunnel, and he entered the Garden State.

Soon his tires came to a screeching stop against the asphalt at the warehouse, and he leaped from his car, his gun tucked into his waistband. He rushed toward the entrance, daring any guard to stop him. They would feel his wrath if they tried to. Tears blinded his eyes as he stormed into the large room where his father, Bugsy, and several other lieutenants were seated around a round table and having a meeting.

All eyes were on Meyer charging into the room abruptly, with Scott outraged to see him there.

Scott stood up with his eyes trained on Meyer coming his way in a heated rage. "What is this, nigga? You coming in here disrupting my meeting with—"

Meyer punched Scott in the face so hard, it almost made his head spin. "You muthafucka!" he screamed.

Meyer struck him quickly again. He wanted to pummel his father into the ground. The two men tussled, with Meyer getting the better of his father.

The underlings came gunning for Meyer, ready to take care of him, but Bugsy sprang into action and pulled out two burners, aiming them at everyone and shouting, "Back the fuck down!"

No one was touching his twin brother.

Soon, father and son were separated. Their clothes were ruffled and they were both breathing hard.

Scott glared at his son and plopped into his chair. He was bleeding, and he was hurt.

Bugsy held Meyer back, while he screamed at Scott incoherently.

"She's dead. Why, muthafucka? Why?"

"Just chill, Meyer," Bugsy said. "Who's dead?"

"He fuckin' killed her!"

Bugsy got his brother to calm down and to explain himself.

Meyer glared at his father and exclaimed, "Penelope's dead! He murdered her because she was having my baby. He killed my girl and my child."

It was new information to everyone in the room, including Scott.

"You ignorant fool! I had nothing to do with her murder. I'm shocked myself," Scott said.

Meyer shouted, "You fuckin' liar!"

"I had nothing to do with it. You need to go talk to your mother. She always wanted her dead," Scott said.

"Bullshit!"

"I made it clear to everyone and your mother that if a hair were even touched on her head, there would be hell to pay."

"I'm 'bout to give you hell now, muthafucka!" Meyer shouted.

Scott told him, "I know she came to you to do the murder, but you rejected it."

Tears continued to stream from Meyer's eyes. He wanted to rip his father apart. He knew Scott killed Penelope. Meyer figured that Penelope had called Scott and confessed everything about their relationship and the baby, and Scott couldn't take the newfound information and had her killed.

Scott composed himself, but he was furious with his son for striking him so boldly and doing it in front of people. His eyes fixed deeply on Meyer, squeezing his words through clenched teeth, he said, "Nigga, if you ever come at me like that again, I'll kill you."

Meyer didn't care for his threats.

Bugsy stood between his father and brother, keeping the peace in the room, knowing these two could easily kill each other.

"Get out of here, Meyer," Bugsy said. "Go for a walk."

Meyer hesitated for a moment, and then he did what his brother advised. He left the room and the warehouse, but his dispute with his father was far from over.

Back in his car and racing away from the warehouse, Meyer called his mother and screamed into the phone he was done with his father, informing her what had happened to Penelope.

Layla would lose no sleep over the girl's death. "Come home," she told him. "We need to have a serious talk."

She was ready to tell Meyer about her and Lucky's plan to start their own organization, and with Meyer on their team, it would be perfect. She was ready to reclaim half of what she'd helped to build. She would not allow Scott to leave her penniless and powerless. She would kill Maxine, and if Scott got in the way, she would kill him too.

"Are you ready to go to war against him and take his crown?" she asked Meyer. "It might mean going to war with your twin brother too."

Meyer thought long and hard about it. "Fuck them! I'm ready. And I got some hired guns to add to our team, Ma. The Greene brothers. They will fuck Pop's whole shit up!"

"That's what I wanted to hear from you, Meyer," Layla said. "That's my boy!"

EPILOGUE

Rehabilitation did miracles for Wacka, and soon he was walking again, though it was with a cane for the time being.

During his recuperation, he'd found out that Maxine had been released from prison, but not before Shiniquia was killed. Word from inside the Louisiana prison was that someone had paid a group of inmates to jump Shiniquia in the shower on behalf of Maxine. To make matters worse, Maxine was now sleeping with the enemy—the same man whose family she'd put out a contract on. Wasn't she supposed to be plotting against him? It made little sense to Wacka. What was her motive? Why put out a contract to kill off Scott West's kids only to come home and become his main bitch? But Wacka told himself it didn't matter why—the bitch was crazy. His only concern was finding Maxine and viciously killing her and the remaining members of the West family.

This time it wasn't business, it was personal.

Deuce opened the champagne bottle and put it to his lips, happily celebrating. Although it wasn't a crucial one, it would hit home with the West organization. Jimmy and his crew followed suit and joined in on the celebration. Payback was a bitch, and it came in the sweet justice of killing Penelope.

"What I tell you niggas? You follow big money and you never know where it might take you. It ain't Scott or his kids, but that bitch was payback for my sister," Deuce said.

After two failed attempts on Scott's life, Deuce thought they needed to touch something Scott loved. The streets were talking, and hearing about Penelope and her pregnancy, they knew how to hit Scott and his people. It was a calculated murder of a pregnant woman, but Jimmy showed no remorse when he made the noose and strung her up to hang. He'd stood there coldly, hearing her plead and beg for her life and her baby's life, but her cries had fallen on deaf ears, and he watched her asphyxiate.

But what they were actually celebrating was waiting for them down in the basement. Deuce and Jimmy left the room and descended into the concrete room where there was a man tied to a chair. So far, he was unharmed. He glared at them, remaining defiant. He knew he was about to die.

Deuce grinned in the man's face and taunted him with a hard stare and uttered with contempt, "The infamous fuckin' Whistler. I bet in a million years you never saw yourself in this predicament—outsmarted by some low-level thugs."

"If you gonna kill me, just do it already," Whistler growled at him.

"Kill you? It would be my pleasure, but I'm ready to talk to you man to man, nigga, because I feel you can be an asset to me. I'm finding Scott harder to kill than expected."

"The feeling is fuckin' mutual," Whistler replied.

Deuce chuckled. "Yeah? Well, I hear you two aren't on the best of terms anymore. He wants you dead. Were you really fuckin' his daughter? I've seen the bitch—nice piece of ass. I woulda fucked her too."

Whistler remained quiet.

Deuce wanted Whistler to join DMC and help take down his former friend and boss, the man who put a contract on his head.

"You have a choice. So what's it gonna be?" Deuce asked.

For Whistler, it wasn't a hard choice to make. He replied, "I'm in."

"My nigga," Deuce said.

BUT WAIT!
THERE'S MORE

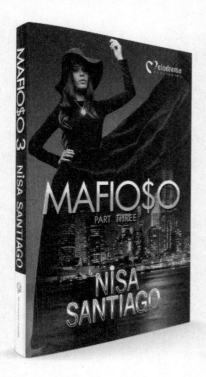
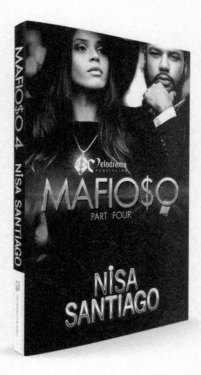

THE SERIES BY
NISA
SANTIAGO

EXCERPT FROM
MAFIOSO - PART THREE

My prodigal son, you telling me where I can and can't be? I'm here to see an old friend," Layla griped back.

"Pops is here, and he's not going to like it at all."

"You think I give a fuck about his feelings? And you have the audacity to side with him after he embarrassed me and went off wit' that bitch? I fuckin' gave birth to you, and you bend your knees for him and—"

"Just leave, please, Ma. I'm beggin' you," Bugsy said.

She slapped him. Immediately, there was a minor scuffle in the lobby between her men and his. It was quickly broken up by the hospital security guards. Layla frowned at Bugsy. What a waste. He had so much potential, but he would rather help out his father than the woman who gave birth to him.

Suddenly, Scott loomed into view of everyone, and he was in no mood for Layla's bullshit. This was the first time they'd seen each other since he tossed her out on the street and she stole his money.

"Why the fuck are you here?" he roared at her.

Layla stood her ground and glared at Scott. She looked intently at his face, and she could see he was visibly upset and saddened by Maxine's condition. It almost looked like he had been crying. Scott, crying? She felt it was impossible, but his face looked flushed, and his eyes were puffy. Seeing this made her even more upset. The audacity of him. Did he ever cry over her, or for her?

"I know you ain't crying over this bitch." She inched closer toward him. If looks could kill, then he would have been massacred.

"Fuck you, bitch!" he snapped back.

"No, fuck you!"

"Don't fuck with me, Layla," he said.

"You love that stupid bitch!"

Scott clenched his fist. "Leave, before I make you leave," Scott said sternly.

"I got the right to see my best friend. She's my friend, and she's hurt," Layla said, dabbing her eyes with a handkerchief and putting on a show for everyone.

"Friend? You're no friend of hers."

"And you think you're better? You fucked me while you were with her, and you were lovin' this good pussy. You let that bitch rot in jail for over twenty years for me, Scott. Don't you forget that shit," she said, airing all their dirty laundry.

Scott wanted to murder Layla. The bitch had some nerve sashaying into the hospital after she'd stolen from him. Had Maxine not pleaded with him to spare her life, he would have killed her in his rage. He was tired of her, but the hospital wasn't the place, and this wasn't the time. Fifty million dollars she took from him. It made his blood boil.

He stood there with a hard scowl. "I want my money back."

Layla didn't take him seriously. It was her money too. She smirked.

"Two weeks, bitch. And every penny better be there, or you'll be sharing a grave with Bonnie."

IT'S ABOUT TO GET DIRTY

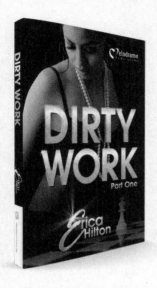
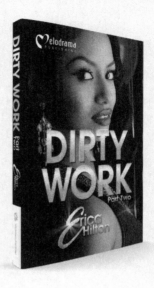

Poisoned Pawn

Harlem brothers, Kip and Kid Kane, are like night and day. While Kip is with his stick-up crew hitting ballers and shot-callers, the wheelchair-bound Kid is busy winning chess tournaments and being a genius.

Kip's ex, Eshon, and her girls, Jessica and Brandy, put in work for Kip's crew as the E and J Brandy bitches. Eshon wants Kip, but Kip is always focused on the next heist—the next big come-up.

When given an assignment by the quirky Egyptian kingpin, Maserati Meek, Kip jumps at the chance to level up to bigger scores. While doing Maserati Meek's Dirty Work, Kip and his crew find that doing business with crazy pays handsomely. But at what cost? Insanity leads to widespread warfare, and the last man standing will have to take down the warlord.

Tired of Being Broke?
Join the *Club*!

Ever wonder why it seems like the cheap girls of the world belong to an exclusive club? Wonder why they have a Zen-like nature while you're struggling to make the rent? Answer: Money.

It's high time to save more and stress less. Step up and accept the challenge. Initiate yourself into the Cheap Girls Club.

Most wealthy people are cheap and know there's more than one way to be charitable. In this how-to manual for financial fierceness, Winslow explains how she found value in being six-figures in debt. Through honest, inspiring stories she spills the tea on what she did to get on the right path to financial freedom.

Learn the secrets of how the wealthy look at money differently. Learn to be Cheap! #CheapGirlsClubChallenge